BODYMORE MURDERLAND 3

Lock Down Publications and Ca$h
Presents

Bodymore Muderland 3
A Novel by *Delmont Player*

Lock Down Publications
P.O. Box 944
Stockbridge, Ga 30281
www.lockdownpublications.com

Lock Down Publications
Like our page on Facebook: Lock Down Publications @
www.facebook.com/lockdownpublications.ldp
Book interior design by: **Shawn Walker**
Edited by: **Nuel Uyi**

Stay Connected with Us!

Text **LOCKDOWN** to 22828 to stay up-to-date with new releases, sneak peaks, contests and more...

Thank you!

Submission Guideline.

Submit the first three chapters of your completed manuscript to ldpsubmissions@gmail.com, subject line: Your book's title. The manuscript must be in a .doc file and sent as an attachment. Document should be in Times New Roman, double spaced and in size 12 font. Also, provide your synopsis and full contact information. If sending multiple submissions, they must each be in a separate email.

Have a story but no way to send it electronically? You can still submit to LDP/Ca$h Presents. Send in the first three chapters, written or typed, of your completed manuscript to:

LDP: Submissions Dept
P.O. Box 944
Stockbridge, Ga 30281

DO NOT send original manuscript. Must be a duplicate.

Provide your synopsis and a cover letter containing your full contact information.

Thanks for considering LDP and Ca$h Presents.

Dedications

This book is dedicated to my father—Timothy Player [rest in power, Pops], my grandfathers—Knight Player and Frank Carter [R.I.P], my brothers Detauwn Jarrod and Antauwn Timothy Player and D D; the Honorable Minister Louis Farrakhan for showing me a better way, making me want to change lives, and supporting my FOI walk in the Nation of Islam where I continue to gain true knowledge, wisdom and understanding. All praise be to Allah! And to the only woman to ever read my work and reach out: Florida's own, beautiful mother of three—Octavia Bowman. Your letter meant the world to me. It's proof that words matter. Thank you! To the fine Tiara Christian. I'll see you soon. And finally, to Jefferson street's own Ms. Nenny. I told you I'd do right. My word is bond. And my beautiful M.G.T. sisters!

Acknowledgments

Of course, I have to first acknowledge Allah. Because without Him none of this would be possible. I'd like to extend my gratitude to my cousins and the good men who took the time to guide me through: Frank Nitti Lance. What we've been through can't even be explained. Loyalty forever!

Anthony 'Bucky' Fields—Southeast D.C.'s truest on both sides of the wall. What more can I say?

Paul-Paul Rhodes—if I ever did anything wrong, forgive me, bruh.

Allen 'Big Al' Griffin, I appreciate you, sporty.

Uncle Walter Lomax—for being an amazingly great mentor.

My man Shaka in the wheelchair—for igniting that fire to know more.

My cousins Wheat, D'Black & Fat Max—for always being there.

Warren ['Lil'Dinky' Stuckey] Muhammad—for giving me a true understanding of the teachings of the Most Honorable Elijah Muhammad.

Phillip Cook—you're still crazy like that glue.

Lil'Clyde & Andre Chapple—for showing me the way.

Pierre Wilson Sr., I love you Cuz.

Robert X ['Cead' Crowder]—I thank Allah for you, brother.

Kerwin Ebb—for leading by example and never turning back.

Marcus 'Lil'Moon' Alexander, thanks for being you.

Big Christian Mark, you're amazing.

Napoleon, thanks for guiding me towards Jesus.

Zimbabwe—for always schooling me even when I was bucking.

Lamarr Harris—I miss you, bruh.

Jamaine J. Jeter—I forgive you, lil'bruh. I really do.

Randall 'Black Randy' Bagley, aka Masood—walk out on what you know and spoil our baby every February 16th.

Acheme Witherspoon—walk slow, think fast and continue to evolve.

Black Reds [Chase]—for upping my work-out from juvenile to adult.

Percy Pair for J & Curtis Brown for M&M.

Sufyan, Azziz & Thomas [Fat Tom/ Wise True] Cook for *everything*!

The bro Cash and Lockdown for giving me this platform.

My nephews Lor'de & Jordan and my little men Darrien & Ahmad for breaking the cycle.

And finally, Jason Murdock, Daniel Carter-El and Jodie Hill for carrying the torch!

Prologue

"Y'all lil niggas ready to earn y'all bones?" Damon 'Lor'Homie' Holmes placed his Mountain Dew inside the cup-holder and glanced over his shoulder as Al-Qamar pulled over. "I said are you lil niggas ready to earn y'all bones or what?" Lor'Homie repeated, turning completely around when nobody responded.

"Hell yeah!" one of the young boys exclaimed, as his sidekick shook his head.

"That's what I like to hear," Lor'Homie said. "Y'all remember who y'all are gunning for, right?" Lor'Homie questioned.

They'd already circled Central Avenue a few times, surveying the layout, pointing out the targets.

"Yeah," the sidekick spoke up, nodding. "The brown-skinned, pigeon-toed nigga with the slight hump in his back that use to come through the block with Charm from time to time."

"The light-skinned nigga with him too," Lor'Homie added, getting out of the car on the corner of Aisquith and Fayette to get the wheelchair out of the trunk.

"What about our faces?" the young boy asked, looking around after climbing from the back seat of the car. "Shouldn't we have masks too? I mean, what if they see our faces?"

"Don't even worry about that. Y'all good," Lor'Homie assured." "Al-Qamar and I came over here last night and drilled the straws out of both police-poles and cut the camera wires."

"What about the ShotSpotter?" the sidekick followed up.

"Yeah, that too," Lor'Homie lied. Honestly, the last time he'd been in East Baltimore was when he and Shaggy had to do a deal with the missing finger nigga 'Mike-Mike' and a couple of them 'Hot Boys'.

Once Lor'Homie realized that Young Danny's and Murdock's set up was too tight to turn a simple hit into a quick come up, he considered hitting them individually. However, Young Danny's routine was too unreliable to find a good enough leak to plan ahead, and Murdock's was too calculated to plan behind. Murdock as what Lor'Homie liked to call a hard target. He didn't make many mistakes. The nigga slept light, walked easy, checked for reflections, watched for shadows, and moved on the side of caution. So, he wasn't just about to let a nigga walk him down. If Murdock had a soft spot, Lor'Homie had yet to find it.

"Look, don't do nothing until you see us at the other end of the block," Lor'Homie instructed, removing the wheelchair from the trunk of the car, before unfolding it. "Which one of y'all taking the chair?"

Lor'Homie looked from one young boy to the other.

"Me," the older of the two spoke up.

"A'ight." Lor'Homie stepped back. "Sit down," Lor'Homie waited until the young boy was comfortably in the wheelchair, before turning towards the car. "Give me that *Final Call*," Lor'Homie requested, leaning inside the car.

Al-Qamar picked up the *Final Call* newspaper with the two Glock 40's tucked securely inside, and handed it to Lor'Homie before he turned back around and laid the news paper across the young boy's lap.

"Don't fuck this up."

"I'm telling you, big homie, we got this," the young boy assured.'

"That's what's up," Lor'Homie nodded. "Don't forget, no matter what happens, stay on the targets—Don't let up," Lor'Homie added, climbing back into the car. "We're going to go all the way around and come down Orleans again. Wait for us."

"Already." The young boys nodded in unison.

Al-Qamar hit the horn twice, made an illegal U-turn, and shot down Caroline. "You think they're ready, Dummie?" Al-Qamar questioned, as Lor'Homie picked up the duffle bag off the floor.

"It doesn't matter. They're bait," Lor'Homie dug an SGM Tactical Glock 9mm with a 50-shot clip out of the bag, and laid it on the floor. "All we need them to do is get Murdock's and Young Danny's attention long enough for us to catch them slipping." Lor'Homie continued pulling an Israeli Army-issued Uzi from the duffle bag before tossing it onto the back seat.

Al-Qamar kind of felt bad that they had to sacrifice some loyal soldiers to get one up on Murdock and Young Danny. But then, he remembered that there was nothing morally right about the game they were playing. So, anybody who played with morals was bound to lose in one sense or another.

Al-Qamar hit Orleans, drove down to Central Avenue, and waited for the young boys to show up.

"What's taking these lil niggas so long?" Lor'Homie questioned curiously. "They only had to walk one block."

"You want me to go around the block real quick and see what's up?" Al-Qamar looked over.

"Yeah," Lor'Homie said, sitting the SGM Tactical Glock 9mm back on the floor again.

"It's crazy how all this shit started over a bitch." Al-Qamar made a left at the corner of Aisquith and Orleans.

"This shit didn't start about no bitch," Lor'Homie corrected because he knew what seemed like a sudden falling-out was merely just the end result of something that had been gradually building. "Charm know Cuzzo a hundred. He's just been waiting for an opportunity to do some fuck shit!"

"What a nigga will do to come up! Who he'll cross!" Al-Qamar seemed to be thinking out loud as he took another left onto Fayette.

"There they go right there!" Lor'Homie exclaimed, spotting the young boys approaching Central Avenue. "Go back around!"

Al-Qamar drove up the block, hit the horn to make sure the young boys saw them. He hit Caroline again, and went back around to Orleans to get back into position. "Make sure you cut the whole street off," Lor'Homie ordered, double checking the SGM Tactical Glock 9mm as Al-Qamar neared the corner.

***

"Knowledge is power, Dummie," Daniel 'Young Danny' Carter said sincerely, leaning back up against the trunk of his 2016 Gold Infiniti Q50. "Don't ever forget that."

"Nah, see—I disagree with that," Jason Murdock retorted, locking eyes on a dude in a wheelchair rolling down the other side of the street. "Power is power. That's how a lot of these stupid ass niggas end up with it."

"You can disagree all you want." Young Danny paused. "The fact still remains that knowledge is power. That's why everybody doesn't have it."

"Yeah, a'ight," Murdock mumbled, keeping his eyes on the wheelchair as the kid pushing it steered it in between two cars and rolled it off the curve into the street. He thought about the dude that had been recently going around using his wheelchair to rob niggas. "Ayo, what the stick-up boy in the wheelchair suppose to look like again?"

"Who?" Young Danny questioned. "Willie Bates?"

"Is that the dude using his baby mother to roll up on niggas in the wheelchair?"

"Yeah, but what the fuck does that have to do with what we're talking about?" Young Danny questioned, confused as Murdock continued to calculate why the wheelchair seemed so out of place.

"Man, what does he look like?" Murdock locked eyes with the nigga in the wheelchair.

"I don't know. Dark-skinned, kind of muscular." Young Danny paused to consider what he knew.

"I do know he has, like, a birthmark hair-patch on his neck."

Murdock never took his eyes off of the wheelchair as Young Danny spoke. "I think he's coming, Dummie," he exclaimed, getting Young Danny's full attention as the wheelchair crossed over to their side of the street.

Young Danny turned around just in time to see the news paper fall out of the wheelchair-bound dude's lap to reveal two Glock .40's as his homeboy struggled to get the wheelchair up onto the sidewalk.

"Yu-errlllll!" Young Danny gave off the call for danger a second before the wheelchair-bound gunman picked up the two tones on his lap, jumped out of the wheelchair and took aim, as Murdock tackled him over the trunk of the Infiniti.

The kid with the two Glock .40's started dumping without hesitation, as Murdock and Young Danny fell into the street and began scouring around the car. The kid knocked off the entire back light with one of the guns, and then started working the other as his homeboy wiped out and stepped back out into the street as a means to trap Young Danny and Murdock off.

The first shooter was hitting everything in sight—The trunk, back windshield, and back side window.

***

Murdock tried to get his tone out as the back tire exploded and the car lowered a good six inches.

"What the fuck are they doing?" Lor'Homie pulled the 'Call of Duty' full-face mask over his head, as they neared Central Avenue. "I told them stupid niggas to wait on us!" He continued hearing the sound of some heavy artillery. The kind of heavy artillery they got from their African gun dealer—the same African gun dealer Charm and them used.

Al-Qamar pulled the Ford LTD across Central Avenue a second before he and Lor'Homie hopped out, ready to work. By then, Murdock and Young Danny's support group had finished one of the young boys, and was chasing the other one right towards them.

"It's go time!" Lor'Homie ordered, scanning the block for Young Danny and Murdock as Al-Qamar rushed around the car and let the Uzi go. Lor'Homie saw their other lil' homie and one of Murdock and Young Danny's hitters go down, but somehow was able to remain focused. He was on a mission. Lor'Homie spotted Young Danny and Murdock halfway down the block, raised the SGM Tactical Glock 9mm and started running down the middle of the street in their direction, emptying the clip.

Murdock and Young Danny not only saw the two additional hitters, they heard them and jumped into Young Danny's bullet-riddled Infiniti and began exchanging gunfire. But Lor'Homie didn't give a fuck. The shit he was throwing was landing like meditation balls.

"Get us the fuck outta here!" Murdock ordered as something the size of a grapefruit knocked half of the dashboard up.

Young Danny ducked low until he got the key in the ignition and started the car. Then he threw that bitch in drive and stepped on the gas.

Young Danny hit the car in front of him, and shrieked when he witnessed what he believed to be a bullet peel the paint off the entire side of the car as it breezed by.

Lor'Homie saw Young Danny's car hesitate, and kept dumping. It was over. The silly nigga had penned himself in. But, just as he came upon the driver's side door, close enough to see the fear on Young Danny's face, the SGM Tactical Glock 9mm jammed long enough for Young Danny to force the parked car in front of him forward, side-swipe two more cars, and take off down the street on a flat tire.

Lor'Homie yanked on the lever until another bullet slid into the chamber. Then, he ran after Young Danny's Gold Infiniti again and let the SGM Tactical Glock 9mm ring off until the fleeing car disappeared around the corner on three wheels, with sparks flying everywhere.

Lor'Homie jogged back up the block, surveying Al-Qamar's work.

"Let's go, Dummie!" Lor'Homie hopped back into the car and leaned out the window to slap the door. "Come on, let's go, nigga! Them niggas riding on a rim!" Lor'Homie knew that Young Danny and Murdock couldn't have gotten too far on three wheels.

Al-Qamar jumped back into the driver's seat, threw the Ford LTD in drive, and floored that motherfucker down Orleans, as Lor'Homie stuffed the other 50 clip into the SGM Tactical Glock 9mm. "Don't let them niggas get away!"

"I'ma cut them off at Fayette and Broadway," Al-Qamar said. "You wore Young Danny's shit out."

Lor'Homie cocked the SGM Tactical Glock 9mm and kept his eyes on the road. He didn't give a damn about no 'vehicular homicide'. He was trying to catch a body—two bodies to be exact.

"Uh shit, Dummie!" Al-Qamar snatched the mask off his face the moment he turned the corner and saw Young Danny's Infiniti crashed head-on into a police car.

Lor'Homie snatched his mask off too, before tossing the SGM Tactical Glock 9mm to the floor and kicking it under the front seat. "What the fuck!" Lor'Homie mumbled, trying to figure out what happened.

A second police officer slowly waved Al-Qamar around the accident scene as he talked on his shoulder radio. They could see blood and shit inside, but no bodies. Young Danny's Infiniti Q50 was fucked up. There were bullet holes everywhere. The passenger side door was hanging off, the windows were shot out, the alarm system would not stop going off, and the back rim was destroyed because the tire was completely gone. That bitch was basically totalled.

When Al-Qamar and Lor'Homie finally came to a stop at the corner of Wolfe and Fayette, they saw Young Danny and Murdock sitting on the curve in handcuffs, smiling at them. "Fuck!" Lor'Homie exclaimed, punching the glove compartment because he knew they'd fucked up.

Not only would they now have to worry about contending with Young Danny and Murdock. He'd also have to hear his cousin Nizzy's mouth when he got back around the way.

Chapter 1

"This should be it right here," Detective Baker informed Detective Gibson from the passenger seat of the dark-colored Crown Victoria, as he carefully eyed the paint-chipped numbers of the row home.

Detective Gibson pulled into the first available parking space a few houses down, and shut the Crown Vick off before climbing out of the car behind her partner. "Not much has changed around here, huh?" Gibson questioned, surveying the neighborhood.

"It sure doesn't look like it," Baker agreed, noticing the corner boys as they made their way towards the house. "Same game, new players," he added, watching his partner climb the steps and approach the front door. "The only difference now is that money justifies and excuses all sins with these young punks nowadays."

"That and the fact that they want the respect without the consequences." Gibson shook her head before knocking on the door. The streets of Baltimore had really changed since the days of gangsters like Gregory Gather and Shorty Boyd. The babies out there today were more vicious and twice as treacherous. They'd publicly set you up, take you out, and even take you down without hesitation and be right back on the corner—'cooling', as they liked to say—because the truth is, they didn't care who knew about it. And honestly speaking, nobody else did either.

In fact, just that morning, after a tip from one of their well-known snitches, Detectives Gibson and Baker had casually waded through some knee-high weeds of an abandoned lot into the stench of death to find the body of a recently released gangster, who just didn't seem to understand or respect the fact that times had changed. These young boys were playing by a different set of rules or a lack thereof.

"That's why the governor needs to invest more money into programs like Safe Streets and Half Court, because all these baby-bookings solutions don't seem to be working!" Detective Baker exclaimed.

"You won't get an argument out of me." Detective Gibson tapped on the door again. Gibson had watched with alarm as the homicide numbers climbed, and the city became more hostile and more frightening.

Especially since the Freddie Grey riots. There were days when she wondered how she and her partner survived. Days when she could not help but acknowledge the deeply rooted segregation and economic separation. Days when it was so thick in the air that she could feel it. Still, she truly loved Baltimore. It was the type of city that keeps you up at night tossing and turning, trying to figure out what could be done to save it.

""Who is it?" what appeared to be a husky male voice questioned from the other side of the door.

"Detectives Gibson and Baker from the Baltimore City Police Department, sir," Gibson replied friendly, knowing that men typically did not view women as a threat. "Would you mind opening the door?"

The locks on the door began to rattle. A few seconds later, the door swung open to reveal the same bald-headed, familiar-looking, light brown-skinned gentleman from the hospital claiming to be Nicole Johnson's fiancé.

"Afternoon, sir," Gibson instantly began to try to place him again. "Would Miss Johnson happen to be home?"

"What's going on?" Keystone questioned.

"We just have a couple follow-up questions and updates on the investigation concerning her kidnapping case." Gibson mixed a little bit of truth in with the falsehood.

"Why don't you come in?" Keystone stepped to the side to welcome the detectives inside. "Nicole's in the basement doing laundry, but I'll go get her for you."

"Thanks," Detectives Gibson and Baker entered the house, surveying the front room as Ms. Johnson's fiancé secured the door before leading them into the dining room.

Keystone was doing everything in his power not to show his hate for law enforcement. Especially, since he'd already known they were eventually coming.

"Nice place you got here," Gibson admitted sincerely, admiring the color-coordinated layout. The inside of Nicole Johnson's home made you feel welcome. It reminded Gibson of a home she'd thought about buying some years ago up on Federal Hill. "I love the coloring."

"Yeah, my wife's an interior decorator." Keystone walked over to the top of the basement stairs and called out to Peaches, as Baker eyed him curiously.

When Peaches answered, Keystone informed her that the detectives were there to see her. "So what's this all about?" Keystone questioned, turning his attention back to the detectives. He of all people knew the game they were playing. "My wife has already dropped all the charges."

Gibson decided to be straight up. "Well, to be honest with you, Mister ummmm—" Detective Gibson waited for Keystone to fill in the blank, but he never did, so she continued. "We're looking into a double homicide." Gibson looked for any sign of jitteriness, but found none.

"Double homicide?" Keystone gave Gibson a strange look. "What does that have to do with my fiancé's case?"

"Probably nothing," Detective Baker spoke up. "You see, both of the suspects who were arrested in Ms. Johnson's case were found shot to death in a burning house the day after they were released."

"That still doesn't explain why you're here," Keystone challenged. He knew the game all too well. Even a dumb detective knew how to get from a dead body to a living suspect.

"Well, we tend to investigate backwards," Detective Baker smiled.

Keystone didn't smile. Detective Baker continued. "That way, we can get a better feel for who our victims were. It's a little thing I like to call *the process of elimination*."

"From the way you were talking at the hospital, you kind of gave me the impression that you already knew exactly who they were." Keystone reminded them just as Peaches appeared from the basement.

"Sorry," Peaches apologized, wiping her hands on a cloth. "I was putting a load in the washer."

"That's fine," Gibson assured, removing a small writing pad from her breast pocket. "How's everything been coming along?"

"Fine," Peaches replied. "But what's this all about?" Peaches inquired, walking over to stand next to Keystone. "I know you didn't come all this way to simply check on me."

"We would just have to ask you a few routine questions concerning your whereabouts on the night of—"

"Hold up, hold up," Peaches interrupted. "Why would you need to know my whereabouts?"

"Well, ummm, the two suspects in your case were killed a few nights ago," Gibson revealed.

"Okay, and," Peaches fired unfazed, "what does that have to do with my whereabouts? I dropped all the charges weeks ago."

"Well—ummmm—for starters, both of the men you identified as your kidnappers were found bounded, tortured and shot to death execution-style in a house on Dukeland Avenue," Baker chimed in.

"And?" Peaches rolled her eyes.

"Look, I understand that you don't give a damn and all, but—"

"Forgive us, Ms. Johnson," Detective Gibson interjected, cutting her partner off before he said something stupid. "I know this has been a touchy time. But, we have to do our job. I promise you it's just routine."

"Look, detective," Keystone spoke up, "didn't you'll say that these guys were linked to all kinds of unsolved crimes?"

"Yes, but we still have to investigate," Gibson decided to step in because Baker had a way of rubbing people the wrong way, and she could sense Ms. Johnson's mounting frustration.

"Yeah, well, investigate God," Peaches retorted smartly. "He's the one who doesn't like ugly."

"Yeah," Keystone seconded. "Maybe somebody finally caught up to them. Crime pays in more ways then one, you know!"

"Whatever the case, we still have a job to do," Baker said, seriously tired of the song and dance.

"Look, Ms. Johnson," Gibson said softly, "as happy as I was to see these guys laid across a slob of steel downtown in the city's morgue, that doesn't stop me from doing my job and investigating any possible leads."

"Well, don't expect me to lose no sleep." Peaches gave Detective Gibson a hard look.

"Fair enough," Gibson nodded, and went on to do all the questioning. She asked Ms. Johnson where she'd been on the night in question. She questioned Ms. Johnson about her alibi, and wanted to know who could confirm it. Gibson further inquired about somebody seeking vengeance on her behalf, and so on.

Detective Baker eyed Ms. Johnson and her fiancé closely, as Gibson went through all the formalities. He knew that everyone lied. Murderers lied because they had to, witnesses lied because they wanted to, and dummies lied for the sheer joy of it, gangsters lied to uphold a general principle that never allowed them to provide accurate information to the authorities under no circumstances, and women lied because they were the best at it.

"Thank you, Ms. Johnson. That'll be all for now," Gibson flipped her note pad closed, and removed a card from her pocket. "If you think of anything else, please don't hesitate to give me a call." Gibson placed her card on the dining room table.

"I won't be thinking of nothing else, you can believe that!" Peaches picked the business card up and kindly handed it back to the detective.

"If it makes you feel any better, Ms. Johnson," Baker spoke up, as Gibson accepted her card back. "Our prime suspect is a big time heroin dealer and gang leader, who we have reason to believe placed a twenty-five thousand dollar bounty on the lives of both Larry High and Bobby Steelz after word got out that they may be responsible for the murder of his younger brother and two of their main suppliers during a home invasion out in Maryland back in early May."

"It doesn't," Peaches assured.

"Have a nice day, detectives," Keystone gestured towards the door, and waited for the detectives to move. When they did, he led them out.

"You know, detectives," Keystone stopped to open the door, "if you really want to make her feel better, leave us the hell alone."

Keystone stepped to the side to allow the detectives to exit.

"We'll be in touch," Gibson said, spinning on her heels, as she followed Baker out of the house. She stepped outside and smiled. She truly loved this city. Its beautiful landscape and crazy people. Even the ones who thought they could pull the wool over her eyes. Detective Gibson walked on down the street to the car in silence and climbed into the car. "She's hiding something." Gibson slid behind the steering wheel. "I don't care how solid her alibi is."

"Uh, she's doing more than hiding something—She's protecting somebody," Baker confirmed. "Did you realize exactly who her fiancé is yet?"

"I kept trying but I just couldn't place his face."

"That was Kerwin Ebb," Baker disclosed.

"It damn sure was!" Gibson proclaimed, snapping her fingers. How in the hell had she missed that. She should've recognized Kerwin Ebb immediately. Especially since he and his childhood friend—Joe Edison—had avoided prosecution when they were picked up and questioned about a string of felony murders less than eighteen months ago. "I can't believe I missed that."

"Well, had I not spotted his name on a piece of mail— I'd missed it too," Baker admitted. "He's picked up a lot of weight."

"When the hell did he begin to lose his hair and get all that gray?"

"He's getting old. But that's him already," Baker assured, thinking about how they were unable to hold Ebb and Edison on the charges and prove the case. "You know after the last case, I'd really began to think that we'd messed up. For a moment, I thought Ebb had cleaned up his act." Baker almost seemed disappointed. "But, I guess he's just gotten better at being bad."

Gibson didn't want to say, 'I told you so'. But, she'd never bought into Ebb's little act of innocence. Not even after more than half of the neighborhood came forward to say that he was homeless. That was just the history of West Baltimore. They would rally together and rise to any ocassion to protect their own, even if it was for the wrong reasons. It was a waste of great potential. "So what do you think? Ebb's at it again?" Gibson started the car.

"I don't know—It's possible," Baker admitted, honestly thinking about the lab report. "Ebb's old school." Baker pulled the seat belt across his chest and buckled himself in. "He lives by a set of principles that you just don't see much of today," he continued. "You know these young punks today will kill for anything except a righteous cause. That's why I can't see Ebb on this one. Not if he had to bring someone else along. He's a loner. And we know from the lab report that this wasn't a one man job."

"Well, Edison's dead," Gibson mentioned Kerwin Ebb's partner in crime. "What about Big John or his brother Gorge?" You know they aren't no strangers to torture."

"It's definitely a possibility," Baker agreed. But the truth of the matter was that the Harrison brothers weren't the only gangsters who would gladly help Ebb revenge a sin against his family. Baker knew that personally. "It could've also been any one of the other Cherry Hill guys he used to run with. You know they're like one big family out there."

"So what now?" Gibson peeped into the rearview mirror, as she slowly pulled out. "How do you want to play it?"

"We follow the evidence and see where it takes us," Baker replied, as Gibson drove down the street. Whatever the case, he knew that if Ebb or any other one of his childhood friends were involved, the chances of solving the case were slim to none because, honestly, they just didn't make a lot of mistakes.

***

I had just left my mom's house after getting the news about the little police visit, but I wasn't worried. I knew that there was no way that the police could trace Keystone to the crime scene because he and mom had an airtight alibi, which meant that they couldn't link us together. And besides, like Keystone said, 'If all else failed, it wasn't what the police knew that counted. It was what they could prove." I dropped Deli off at Bucky Love's grandmother's house and drove around for a minute bullshitting. I wanted to go fuck with JuJu. But, I knew that he was ironing out some shit with his son's mother. I was just about to text Young Danny to see if he and JuJu's cousin—Jaxkey—had made it up to the car auction yet, when I recognized Butta's fine, bow-legged, pigeon-toed ass strutting down North Avenue, and quickly pulled over.

"Damn shorty, what's good?" I leaned over the armrest towards the passenger seat window, shooting game. "You looking nice today, baby," I added, slowly taking in Butta's outfit. She had on a sheer yellow, backless top with metal rings down the sides that showed off the black lace bra underneath, a skin-tight, hip-hugging black micro-mini skirt that was really nothing more than a series of leather bands held together by thin strips of cloth. And some yellow leather platforms style heels that had a single strap across the top of her foot just above the toes, another strap that ran up from the outside of the heel and wrapped around her ankles and lower calves about five times before running down across her insteps. "Damn, you gonna ignore a nigga with all that ass?"

"What?" Butta looked over like she was about to go off, and laughed when she saw me. "Boy!" Butta emphasized, bouncing over. "I was about to let your ass have it."

"You was scared as shit," I teased.

"Boy, bye," Butta said. "And what are you doing, looking at my ass anyway, nigga?"

"Shiddd, I couldn't help it," I admitted honestly as Butta used her finger to rake a few strings of her short blond hair back behind her ear. "You out this mother fucker like it's summer time."

"Don't be checking for me, nigga," Butta joked.

"Yeah, I heard that," I cracked a half of smile, looking around. "What's good with you though?"

"Nothing," she replied. "On my way back to the house to wait on your boy. Why? You gonna drop me off or something?" Butta added, giggling like a school girl.

"Yeah, a'ight," I replied, knowing damn well that Butta knew just how turnt up shit was between Nizzy and I because the streets were definitely talking. "I'll drop your ass off alright."

"Y'all two cranky, stubborn ass niggas killing me with the dumb shit," Butta shook her head and continued. "After all the shit y'all been through. And for as long as y'all have known each other. Y'all gonna really let a couple hundred dollars come between y'all?" Butta rolled her eyes and waited for an answer that would never come.

A couple hundred dollars, I thought. Maybe Nizzy wasn't as pussy-whipped as I'd first suspected. "You right," I nodded in agreement, bullshitting because too many lines had been crossed, and too many things had been said. Shiddd, not only that, but blood had been drawn, and bodies had even dropped. "Niggas just ego tripping. We'll be alright." I lied because, honestly speaking, there just wasn't any coming back from something like that in the concrete jungle. Once the lions conquered every other animal, they always began to feed on each other. "What's up though? You want a ride or what?"

"A ride *on* what?" Butta bit her bottom lip seductively.

"Girl, you crazy as shit," I shook my head and opened the door. "Get in."

Butta opened the passenger side door and slowly climbed into the car. I couldn't lie. I'd been wanting to smash Butta. But, because Nizzy was my nigga, I'd never crossed that line. But now, all bets were off. "Where you coming from?" Butta inquired.

"Taking care of some business over east," I replied sincerely.

"Mmmmh—hhhhm," Butta twisted her sexy, little, glossed-covered lips up.

"Mmmmh—hhhhm what?" I played along, although I was serious. I'd really been over east looking into something.

"You know what?" Butta looked at me knowingly. "Just don't let my sister find out."

"Man, I'm not paying your crazy ass sister no mind," I assured, slowly eyeing Butta from head to toe before licking my lips. *I'd bet any amount of money she don't got no panties on*, I thought.

"Yeah, you the one got her like that."

"Fuck outta here. Shorty been crazy. Keying up niggas cars and shit."

"Yeah, that's 'cause your ass got that big ass dick," Butta smiled. "Don't look at me like that, nigga. You know my sister tells me everything."

Butta paused, as if waiting for me to play her little game. But I remained silent and refused to feed into the bullshit. "Like how you love to fuck a bitch all night off the Molly."

"What?" I laughed.

"You heard me," Butta leaned over dangerously close and continued. "Don't get all shy now, nigga!" She cooed in my ear teasingly. "You aren't shy when you're slinging that big ol' dick."

"Your sister giving you bad information," I lied, remembering the night in question. Butta's facts were a little off, though. Actually, I'd given Ty'shea some Molly and fucked the shit out of her—and another bad ass red-bone named Keisha—for three straight days at a motel out in West Virginia.

I couldn't lie, though. Although Ty'shea was one of the baddest thots I'd ever fucked in West Baltimore, when the bitch Keisha peeled off her clothes and stood in front of me naked, I knew I'd struck gold. And for the next seventy-two hours I treated her body like an anamorphic sculpture. Viewing it from all different kinds of positions until all its beauty was revealed.

"Yeah, I bet you don't," Butta continued to smile. "Anyway, I know you got some pills on you. Since you coming from taking care of some business over east and all."

"Some pills?" I repeated. Like I hadn't been fucking with the pills since Deli's coming home party.

"Yeah, nigga! Some pills. Molly, ex, Valiums," Butta spat. "Don't play dumb."

"I thought your sister told you about what I did to bitches who play with me and Molly at the same time?" I eyed Butta questionably.

If she wasn't trying to get slutted out, now would be the best time for her to pump her breaks.

"She did," Butta replied nonchalantly. "But, I've always been the type of bitch who doesn't believe a dick is that good until I get up on it myself."

"Say no more. That's what it is then." I nodded and headed for the nearest motel. It was time to find out if revenge was the sweetest joy next to getting pussy.

By the time we got the motel, the Patron we'd picked up at the bar—and the Molly I'd given Butta—had her reclined in the passenger's seat playing with herself in 'go mode'. I kept peeking over, ready to take cold-hearted advantage of Butta as she used her fingers to slowly follow the trail of honeybees that ran up the inside of her thighs.

I knew that Nizzy was crazier than the nigga 'Django' when it came to his bitch. So, I was about to see if he'd still be able to use his emotions to think once word got out that I'd knocked the bottom out of Butta's pussy.

Inside the motel room Butta popped two more Molly's and put on the nastiest striptease I'd ever experienced while I grizzled mouthfuls of Patron. When she started squirting all over the place, giggling and licking her own pussy juice off of her fingers, I knew it was time to fuck.

"Damn, you're sexy as shit!" I admitted truthfully, as Butta stood in front of me in nothing but her criss-crossing heels and a diamond-studded waist chain. "Get on the bed."

I never took my eyes off of Butta as she strutted towards the bed. "Nah, nah, hold on," I requested, removing my phone from my pocket. "Keep them heels on and do that sexy dance move again," I ordered, trying to turn the camera to my phone on to record the action.

"Boy, don't even play like that," Butta crawled across the bed to the edge and laid on her stomach. "You know you can't record this."

"It's going to be for my eyes only," I lied and tried to encourage her with a passionate tongue kiss. "You know, a nigga been dying to see what that pussy was hitting for on the low." I tried sounding convincing, breaking the kiss to lean forward. Then I ran my hand down her back, over the curve of her phat ass and in between her legs to tease her wet pussy and tight asshole. "I swear it's only going to be for me, Butta."

Butta started breathing all hard and shit, as I carefully slid two fingers in and out of her wet pussy and played with her ass with another finger. "Please let me record you, Butta." I teased her clitoris. "You know I've never had a bitch badder than you," I added, skilfully running my fingers back and forth between the silky-soft folds of her wet pussy lips. "I just wanna be able to remember this moment forever," I declared. Butta's pussy was dripping, leaking even. "Your pussy super wet!"

"Charm, I swear—" Butta began before pressing her face into the mattress, panting. At that moment, I knew I had her.

"I know, baby, I got you. I promised," I whispered, as I felt her pussy throb with impetuous desire. "Come on, get up," I commanded, lightly slapping Butta on the ass. "I wanna see that mean ass walk again."

When Butta stood back up, my mouth began to water. It was almost like I was seeing her for the first time. My mouth quickly found its way to one of her hard nipples, and went to work. I wasn't trying to give her a chance to think straight. Because I didn't want her to back out on me now.

"Mmmmhhh," Butta moaned, taking my head in her tender hands, as I nibbled and sucked on her bullet-sized nipples and gently toyed with her clitoris. "You better not show nobody, Charm, I ain't playing."

"I swear." I continued to tease her nipples, going from one to the other, circling them with my tongue. "Walk back across the room for me," I encouraged. It was clear to see that the drugs were starting to have an effect on Butta because she kept trying to force my head down between her legs.

Once I recorded her strutting around the motel room, I made her get on the bed with her legs wide open and play with herself for the camera. Then I slid my hands behind her knees, and held them up while I skilfully licked her from her asshole to her clit and felt her instantly start cumming.

I watched in amazement as Butta's pretty little pussy reflexively opened up to reveal the fattest little clit I'd ever seen. "That's right, baby, open up for daddy," I encouraged, quickly dipping my head to tease her clit with the tip of my long tongue. "Let me get that pretty pussy." I felt Butta shiver and cum again, as I slowly ran my tongue around her thick, dark red pussy lips in small circles.

"You gonna let me get this pussy?" I questioned, softly kissing each honeybee that ran up the inside of her beautiful thighs towards the honey jar that I now knew outlined her phat pussy and made it appear to be sitting inside the bottom of a jar full of honey.

"Huh?" I stopped devouring her pussy for a moment. "You gonna let me beat that pussy up?"

"Yes," she agreed, almost timidly, grabbing my head, trying to force feed me.

"I can't hear you," I warned, aggressively attacking her pussy and clit for a few seconds. Then I switched tempo, gently sucking on her clit before darting my tongue in and out of her pussy. If I didn't know nothing else, I knew my way around a pussy. Ms. Candy had made sure of that.

"Yes," Butta groaned loudly through clenched teeth. "You can have whatever you want. Just keep eating this pussy!" she begged, grinding her pussy into my face as she held my head in place.

Smiling inside, I paused for a moment to reach over and sit the phone on the nightstand with the camera still recording. I fixed it so that the camera would be facing the bed to make sure I got everything that was about to happen. Then, I went back to work.

I ate Butta's pussy and ass feverishly through three orgasms. Then I stood up and frantically ripped my joggers off, as she crawled back across the bed and laid on her stomach at the edge, so that my dick was dangling in her face.

"Now, I'ma show you why your boy so crazy about me," she grinned up at me, kissed the head of my dick, cupped my balls, and straight up tried to inhale my shit to the root. I knew right then and there that Butta was a top-notch dick sucker because only professionals knew how to handle the dick and balls stylishly. After all, it was a package deal.

"Yeah, un-hunh," I managed with a proud smile when Butta was forced to regroup after slightly gagging. "I ain't Nizzy."

"Yeah, but I'ma still slay you," Butta assured, spitting into the palm of her hand before taking a hold of my dick with her butter-soft hands. After looking up at me again with a mischievous smile, Butta turned her full attention back to the task 'in' hand. First, she used her hand like a virtuoso to slowly, yet firmly, run spit all up and down the length of my dick with an underhanded twist.

"You like that big motherfucker, don't you?" I questioned rhetorically, reaching across Butta's back to slap her on the ass again.

"Mmm-hmmm," Butta sighed, bit her bottom lip and continued to long-stroke my dick with care as her ass cheeks wiggled like a jellyfish. "I bet my sister couldn't take the whole thing?" she challenged, staring at my shit in awe.

"It depends on where it was going," I said as Butta slightly twisted her body to the side, repositioned herself and took me down her throat to the root. "Nasty bitch!" I growled through clenched teeth, as my toes curled to their breaking point.

"Mmmmmmh," Butta moaned and continued to go to work. I stood there and watched in wide-eyed amazement as Butta's pretty little mouth and soft lips slowly slid up and down the length of my dick from head to nuts over and over again. I'd never felt anything like it in my life. And when her slimy, little tongue slipped out of her mouth to tease my balls while my dick was still stuffed down her throat, I almost collapsed.

"Uh bitch, you're tryna to make me fall in love!" I exclaimed, shaking like I'd been struck by lightning.

Butta moaned, sniffled and kept bobbing her head like a piston. *Damn!* I thought, as my knees threatened to buckle from Butta's polish game. I'd never had a bitch deep-throat my shit like Butta, although I'd been sucked off by some serious 'Head Doctors'. Bitches like big butt Linette, white girl Donna from South Baltimore, and old head Judy.

"Shit!" I exclaimed over the sounds of Butta's loud sucking and smacking noises. I just loved the way Butta would look up at me submissively every time after she deep-throated. I swear to God. I balled my fist up and shivered when Butta had the nerve to deep-throat my dick and just hold it down her throat. "You're going to make me fall in love." I gripped the back of Butta's head strongly. No bitch had ever gotten me completely down her throat like that.

Butta murmured something, then started somehow working her magic again. Her butter-soft throat muscle felt like they were massaging my dick. I was in heaven. No! Fuck that, I was in love. "You're mine now!" I let out a sharp breath, picked up the camera phone and carefully filmed as Butta bobbed her head in slow and deliberately long, deep nods. She kept stuffing my dick down her snake-like throat repeatedly, as her nose began to run.

"You gonna let me bust in your mouth?" I questioned, and Butta nodded without hesitation. "You gonna swallow?" I continued, knowing that there was no way in the world that she could suck dick that good and not swallow.

"Of course," Butta replied, after removing my saliva- covered dick from her mouth to slowly lick it as she caught her breath. Butta stroked my dick and looked directly into the camera phone. "If you can keep it up all night, I promise I'll swallow it every time you cum."

That was all I needed to hear. I reached for my joggers, ruffled through the pockets, pulled out the rest of the Mollys, popped two, and it was show time.

Butta was a 'head surgeon'. She did things to my dick with her mouth, tongue and throat that I'd never heard of before. And the nasty bitch never took her pretty, teary brown eyes off of me. She waxed my shit for a while, only coming up long enough to swallow her own saliva, catch her breath, sniff, wipe at her running nose, and talk some shit about her sister not being able to deep-throat me like her. Butta spat on the head and swirled it around with her tongue, keeping it thoroughly wet as she held it at the base. I couldn't believe it. I'd only seen porn-star bitches give head like that.

Butta was something special. I especially loved when she carefully caressed my balls, grinned, opened her mouth wide and slowly slid me over her greedy tongue until I disappeared down her tight throat again. I almost dropped the phone three or four times.

"Uh, no, you ain't, nigga," Butta said, snatching my dick out of her mouth, shaking my hand off the back of her head as I began to feel that familiar rush of pleasure in my lower stomach. "I told you—You're gonna beat this pussy up with that big ol' dick first," Butta said, wiping her nose and mouth as she rolled back over onto her stomach, twisted around and rose up to her hands and knees. "Then, after that I'll swallow everything 'cause I ain't trying to get pregnant," she added, looking back over her shoulder, sexy as shit.

I just stood there in awe as Butta slowly fell face first into the pillow and reached back to spread her ass cheeks apart, so that I could see everything she had to offer as clear as day. Her pussy was pretty with dark pink lips, and her asshole was nice and tight. Honestly, it was the prettiest sight ever, and I realized at that moment that I'd struck gold twice. First, fucking with Ty'shea, and now with Butta. *Pretty pussy must run in the family*, I thought, unable to resist leaning forward to stuff my face between her cheeks to get another quick taste of that sweet pussy from the back. I was almost helpless.

"Sssss—" Butta arched her back, shook and begged me to fuck her.

Slapping her across her nice ass once again, I straightened myself up, used her hips to pull her back to the edge of the bed, and aimed my dick at her phat pussy as she wiggled her ass at me.

Then, I slowly sank myself into her lava-hot, juicy pussy, stretching it wide open. I could feel Butta trying to run, but I gripped her hips and held her in place as I went balls-deep.

"Ahhhh!" Butta sighed, letting out a long broken moan and deep strain as she balled the bed sheets up in her fist. "Ain't no way in the world Ty'shea was taking all this dick, shit!"

"Damn girl," I hissed, wishing I'd gotten a hold of her before Nizzy. "You got some good ass pussy," I admitted honestly. However, Butta only continued to whine, whimper and try to run as I punished her tight little pussy. Butta's pussy was amazingly deep, almost gutless and so fucking wet, just like her sister's. Nizzy still wouldn't have been able to convince me that Butta was wifey material. But, he'd damn sure be able to tell me that her pussy and head game were next to none.

Butta tried to press her face down into the pillow to muffle her moans, but I wasn't having it. Not while I was recording. I wanted to make sure that when Nizzy saw the footage, he'd know that I had gutted his bitch. So, I reached down and grabbed a handful of her short blond hair, pulled her head up and continued to fuck the shit out of Butta.

"Please, Charm," Butta begged in a broken cry, trying to run again as I slowly knocked the bottom out of her pussy. "Your dick too big."

"Whose pussy is this?" I asked, zooming in with the camera close enough for Nizzy to be able to see the streaks of cum coating my wet dick, as I slowly slid in and out of Butta's juice box. "Whose pussy is this?"

"Mmmmmh," Butta moaned, bringing the bed sheets up to her mouth, shaking her head. Her pussy was so soaked that pussy juice was now running down the back of her legs.

"You better tell me whose pussy this is or I'ma stop," I coaxed, slapping her on the ass, as the squelching noises continued to fill the air. "Whose pussy is this?" I held the camera phone in front of Butta's face. "Whose is it? Nizzy's or mine?"

"Yours!" she admitted, dropping her head in defeat. "It's all yours, daddy."

"Nah, say my name, bitch." I pulled out until only the head of my dick remained inside Butta's pussy.

"I'ma bout to cum again!" Butta cried out.

"I said say my motherfucking name!" I ordered, intentionally going balls-deep.

"Ahhhh, Charm!" Butta shouted. "Charm, shit! You're putting a hurting on this pussy."

"It's mine?" I rolled my hips, hitting Butta's soft pussy walls.

"Yesss," Butta submitted.

"Can I have it whenever I want?"

"Yes."

"Look into the camera and tell Nizzy!" I demanded, slowing down to give Butta long, deep strokes.

"Charm," Butta pleaded, looking away from the camera, embrassed.

"A'ight, we're done then." I began to slowly pull out.

"Okay, okay," Butta surrendered after I withdrew about half of my dick from her pussy. "You can have it whenever you want!"

"Nah, look into the camera and say it," I insisted, knowing I had her right where I wanted her.

"I swear to God, Charm, you better not show nobody this shit," Butta blushed, looking into the camera. "You can have this pussy whenever or wherever you want, just keep fucking me."

I mushed Butta's face into the mattress before bringing the phone to my face to taunt Nizzy. "Yeah, nigga, you already know what's about to happen next," I teased with a smile, sitting the phone back on the nightstand.

"Can I call my nigga over here?" I winked at the camera and started hitting Butta from the back voraciously. "Huh?" I slapped Butta on her ass and pulled her head back up. "You gonna let my nigga get some of this good ass pussy?" I asked. Wasn't no fun if the 'Dummie Squad' couldn't get some.

"Yes," Butta exhaled and shook. "Whatever you want, daddy. Just keep making me cum."

I smiled because I knew that this was how it always began before we were slutting a bitch out. First we double-teamed her.

Then, we started passing her around, running trains with the whole squad, sending her on 'Dummie' mission and shit.

After calling Murdock and informing him of where I was, I got busy up in that bitch. I don't know exactly what my phone picked up as I flipped, tossed and chased Butta's pretty little ass all over the room. But, I was sure that it picked up the sounds of our urgent fucking and skin slapping, as I began to put passion marks on Butta's titties and tried to pound her now loose pussy into exhaustion.

By the time Murdock arrived, I had hit Butta in every position imaginable, placed hickies all over her body, and talked her into letting me fuck her up the ass in the shower. So, if Nizzy paid attention to her for the next week, he'd probably notice her walking a little funny. Butta kept her promise and swallowed everything too.

Now, I was laid back in pure sexual bliss, watching my nigga, about to do Butta dirty. If revenge was the sweetest joy next to getting pussy, as one of them old rappers once said, then the combination of them both had to be the first.

I reached over and picked up my phone as Butta got down on her knees and began blessing Murdock with that bomb ass slow-neck.

"Yeah, Dummie, I already know," I confessed when Murdock looked over at me speechlessly. "You haven't seen anything yet," I assured, continuing to record. "Wait til' you get up in that pussy."

Murdock just smiled and stood there in a sexual trance before his eyes went wild in amazement as Butta deep-throated him. "What the fuck!" Murdock looked down at Butta and gently ran his hand over her head, and I knew it was going to be a long night.

***

When the guard informed Billy Lo that he had an attorney visit, he got up and hit his funky-four—arms, nuts, ass and feet—before putting the *gun* (toothbrush) in his mouth to kill the smell.

He had been working day and night to get his legs completely back up underneath himself, so that he would be ready if administration agreed to Susan's request to house him out in general population. Billy Lo had filled out request form after request form, like Susan suggested, and sent them to both the warden and security chief's officer. He'd even had Shaneeka follow up with a number of emails and phone calls. But, as of yet, Billy Lo hadn't heard anything.

"Are you about ready, Izzard?" The normal guard stuck his head into the room.

"Yeah, I'm coming now." Billy Lo grabbed his cane, picked the legal papers up off of the bed, and made his out of the room.

"You need a hand with that?" the guard questioned, offering Billy Lo some assistance as he struggled to find the best way to use his cane and balance the legal papers.

"Nah, I'm good," Billy Lo assured, somewhat agitated. He hated when people treated him like he was handicapped. He didn't need any help, nor did he want any, especially from a fucking pig. He knew that behind all the phony smiles and fake well wishes, the dude was just like any other cop—an opportunist looking to serve the enemy on the backs of his own people. "I can handle it." Billy Lo tucked the legal papers comfortably under his left arm, and held the cane with his right hand so that he could keep the full weight of his body off of his right leg, and headed on towards the visiting area.

"Move, nigga!" A young dude came flying around the corner, almost knocking Billy Lo over. "Fuck out the way!" he added, running down the corridor.

Billy Lo just looked back, eyed the kid and smiled. The jail had definitely changed since the 90's. It wasn't nowhere near as treacherous but it was definitely just as wide open. The only difference, it seemed, was that a lot of lames were hooked up in one 'sucker lives matter' movement or another. The shit was sickening, especially since Billy Lo came from an era when suckers were really suckers, and lames got what their hands called for. Now, it was like men were allowing them to skate though untested for a few crumbs. All the same, Billy Lo couldn't wait to make it out into general population to get into the mix of things. He needed to do a little shaking and baking himself, and knew that being trapped off in the medical ward wasn't helping him. Billy Lo acknowledged a few familiar faces, and continued to make his way towards the visiting area for his attorney visit, as his escort made small talk.

Every time Billy Lo laid eyes on Susan Kerin, he couldn't help but smile. For an older, white petite woman, she was a fucking pitbull in a skirt. Not to mention a fine one at that. Susan had the cutest little face and smile Billy Lo had ever seen on a white woman, and he was glad that he'd hired her when he was on the run. She was proving to be worth every fucking penny. If she wasn't flooding the state's attorney office with request, she was hunting down potential witnesses or hitting the judge with motions.

"Good morning, Anthony," Susan greeted Billy Lo amiably, standing up in her jazzy little business suit to shake his hand.

"Good morning, Miss Kerin," Billy Lo replied, placing his papers on the table before accepting Susan's soft, little extended hand. "So what's going on?" Billy Lo questioned, slowly taking his seat. "I thought you weren't coming until next week."

"Well, first, I wanted to deliver the discovery packet you seem to keep having trouble getting." Susan sat down, leaned over and removed a large manilla envelope from her briefcase. "This is your copy," Susan added, pushing the envelope across the table as the guard busied himself shackling Billy Lo's left leg to the custom-made metal-ring attached to the bottom of the table. "It has all the initial statements, police reports, crime scene photos, and so on."

"What about the identity of the so called C.I.?" Billy Lo questioned, flipping through the papers as the guard exited the room and stood outside by the door.

"It's all in there," Susan confirmed, tossing her long, dark brown hair over her shoulder. "But you already knew who it was."

"Yeah, I know." Billy Lo nodded. He'd known all along that it could only be Charm or Herbert. He just had to confirm exactly which one it was. "I just want to see what all they had on him."

"Listen, we have an early court date scheduled for next week. The eleventh, I believe it is," Susan paused to stroll through the schedule on her cell phone to be sure.

"Why?" Billy Lo questioned curiously, laying the stack of papers down on the table.

"The state wants to push our trial date back. But that's very normal in a death penalty case." Susan appeared to find what it was she was looking for on her phone screen. "Yeah, it's the eleventh," she confirmed, looking back up. "Honestly, we might not start trial until well into some time next year."

"Some time next year?" Billy Lo repeated with disappointment all over his face. "Mannnnn," Billy Lo exhaled, running a hand over his face. He wasn't trying to hear nothing that had anything to do with him sitting over the jail another year. Especially if he couldn't get out of the medical ward into general population.

"They're going to try and act as if they want to be sure you're competent enough to stand trial," Susan warned.

"That's bullshit!" Billy Lo exploded, raising his voice. He was ready to get in the ring and go the whole twelve rounds if need be. "The little psychologist chick already cleared me for trial."

"I know," Susan agreed. "And trust me when I tell you that I am going to fight them on this because I know it's just a stall tactic," Susan informed. "The state knows it has a shaky case. The strongest evidence they've against us is a crooked cop, plus the DNA recovered from the cheap motel room which you could've been in at any time. And the fact that you were arrested in a costume they allege favors the one used in the St. Mary's Catholic Church shooting at the bus terminal. Besides that, there's nothing linking you to any crime."

Billy Lo loved when Susan talked that 'us' shit. It let him know that she was on some team shit.

"The older woman they claim to have from the mosque doesn't remember much, from what I gathered, and the child can't identify you, because you were dressed up. Allegedly, of course." Susan's lips curved into a cute smile showing her white teeth. "And I just discovered that Catholic men and women don't usually enter the same door at the church."

Billy Lo smiled back because he knew that she was on top of shit. Plus, she already knew the deal. Billy Lo had told her the truth in so many words. In fact, during their first meeting, when Billy Lo was still on the run, he'd sat in her office in Rockville, Maryland and told her some shit about making their relationship worth her while if she should ever have to represent him in a court of law.

What about a probable cause motion?" Billy Lo questioned. "Because they would not even have gotten half of that shit if it wasn't for Herbert's crooked ass."

"I can give it a try." Susan didn't sound too confident. "But, honestly speaking, Anthony, his information was reliable."

"But he was under investigation, trying to save his own ass," Billy Lo argued.

"Yeah, but the state won't spend it that way, Anthony," Susan countered. "They'll act like he was doing his civil duty."

"What about the judge? How much were you able to find out about him?"

"Not much, former prosecutor. Cold as ice, impossible to read. He used to play poker with my boss—which tells me he's good at concealing his feelings. But, I told you I was only concerned about one thing."

"What's that?" Billy Lo questioned, kind of absent- minded.

"If he would allow me to try my case," Susan reminded. "That was what all the calls and inquiry was for. And from what I gathered he'll."

Billy Lo thought for a minute. There had to be another way that they could force the state's hand. The safest defense was the defense the jury never had to hear. "Did you talk to India yet?" Billy Lo inquired, unsure, wondering if the other angle he'd given her would work. "Cos I haven't been able to catch her." Since Zimbabwe and Little Dinky had been released, it was hard to get the scared ass new working man to recharge his cellphone battery for him. So, he had to limit his calls.

"I did," Susan replied. "And you may be right. We definitely may be able to use her. At least, to show the court just how hard up the lead detectives are to get you."

"What about the general population thing?" Billy Lo asked. "Any luck with that?" Billy Lo wasn't trying to keep being stuck in the medical ward. It was stiff ass shit over there.

"As a matter of fact, that's another reason why I came to see you personally." Susan was already two steps ahead of him. "I had a long phone conversation with the warden last night about you. You remember I told you that his biggest concern was Herbert? You know, being that he was one of his officers back in the day and all."

"Yeah," Billy admitted, remembering her saying something about Herbert being a corrections officer as well as a bounty hunter. "But honestly, once you said he wasn't trying to let me off, I kind of only heard half of what you were saying."

"Well, in the future, when I am talking, you better start paying attention." Susan gave Billy Lo a stern look. "Anyway, are you listening now?"

"Of course," Billy Lo smiled.

"Well, you should be going to g-pop soon because Herbert was found dead in a cheesy, roadside hotel over the weekend."

"What? Hold up! Herbert's dead?" Billy Lo perked up, surprised.

"Apparently," Susan confirmed. "From what little I was able to gather yesterday, it appears to be some kind of homophobic, love triangle gone wrong. There were sex toys, DVD's, whips and some things I never even heard of found in the room."

"Wow!" Billy Lo exclaimed, thinking out loud. *That bitch Peanut a savage!* Billy Lo thought.

"So, you just relax and give me a couple of days to file the necessary paperwork with the warden, and I'll have you in g-pop."

"You know you're my favorite white girl, right?" Billy Lo smiled. He couldn't believe that Peanut had carried that mail already. Black had raised her right.

"I better be," Susan blushed, standing up to leave. "And do me a favor, Anthony."

"What?" Billy Lo watched Susan gather her things.

"When you get in population, please stay out of all the darn mess going on around here. Lord knows we got enough mess to worry about."

Susan double checked her briefcase and made her way to the door, rambling on. "Every time I turn on the news there's something going on over here. Gang extortion, drug and prostitution rings, stabbings, snitching, baby making, every got darn thing!"

"I heard that," Billy Lo said, as Susan paused at the door.

"And stop looking at my ass too!" Susan warned, looking over her shoulder before tapping on the door to signal for the guard.

"Come on now, Susan, a nigga locked up. What do you expect?" Billy Lo grinned and threw his hands up like he couldn't help himself. Truth be told, he couldn't. Susan's black slacks were hugging the hell out of her little tight ass and nice hips.

"I'll see you next week, Anthony." Susan shook her head and exited the room.

Delmont Player

Chapter 2

"I think the guys I got to snatch Charm's mother are dead—But, the move definitely did exactly what we needed it to do—Charm went straight at Nizzy," I said before going on to explain the next phase of my crazy game.

Now that blood had actually been drawn, and both Charm and Nizzy were at each other's throats, it was time to really turn the heat up another notch. That was why I'd negotiated something sweet with Roofy and brought my little brother—'Gooh'—and his man, 'Stinkface', into the mix. They were young, ruthless, and ready to fall for me if need be.

"I can respect everything that you're saying, Peanut," Zimbabwe interjected. "And seeing how far you're willing to go to exact your revenge proves just how treacherous you can be. But, this isn't as personal for us as it is for you and Billy Lo. So, I've to ask. Does any of these moves involve money? I ask because Little Dinky and I just came home and we aren't about to get caught up in a game that has nothing to do with us." Zimbabwe paused for a second. "I mean, we're going to represent Billy Lo, regardless. But, at the same time, we're trying to get back on our feet."

I smiled at Zimbabwe. I'd liked him from the moment we met. He just seemed like one of them older gangsters that you rarely encountered nowadays. He and Little Dinky's pretty boy ass. Shiddd, honestly, if it wasn't strictly business, Little Dinky's old ass could get it.

"Uh, everybody's going to eat," I assured, looking from Zimbabwe to Little Dinky. "I already got Nizzy's barber shop schedule. And my little brother got the blueprint on their entire East Baltimore operation."

"Yeah," Gooh spoke up. "I been copping weight directly from one of their lieutenants for a minute now. So, I know exactly where the trap house at. And that coochie wet!"

"What?" Little Dinky looked at Gooh, confused.

"That coochie wet just means that the lick is sweet—The guy's guides are down—He's wide open," I rationalized, shaking my head with a slight giggle, cutting my eye at my little brother. *Please don't start talking all that, 'popping a nigga's coochie shit,* I prayed silently.

"So, you've already been inside?" Zimbabwe questioned.

"Yep," Gooh nodded. "Several times."

"How many people inside? Where are the guns located? Who picks up the money? Who lives next door?" Zimbabwe started firing off questions rapidly.

"Huh?" My little brother looked at me. "Peanut, what's up?"

"Yeah, Peanut, what's up?" Zimbabwe turned his attention back to me. "What type of boy scout shit is this? Shorty talking about he got the blueprint, but he doesn't even know how many niggas are usually inside."

"Nah, it's not that kind of spot," Gooh argued, but I waved him off because I knew that Zimbabwe had come up during different times. He didn't understand these young boys the way I did. And he probably had less tolerance for both them and their lingo.

"Times have changed, Zimbabwe," I said. Sure, my little brother wasn't as quick on the draw. But, he was damn sure reliable and obedient.

"Yeah, well, I haven't," Zimbabwe retorted. "I don't walk into anything blind."

"Hmmph, okay," I considered the statement. "I can respect that," I added, nodding in agreement. Bravery was nothing without iron discipline.

"Respect what? He didn't even give me a chance to answer," Gooh defended.

"I shouldn't have to, soldier," Zimbabwe addressed Gooh. "It should be like second nature. You should already know what we're walking into and how we're going to walk out."

"Mannnnn," Gooh exclaimed, as if he was losing patience. But, I understood that as long as there were those who remembered what 'was', there would be those who refused to accept what 'is'.

"Listen," I looked from Zimbabwe to Little Dinky, "I know that y'all love and trust Billy Lo or y'all wouldn't be here. So, all I'm asking is that y'all trust my judgment. At least until I show y'all that I don't deserve that trust. I didn't just start doing this."

Zimbabwe stared at Little Dinky until he smirked and nodded. "We're in," he said. Once again, we were back in business.

We went over everything we knew in great detail, including anything that could possibly work against us. We saved a few good ideas that I knew would come in handy at a later date, and utilized all the information that my little brother provided. After that, I just opened the floor up to Zimbabwe.

"I got to tip my hat off to you, Peanut, I misjudged you," Zimbabwe admitted after a quick history lesson. "But, I can see why Billy Lo trust you. You been making some major moves to put yourself in a position to win. I like that."

"My daughter's father use to say—" I stood up to stretch. "To best your enemy, you have to—"

"Become your enemy!" Zimbabwe took the words right out of my mouth and completed my sentence.

"Exactly," I smiled. If he only knew the half of it! "So everybody's ready to do this, right?" I slowly scanned the room as everybody nodded. "Good, then y'all can start making house calls next week," I added. Billy Lo and I had put together a solid crew. I mean, they weren't the 'Four Horsemen—Black, Mumbles, Lil'Dray and D.W.—but they were definitely a force to be reckoned with.

***

"If it's a girl, I wanna name her after your sister," Ebony said as we laid in the bed watching 'Scarface' after I'd rubbed Intensive Care Vaseline all over her stomach, hips, ass and thighs. It was an old-school remedy my mother had taught me for beating stretch marks. "But, I'ma make her middle name, like, Jasmine, Jadah or J'nai."

"J'nai," I repeated, tracing what appeared to be the beginning of a black line running up the center of Ebony's belly. It felt strange to know that I was actually having a baby, especially since all the homies always joked about me shooting blanks. "I like that. It's pretty."

"I love you, Calvin," Ebony said, caressing my head.

"I love you too, baby," I tilted my head up to kiss Ebony softly on the lips. "Both of y'all," I added, gently kissing her on the stomach. A baby had to be the most beautiful and precious thing in the world. A straight gift from God.

"Oh, baby, look, watch this part right here." I said as Al Pacino went off on Sosa over the phone. "Hey! Hey! who the fuck you think you're talking to, huh? Your Fucking bellboy or something?" I mimicked Al Pacino, juggling my phone. "Tony, my motherfucking nigga, baby! Fuck Sosa!"

"Why you love this damn movie so much?" Ebony questioned, as I rewinded the part again.

"What cha mean?" I asked, not truly understanding the question.

"I mean, you watch this shit everyday," she argued. "So what is it that you love about Tony so much?"

"The fact that he never broke his own rules for those he loved or feared the most," I replied honestly. Because, throughout the entire 'Scarface' movie, Tony never went against the shit he stood for.

For a second, we laid there in silence, both lost in our own thoughts until my cell phone vibrated inside my pocket. Reaching into my pocket, I pulled out the phone and looked at the screen. When I saw the new 'Dummie Squad' code for 'Nizzy', I knew what time it was.

"Yo, I gotta go make a run real quick." I kissed Ebony on the forehead, showed her the phone and rolled out of the bed. She didn't ask no questions. She didn't have to; she already knew what it was.

"Be careful, Calvin," Ebony pleaded.

"You already know." I got dressed with lightning speed. Then I walked over to the dresser, grabbed my tone, and stepped out of the house on a serious mission.

Twenty minutes later, I was coming through the back door of our new trap-house on Gold Street. My niggas— Delvon 'Deli' Whack and James 'JuJu' Tanner—were already inside waiting. Odie 'O' Hill was up the street inside Ms. Candy's, playing his part. Nizzy thought that he was doing something slick by hitting JuJu's and Deli's phones with the 'old' Dummie Squad code for war. He thought that all of us would come running to Ms.Candy's spot. But a lot had changed. Codes and trap-houses were just a few of them. So, what Nizzy was about to learn the hard way was that he'd have his hands full fucking with us with this beef shit.

"How it look out there?" I asked, peeping out the window.

"It's a tinted out Blazer parked near the top of the block and a blue lemon hoopty sitting across from Ms. Candy's," JuJu explained.

I couldn't really see the Blazer, but the lemon stuck out like a sore thumb. Almost as if Nizzy wanted us to see it. "You sure that that's them?" I questioned, letting the curtain fall back into place. Nizzy was really underestimating us.

"I don't know about the niggas in the Blazer," JuJu admitted. "But, you can see Al-Qamar sitting inside the lemon clear as day."

"That's what's up," I said, wondering who the fuck was in the truck. "So, what are you thinking? Two, maybe three shooters?"

"Probably," Deli answered. "Ain't no telling though. It could be some niggas in the back that we can't see because of the tints," Deli added. "I don't think Al-Qamar here to put in no work though. He's probably just over seeing the hit. That's why he sitting down here watching."

"Right, right," my voice trailed off. I hadn't seen Al-Qamar since I chased Nizzy into the vestibule of his trap-house around on Warwick and got tasered by Lor'Homie's whore ass. "Go down the basement and grab that trash bag I dropped off Sunday real quick.

This Nigga Al-Qamar was really getting out of hand. First, the situation with me; then, the shit with Murdock. Al-Qamar was really feeling himself. But now, I was about to show him my teeth.

"You serious?" JuJu looked at me questionably.

"Yeah," I nodded. It was time to show these niggas something. "We're going to play this shit like them niggas ten deep up in that truck."

"Fuck you got in the bag?" Deli inquired, noticing how JuJu was staring at me with concern written all over his face. "Body parts?"

"Something like that." I winked as JuJu disappeared down the basement stairs.

JuJu appeared out of the basement two minutes later, lugging the trash bag over his shoulder before tossing it on the couch. "Wait til you see what this crazy nigga got, Deli." JuJu informed, stepping back.

"Don't pay him no mind, Dummie," I grabbed the bottom of the trash bag and used it to pour all the guns out. "You gonna love these joints."

"Uhhhh, shit, Dummie!" Deli exclaimed excitedly, snatching up the Knights Armament SR-25 Assault Rifle 7.62mm. "Where the fuck you cop this bitch at? This—that!"

"Who else? That crazy African nigga Ugun, Ugunoba or whatever his name is," JuJu said. "He's the only mother fucker moving this type of heavy metal."

"Nigga, are you going to grab one or not?" I questioned, picking up the Saiga-12 shotgun with the rotating bolts Ugun had been bragging about.

"I'm telling you, Dummie, something off about that crazy nigga," JuJu said, reaching for the 16-shot Smith & Western SW1911. "He always talking that white supremacist, recruitment, training and organizing shit."

I knew JuJu was right. Ugunoba was a weirdo. But, that nigga knew everything there was to know about guns, explosives, war preparation, tactical skills and government intelligence. You name it, and Ugun knew it. "Man, that's all that military shit in his head. But, yo solid, Dummie."

"I didn't say he wasn't solid," JuJu defended. "I said that nigga wasn't stable. Yo be coming through with them dumb ass, long dreads, jumping out with no shirts and shit on. That nigga be throwing me off. And why the fuck he ain't never got no damn shoes on?"

"Dummie ain't lying," Deli seconded, making me laugh to the point of tears. "Your man definitely off the chain. Especially when he gets to breaking down politics, domestic and foreign terrorism. You know this nigga had the nerve to tell me that the white man's greatest fear was 'genetic annihilation' or, as he put it, 'Black American'."

"Y'all better leave my man alone before I fuck around and put him on y'all!" I warned, unable to stop laughing, feeding the shotgun shells.

"That nigga know his firearm though. Don't he, man?" JuJu pressed on the thumb safety Ugunoba said a lot of people mistook for a lemon-squeeze.

"You already," Deli replied.

"Fuck all that! Are y'all niggas ready or what?" I asked no one in particular, cocking the shotgun as Deli toyed with the SR-25 like he couldn't wait to let that motherfucker go off.

"Let's do it." JuJu gripped the top of the .40 and slid it back to slip one into the head (chamber).

"Text O and tell him that it's go time," I instructed Deli before turning my attention to JuJu. "Me and Dummie got the Blazer," I continued. "As soon as you hear this bitch go off," I gestured towards the Saiga-12 shotgun in my hand, "run out there and let Al-Qamar have it. Get that bitch good too." I didn't like the way Al-Qamar was sitting out there stunting like he was a serious shot-caller or something, especially after that shit he and Lor'Homie tried to pull over east with Young Danny and Murdock. My niggas had been forced to crash into a police car and got arrested to escape possible death.

"I'ma wear that nigga out and meet y'all back at my aunt's house." JuJu nodded.

"I told O to post up outside, like, he's waiting for us to show up any minute now," Deli said.

"A'ight, break that phone up!" I ordered, remembering how the police had been using niggas' phones against them lately. "Now, let's go ring these niggas' bells," I added, praying that Nizzy and Lor'Homie were dumb enough to be inside the Blazer. I mean, I knew that—like all the 'Dummie Squad' originals—Nizzy and Lor'Homie were 'trained to go'. But I was hoping that at least one of them was thinking with their emotions.

We hit the back door on a mission. It was time to remind Nizzy why you never sent hyenas to hunt lions. In the dark alley, no words were exchanged between Deli and I. We just slipped into our angry-face 'Dummie' masks, gave each other a knowing look, and moved out to conduct our business.

Deli and I crept out of the alley into position across the street from the tinted-window Blazer and got down behind a parked car. O was already standing on Ms. Candy's front steps, anxiously looking up and down the block as if he was waiting for us.

"Go time, Dummie." I tapped Deli's leg before quietly beginning to move towards the front passenger's side wheel, with my heart pounding.

Deli stayed crouched down as I slowly eased up beside the wheel and peeped over the hood. After taking a look, I looked back at Deli and signaled for him to get ready. As he moved, I pulled both bolts on the Saiga-12 one time and got ready to work.

Once Deli eased as far as he could and nodded, I came up and sprinted around the front of the parked car, and ran right up to the back passenger side door as Deli broke around from the other end of the car, holding the SR-25 Assault Rifle waist-high a second before my shotgun exploded.

After the back window burst, I smashed the nose of the shotgun through the back window and emptied that bitch amidst screams and hollers. Then, I stepped back as Deli stood about five feet away from the Blazer with all his weight on his right leg, as he held the SR-25 'Scarface' style and aired the truck out. I knew whoever was inside didn't have a chance.

Then, I heard the sound of a cannon and looked up the block to see JuJu standing on the hood of Al-Qamar's lemon, dropping his nuts. JuJu fired shot after shot from the 16 shot Smith & Western SW1911 down through the windshield as Al-Qamar appeared to be trying to climb into the backseat.

Once the shooting stopped, I took off running. Nobody had to tell me that it was time to go. I just hoped nobody had to tell JuJu or Deli either, because I never looked back.

***

"Come on, Mr. Earl, hook a nigga up with one of them fine ass sisters of yours," Lor' Homie continued to talk trash to the owner of 'New Identity's Barbershop & Beauty Salon as he and Nizzy got their weekly haircuts. "That's the least you can do."

"And I'm doing this just because you always come to my shop and sit in my chair, right?" Mr. Earl questioned, laughing.

"Ain't no secret," Lor'Homie turned his open palms up. "Fair exchange ain't never been no robbery."

"Well, in that case, it may be time for you to find another barber," Mr. Earl exclaimed, still laughing.

"Man, Earl's sisters will run circles around you, youngster," Tall Jermaine spoke up. "They aren't them little girls you be chasing up and down the avenue. Them grown women right there." Tall Jermaine paused to scratch at his salt-and-pepper beard.

"Fuck outta here," Lor'Homie retorted. "Cuzzo, please tell these old, stiff niggas about me."

"I ain't got nothing to do with that fool!" Nizzy fired, making the entire shop laugh, as his ring-tone sounded.

"Damn, Cuzzo, I thought blood was more important than a barber," Lor'Homie said.

"Not when I'm getting my shit cut," Nizzy continued to laugh, reaching underneath the smock to retrieve his phone. "Wohh!"

Nizzy answered the call. "Yeah, what it do, Dummie? Huh? The police did what?"

"What's up, cuzzo?" Lor'Homie inquired curiously from Mr. Earl's chair, as the expression on his cousin's face instantly changed.

"Hold up, Cuz," Nizzy waved Lor'Homie off and jammed a finger into his ear, so that he could clearly hear and understand exactly what it was that one of their lieutenants was screaming into his ear. "Say it again now—What?—When this happen?—Fuck!—How many of them was it?" Nizzy questioned with blood in his eyes. "A'ight, we're on our way."

"What's up?" Lor'Homie and another soldier named Berry asked in unison, getting to their feet when Nizzy ended the call.

"I'll hip y'all in the car," Nizzy assured, not wanting to discuss family business in a room full of nosey outsiders. "But, we need to get around the way now!" Nizzy hopped out of the chair quickly.

"You know I'm not finished, right?" Tall Jermaine said, standing there, holding the running clippers as Nizzy snatched the smock off.

"Yeah, I know. Don't worry about it though." Nizzy dug into his pocket, pulled out a knot of bills and piled off three crispy twenties. "I'll come back later."

"Come on now, youngster. I can't have you running around the streets like that. Motherfuckers going to think that's my work." Tall Jermaine argued as the empty barber's chair slowly spun around in circles. "At least let me clear your neck and stuff up."

"A'ight, man, hurry up." Nizzy sat back down in the chair real quick as Lor'Homie and Berry looked at him like he was crazy. "Just hit my neck," Nizzy requested. He couldn't believe what he'd just heard. First, his cousin had cost them one of their most loyal soldiers by sanctioning a sloppy ass hit on Charm without his consent. And now, some crooked ass, plain-clothes cops had just jacked his shipment.

"I got you, youngster. Just—" Tall Jermaine began a second before the door of the shop flew open, and five plain-clothes officers stormed in.

"Baltimore City Narcotics Unit! Nobody move!" the first plain-clothes officer through the door demanded, pushing Tall Jermaine to the floor before pulling Nizzy out of the barber's chair.

"You hard of hearing, nigga?" another officer questioned, pressing a gun against the side of Lor'Homie's head. "Get your punk ass on the floor before I push your shit back!"

"Mannnnn, y'all niggas aren't no real police!" A light-skinned dude with only about a quarter of his bald head cut bucked. It was then that Nizzy noticed that all the officers were covered up for real. "Them badges fake ass shit! My father's a cop! I want to see y'all badge numbers."

"Somebody shut that bitch up!" the slim officer with the wicked limp ordered, pointing towards the light-skinned dude, as he walked over to flip the 'Open' sign to 'Close'; then he drew the blinds.

Another one of what everybody now realized were fake cops walked over to the light-skinned dude and smashed the butt of his gun into his mouth, knocking a few of his teeth out. "Anybody else wanna see some badge numbers?" The first officer who'd come through the door looked around as the light-skinned guy cupped his bloody mouth and tried to pick up his teeth. "Good." He signaled for his crew to continue.

Once the entire barber shop was under control, two of the gunmen went into the back to secure the beauty salon. Nizzy couldn't believe it. These had to be the same niggas who'd just jacked his shipment less than twenty minutes ago.

"A'ight, listen up!" the tall, slim, fake plain-clothes officer with the chrome Mosberg spoke up after the other two robbers in the back seemed to have gotten all the women in the salon to calm down and stop crying.

"This is a simple robbery. Officer Friendly here," he pointed to a short plain-clothes officer tooting two D.E.'s, "is going to run y'all pockets. Once that's done, we'll be out of y'all hair. So, just close your eyes and keep your head down and this shit will be over in no time. But, I'ma let you know right now—" He paused. "If any one of you niggas act stupid, I won't hesitate to split your wig, cut and dry. Got it?" Menacingly, he surveyed the shop. When nobody appeared to want to challenge him, he continued. "A'ight, shorty. Do your thing."

Nizzy, Lor'Homie, Berry, Mr. Earl, Tall Jermaine and everybody else in the barbershop complied as they were grabbed, pushed, threatened and even strip-searched by Officer Friendly, as he took money, phones, car keys, jewels and guns off them.

Nizzy watched closely as Officer Friendly moved slowly and methodically through the shop after stuffing the D.E.'s into his dip. He was opening shop drawers, upending couch cushions and going through coat pockets. He only paused to check for hidden objects in niggas' shoes and shit. Nizzy could tell that Officer Friendly wasn't new to the raid/home invasion style, barbershop robbery game. His movement was too calculated, too professional. So, Nizzy knew that they weren't fucking around with no amateurs.

"Aye, slim," the fake cop with the Mosberg signaled to another gunman as he went to stand by the door. "Dump that trash out and use that bag to get everybody shoes and shit. Especially *his* and *his*."

It was at that moment Nizzy realized that it may be a hit. Why else would the tall, slim nigga single him and his cousin out? *These niggas know too much*, Nizzy thought, peeking up for tell-tell signs that would reveal exactly who the stick-up boys were.

"Nigga, you got one second to put your face back on that floor or I'ma smash it in." Another one of the gunmen walked over with his gun aimed at Nizzy's head and stood over top of him. "It's not good to be sneaky, nigga."

Nizzy laid his head back on the ground just as the robbers came out of the back asking if everything was straight out there.

"Yeah, we're good up here," the tall, slim gunman replied, walking over to peek out the storefront window of the shop.

"Wrap that shit up back there and come on!" he commanded, gesturing with his head. "We're moving out in two."

The robber disappeared into the back again, only to return with his partner about a minute and half later with a clear plastic 'New Identity's duffle bag filled with handbags, cellphones and blow-dryers. He even had fake hair in the bag.

"We're clear in the back," he announced, quickly walking over to Mr. Earl's barber station to stuff some clippers and a few mirrors into the clear duffle bag. "We locked all them bitches in the bathroom," he added, checking the weight of the bag again, before slinging it over his shoulder so he could still maintain authority with his gun hand.

"A'ight, we're falling out," the fake officer who appeared to be calling the shots said, and everybody started moving towards the doors.

"It was nice doing business with you." The rent-a-cop who appeared to be starting his own barbershop and beauty salon paused after clearing out Mr. Earl's barber station to bow before backing up out of the shop, as the ring-leader stood guard at the door with the Mosberg.

"You folks try to have a nice day." The Mosberg-toting fake cop smiled and fired two shots above everybody's head, hitting the wall mirrors before running outside to jump into a waiting mini-van. Nizzy peeked up just in time to see the Mosberg-toting fake cop hanging out of the mini-van as he fired another shot through the storefront window, forcing everybody to cover their heads again as the mini van pilled off.

"Fuck!" Lor'Homie exclaimed, getting to his feet as the mini-van burnt rubber down the block. "I can't believe this shit!" Lor'Homie added, standing in the middle of the shop in nothing but his boxer briefs and socks.

"That wasn't no random lick, Cuz," Nizzy said, slowly getting to his feet, trying to avoid stepping on any of the broken glass that was now all over the barbershop floor. "Them niggas knew exactly who they were looking for."

"Somebody, call an ambulance!" the guy with his mouth bleeding all over the place pleaded, making his way over to the chairs to sit down. "Please, somebody, call the ambulance!"

Tall Jermaine checked on all the customers as Mr. Earl dashed into the back of the shop to check on his sisters and their customer. "Somebody, grab that towel over there," Tall Jermaine requested, walking over to the customer with the busted mouth and large knot on his head, after making sure nobody else was wounded.

"Uh, somebody's going to jail for this!" the guy with the busted mouth muttered.

"Somebody put them niggas on us!" Nizzy argued, dusting his clothes off as he thought about the phone call he'd just received barely a minute before the fake cops came through the door.

"I didn't even think about that, Cuzzo," Lor'Homie confessed.

"Why else you think they only took our shoes?" Nizzy looked at his cousin knowingly.

"Fuck!" Lor'Homie shouted. There were only a few other niggas who knew about the shoe move.

"Mannnn, they took my rope," Berry whined, ready to knock someboy out. "I just spent six bands on that bitch!"

"What?" Lor'Homie eyed Berry. "Nigga, you bitching about a chain? Fuck that chain!" Lor'Homie shook his head. "You can buy another one after your next fight."

"Yo, just go get the car so we can bounce before the police get here!" Nizzy ordered, looking around the shop. He'd never seen so many clueless niggas in his life.

Nizzy couldn't help but laugh. First, at the silly ass dude who'd got to faking and ended up losing a few teeth. Then, at Berry's dumb ass for crying about his bullshit ass cheap chain. And finally, at his cousin who had seemed to have no idea that his feet was bleeding all over the place as he paced back and forth across the glassy floor of the barbershop with one side of his fro-hawk finished.

***

Zimbabwe got out of the car and followed Gooh into the last standing Lafayette projects building. Being that the sucker who pushed weight for Young Danny and them lived on the third floor, Zimbabwe suggested that they take the stairs to avoid too much attention.

When they got to the apartment, Gooh knocked on the door exactly four times before pausing to knock twice, as Zimbabwe kind of stood off to the side out of the door.

"Who the fuck is it?" a voice fired from the opposite side of the door as the peephole got dark.

"It's me, Scooter—Lett-Lett!" Gooh replied, winking at Zimbabwe.

A second later, the locks sounded and a brown-skinned dude with long, overdue cornrows opened the door to let Gooh in. "You're early, homie." Scooter held the door open for Gooh, as Zimbabwe came around the corner. "Whoa yo! Who the fuck is this?" Scooter questioned, looking Zimbabwe up and down.

"Oh, this my man Oakie from up Edmondson Village," Gooh lied again.

"Come on, Lett-Lett yo, I told you not to bring nobody to my spot, Scooter complained.

"Yeah, I know, yo—That's my bad—But, bruh called me this morning trying to get a half of bird," Gooh said, knowing that Scooter was the type of nigga who valued profit over principle.

"Yeah, yo, but still—" Scooter eyed Zimbabwe, toying with his nose before addressing him. "So, you're tryna to get a half of brick, huh?"

"Yeah," Zimbabwe confirmed, carefully looking up and down the narrow hallway. It was easy to see that Scooter liked to get his nose dirty. "So, what's up, homie? You gonna invite us in or what? 'Cause I ain't trying to keep standing out here with all this bread on me." Zimbabwe held up the bag in his hand.

"I'm telling you, Dug, everything's everything," Gooh assured, as Scooter appeared to contemplate his next move. "You know I ain't going to just bring no anybody to you, homie. Oakie like family to me."

Scooter looked from Gooh to Zimbabwe again. It was easy to play big boy and take advantage of a naive young nigga—especially from a strong position of power. But, he wasn't so sure if he could run the same game on the older cat. "A'ight, homie, if you say he's cool, he's cool." Scooter nodded and stepped to the side to allow Gooh and Zimbabwe to enter the apartment.

"Listen though, I'ma have to make a call for the half because I didn't know you were coming, homie." Scooter locked the door and used to steel bars to reinforce it before following Gooh and Zimbabwe the short distance to the small kitchen table.

"That's cool," Zimbabwe replied. "You sure your people can move on such short notice though?"

"Ain't no question!" Scooter exclaimed, smiling as numbers began to roll around in his head. "Lett-Lett, you didn't hip your man to me?" Scooter looked at Gooh.

"Yeah, he's hip," Gooh said honestly, thinking about how much of a bitch Scooter was.

"Yeah, homie, if you want it, I can touch it," Scooter bragged. "You know a half gonna run you fifteen, right?" Scooter added, ready to tax Zimbabwe three extra bands. "So, if you can't cover that, I'm not even making the call."

"I got sixteen right here," Zimbabwe said, sitting the small 'Crown Royal' styled bag he'd walked in with up on the kitchen table. "Call your folks."

"Okay, Oakie." Scooter pulled the bag across the table. "I see you don't do no bullshitting," Scooter continued, pulling a chair out to sit down. "I like that."

"Hold up, Scooter," Gooh stopped Scooter from untying the bag. "What are you doing?"

"I'ma bout to count this paper," Scooter explained, moving Gooh's hand off the bag.

"So what! You think we're about to sit here all day and wait for you to count sixteen thousand dollars?" Gooh challenged. There was no way in the world that they could allow Scooter to open the bag. It would ruin their plans to lure Young Danny or

Murdock into their trap. "Fuck outta here!" Gooh reached for the bag again. He had to keep Scooter from looking inside the bag.

"Then I'm not making the call." Scooter began to get up. He wasn't stupid. He'd been moving weight too long not to make sure everything was on the up and up before he started making calls.

"Nah, it's all good," Zimbabwe reached for Gooh's arm. "If he wants to sit here and count sixteen grand, let him go right ahead. We got all day. Just as long as you make that call."

Gooh raised his eye-brow and looked at Zimbabwe strangely as he released his grip on the bag and watched Scooter sit back down.

Scooter carefully untied the bag, pulled the draw-string, and began to dump the stacks of fake money out onto the kitchen table. "What the—"

Zimbabwe cracked Scooter on the top of his head with a Glock 45 and slammed his face into the table. "Take this bitch in the bathroom, tie him up, and make him call Murdock and Young Danny!" Zimbabwe directed as Scooter's face bounced off the table a second before his body slid out of the chair and crumbled to the floor.

"Ahhhh," Scooter cried out, grabbing the chair, reaching for the table as Gooh tried to drag him towards the bathroom. "Come on, Lett-Lett, man!" Scooter pleaded, holding on to the leg of the table. "Don't do this."

"Let the table go, nigga!" Gooh ordered, yanking on Scooter's legs.

"Bitch!" Gooh let go of Scooter's legs and struck him. "I said let go of the fucking table!" Gooh struck Scooter again.

Zimbabwe watched Gooh drag Scooter into the bathroom before listening carefully to see if the neighbors had heard any of the commotion through the paper-thin walls.

Once he was sure the coast was clear, he began ransacking the small apartment. He opened all the dresser-drawers, tossed all the clothes out, snatched all the stuff out of the closet, flipped the bed, and pulled up the carpet. Finding nothing, Zimbabwe took one of the knives from the knife-set on the kitchen counter, and headed for the bathroom.

"Where we at?" Zimbabwe walked into the bathroom to see Scooter standing in the middle of the bathtub naked with his hands tied behind his back as the water ran. "He make the call yet?"

"Nah," Gooh shook his head. "But he's going to," Gooh added, smiling.

Zimbabwe stood back and let Gooh do his thing. He was curious to see how far the young boy was willing to go to accomplish the mission.

"Grab that phone out of his pocket real quick." Gooh gestured towards the pile of clothes on the bathroom floor. Zimbabwe handed Gooh the phone and waited to see what he would do next.

"Who you wanna call first? Murdock or Young Danny?" Gooh questioned, using a cord he'd gotten from somewhere to wrap around Scooter's lower calves and ankles before tying it into a knot.

"Come on, Lett-Lett yo," Scooter begged. "I haven't ever done you dirty."

"Okay, tough guy." Gooh stood up and stuffed one of Scooter's socks into his mouth. "Have it your way." Gooh kicked the back of Scooter's legs and let him fall backwards into the bathtub which—by now—was more than halfway full of water. Then he began trying to drown him in the tub. "Let's see how long you can hold your breath under water."

"Hmmph!" Scooter's eyes got big as he realized that he would have a hard time fighting to keep his whole body from being completely submerged under water. "Hmmphhhh—"

Gooh forced Scooter's head under the water, silencing him. Water splashed all over the bathroom floor as Scooter struggled and fought not to drown. "You ready to cooperate now, bitch?" Gooh questioned, snatching Scooter's head from under the water to stare into his eyes.

With his eyes bulging, snot running from his nose, and his chest rapidly rising and falling, Scooter nodded to let Gooh know that he would make the call.

"Here," Zimbabwe handed Gooh the kitchen knife. "I don't believe him, just cut his throat."

"Mmmmmm—" Scooter groaned wide-eyed and tried to wiggle free as Gooh accepted the knife, pushed him back underneath the water, and began repeatedly stabbing him in the head until the tub water turned reddish.

"You gonna do right, nigga?" Gooh pulled Scooter's head above the water and waited for him to collect himself. "What's up? You ready to do right now?" he questioned after back-handing Scooter to calm him down.

"Good," Gooh pulled the sock out of Scooter's mouth and used it to wipe away most of the blood now pouring out of his head wounds after he nodded. "If you play any games, I'ma kill you in here!" Gooh warned, tossing the bloody sock into the water.

"How much coke and shit you got up in here?" Zimbabwe tested the waters to see if Scooter had any more fight left inside of him.

"A couple ounces and about five bands," Scooter confessed without hesitation, keeping his eyes on the shiny knife in Gooh's hand until it went behind his back, out of sight, to cut the belt that Gooh had used to restrain him. "It's in the flower pot out on the balcony," Scooter revealed, rubbing his sore wrist after his arms were cut free. "I got two burners in a pillowcase in the corner of the closet too."

"See, was that so hard, nigga?" Gooh reached down into the bloody water and unplugged the bathtub stopper before cutting the cord around Scooters legs.

"Give him the phone, soldier," Zimbabwe urged, stepping forward to press the business-end of his Glock 45 to the side of Scooter's head. "Now you can either get Young Danny or Murdock over here or I can slump you right here, right now!" Zimbabwe suggested as Gooh shoved Scooter's phone into his hand.

"A'ight, man, a'ight," Scooter submitted, accepting the phone.

Scooter nervously dialed Young Danny's number. "He's not answering," Scooter confessed honestly.

"Let me see," Zimbabwe requested, and Scooter instantly showed him the phone screen. "A'ight, try Murdock!" Zimbabwe ordered, pushing Scooter's hand out of his face after confirming that he'd tried to call Young Danny.

Scooter called Murdock and tried Young Danny under Zimbabwe's watchful eyes. "Neither one of them niggas are answering," Scooter finally admitted.

"I'm sorry to hear that." Zimbabwe raised the Glock 45.

"You better text them niggas or something because you're running out of time!" Gooh fired, ignoring Scooter's scary look.

Scooter nodded and slowly began to text Young Danny and Murdock a coded group text about one of his regular customers wanting a half of chicken.

"Let me see it before you send it too, nigga!" Zimbabwe carefully read the text message before pressing the send button.

"Young Danny just texted back." Zimbabwe handed the phone to Gooh. "He's said he's on his way."

"That's what's up." Gooh broke the phone in half and flushed it down the toilet. "What type of car Young Danny going to be pushing?"

"A silver BMW with tints," Scooter said.

"You did good." Zimbabwe stepped forward and signaled for Scooter to put his hands back behind his back.

"Hold up, man!" Scooter complained in surprise as Zimbabwe forced his hands behind his back. "I did what you asked me to do," he argued. "Lett-Lett!"

"Be cool," Gooh instructed calmly. "We're just going to keep you on ice until we get Young Danny. Once that's over with, I'll let you go. That's my word." Gooh lied.

"Nigga, if you don't let me tie your hands, I'ma shoot you in your fucking head!" Zimbabwe warned when Scooter began to resist a little bit.

Once Scooter complied, Zimbabwe secured his hands and gagged him again. Then he sat him back down in the bloodstained tub and stabbed him in the chest until he completely stopped moving and his body laid still at the bottom of the tub.

"I thought you said if he didn't let you tie his hands, you were going to shoot him?" Gooh joked.

"Yeah, but I never said that I wouldn't butcher him." Zimbabwe laughed. "Now, let's check the flower pot and closet."

"Hold up," Gooh paused to look around before twisting his face up. "You smell that?"

"Hell yeah, man," Zimbabwe confirmed, covering his nose as the strong odor hit his nostrils. "What the fuck is that?"

"Ewwww yo," Gooh covered his mouth and nose, pointing at the bottom of the tub. "This bitch ass nigga shitted on himself." Gooh shook his head. "I'm gone."

Gooh couldn't move quick enough. Zimbabwe followed him out of the bathroom and pulled the door shut. "A'ight, look, you check the flower pot and I'll get the guns outta the closet. Then, we're going to sit back and wait for the kid Young Danny to show up."

"It'll be real nice if we can get him to call the rest of them niggas over here one by one," Gooh said, walking over to slide the balcony door open

"We'll see what happens when he gets here," Zimbabwe replied, stepping over the bed to get to the closet. It wasn't such a bad idea.

Zimbabwe was searching for the pillowcase when a loud noise and scream got his attention. Drawing his gun out of precaution, Zimbabwe peeped out of the closet to see Gooh looking over the balcony. "What the fuck was that?" he asked curiously.

"This silly nigga just jumped off the balcony." Gooh stepped back inside.

"Who?" Zimbabwe was confused.

"Scooter," Gooh revealed.

"Scooter?" Zimbabwe repeated, trying to gather his thoughts. It was then that he noticed the trail of blood leading from the balcony to the bathroom. *Shit!* he thought. *How in the fuck?*

"Did you hear what I said?" Gooh asked again, to be sure.

"Yeah, I heard you," Zimbabwe admitted as Gooh's words really began to register. "Did you find the money and coke?" Zimbabwe inquired. Now wasn't the time to panic.

"Yeah, but it's like it's stuck to the bottom of the flowerpot or something."

"A'ight, fuck it. Let's bounce!" Zimbabwe ordered, snatching the sheets off the bed before going over to the stove. There was no way in hell that he was risking his freedom for five grand and a couple of ounces of coke.

"Man, shiddd! I didn't do all this shit for nothing!" Gooh fired, rushing out onto the balcony to grab the flower pot. "I'ma get mine!" he said, coming back through the door, smashing the flower pot to the floor so he'd get to the money and coke as Zimbabwe used the stove to set the bed sheets ablaze.

Once the fire started to spread, Zimbabwe and Gooh exited the apartment cautiously. They split up and dipped down the back stairwell on the opposite side of the building. There was no way in the world that he was about to take a chance walking with Gooh while he looked like a fake ass gardener with dirt and blood all over his clothes.

Zimbabwe held his breath until he made it outside, past the crowd of onlookers now gathering near Scooter's shitty, broken-up body to the car. Then he exhaled and began to relax. "What the fuck happen up there?" he questioned, climbing into the car. "How the hell that nigga manage to get past you?"

"Fuck if I know," Gooh hunched his shoulders. "I thought he was dead."

"Yeah, me too. I put the knife in his heart like three times."

"I know. When I first saw the shadow, I thought it was you. Then I looked up to see this nigga running full-speed." Gooh explained further. "I tried to grab his ass. But I wasn't about to go over the balcony with him. So, I let his dumb ass go."

"Damn," Zimbabwe shook his head before leaning forward to see the smoke and fire now shooting from Scooter's apartment windows. "Somebody must be praying for Young Danny because he was a dead man today."

"Ain't no question," Gooh agreed. "So what now? You still wanna try and grab him?"

"Nah," Zimbabwe started the car and pulled off slowly so that he wouldn't draw too much attention. Little Dinky had told him a long time ago that when you started a fire, make sure that you didn't stick around to watch it burn. "We'll catch up with him another time."

Delmont Player

Chapter 3

"I got to be honest with you, Ock, I never liked the idea from the start." Tariq paused as Adnan blew a thick cloud of smoke into his face after taking a long puff of his imported Cuban cigar. "You should've told Charm that Nizzy still had your protection, and maybe this little beef wouldn't have gotten so out of hand," he added, waving his hand back and forth in front of his face. Since successfully beating cancer, Tariq really had a distaste for smoke, even if it was second-hand.

"We're not even sure if Charm's people are behind this mess. I mean, after all, they were hit too." Adnan took another puff of his cigar and pointed his finger at Tariq.

Tariq shook his head. "Ock, you know I don't care one way or the other. They're both *kafirs*." It was no secret that Tariq didn't have any love for non-believers. "All I'm concerned about are my brothers and our money."

"I say let the *kafirs* war it out," Rashid Salih spoke up. "Either way, it's a win-win situation. The loser dies, the winner expands, and we reap the benefits."

"True enough," Adnan nodded and melted back into the cool soft leather of his recliner before taking another puff of his cigar. "All the same, Ock, the idea that one of these *kafirs* has taken money out of my pocket just disturbs me."

Rashid Salih knew that Adnan could be as unpredictable as a volcano. So, he just remained silent and waited for Adnan to tell him the solution to their problem.

"Ock," Adnan finally broke his silence, "I want you and Tariq to keep an eye on Charm's little posse. Find out what they've been up to." Adnan paused again. "And if they're responsible in any way for our recent loss, then I want them nailed to the fucking cross."

"Enough said," Tariq said, grim-faced. "We're all over it."

Rashid Salih simply nodded and got to his feet. The order had been given. Still, he couldn't believe that Adnan had actually accepted Nizzy's story so easily. Why would Charm hit Nizzy's spot for a measly hundred grand? More so when—just the day before—one of his workers had been robbed and tortured! It just didn't make any sense. At least not to him. But, he decided to keep his mouth shut.

"And Ock," Adnan took one more pull of his Cuban cigar and mashed it down into the silver ashtray, "I want you to put Yah-Yah on Nizzy. Because, if he's playing us, I want to deal with him personally."

Rashid Salih smiled and followed Tariq from the office. That was the Adnan he knew. The one that never left anything to chance.

"Ock," Rashid Salih whispered, pulling Adnan's office door close. "What do you think about this kid Nizzy?" Rashid Salih continued when Tariq looked over his shoulder at him. "You think his confession is a sloppy cover up?"

"I don't know," Tariq replied honestly. "Insha'Allah, we're sure going to find out, though."

***

Nizzy looked out the window as they came over the Viaduct into the heart of East Baltimore in one of Lor'Homie's thots' car. It was time to show his teeth and mash the gas on Charm and them for the stunt he was certain they'd been responsible for pulling at the barbershop last week. The situation had him so vexed that he'd lied to the plug and told them that Charm had strung him for a hundred bands.

"Are you sure it was him?" Nizzy questioned Berry, turning his head just enough to see into the back seat as Lor'Homie floated towards the projects.

"Yeah," Berry nodded. "Cock-eyed Willie and I followed him to house near Douglas Court."

Nizzy, Lor'Homie and Berry drove around until they spotted Young Danny's brand new 2016 silver BMW he had gotten after Lor'Homie tore his Q50 up tucked off behind an old Nissan on Dallas Street.

Lor'Homie slowly backed up, and Nizzy carefully surveyed the block. "Pull in behind that green Honda." Nizzy pointed, looking for any sign of Young Danny, as his cousin turned onto the block and parked.

"So, how you wanna play this, Cuzzo?" Lor'Homie questioned, shutting the car off.

"You already fucking know!" Nizzy said, ready to get his hands dirty. "When this nigga come out, I'ma walk him down. Plain and simple."

Lor'Homie smiled. He loved when his cousin got on his straight gangster shit. "Now, you're sure this nigga didn't see y'all?" Lor'Homie questioned, turning completely around in his seat to look into the back.

"Positive," Berry assured. "He was too wrapped up in the lil' bitch."

"You didn't see exactly which house he went in?" Nizzy asked, looking around for any telltale sign of which house Young Danny may be in.

"Nah," Berry admitted. "But, it's definitely right here somewhere," he added, pointing back and forth between the identical houses.

"All we got to do is wait his ass out," Nizzy said. "He's definitely coming back to get his whip."

"That's what it is then," Lor'Homie exclaimed, turning back around in his seat. "We're gonna sit right here and lay on this nigga until he shows up."

Nizzy and 'em waited for what seemed like an eternity When night began to fall, Lor'Homie was starting to get restless and think that Young Danny had either decided to spend the night or he'd already bounced by the time they showed back up. He knew that there was no way in hell that Young Danny was still up in no thot's house fucking.

"That nigga ain't build like that, Cuzzo, trust me. I done freak off with him a few times. He squirting as soon as he touch the pussy," Lor'Homie assured, trying to convince Nizzy that Young Danny was long gone.

"That nigga still in one of these houses—I just know it." Nizzy said, determined to wait Young Danny out.

"There the nigga go right there!" Lor'Homie fired, breaking the silence as Young Danny came strolling out of a house down the block, on the opposite of the street, all smiles—damn near two hours later.

"This dumb ass nigga man," Nizzy referred to Berry spotting Young Danny.

"Shit!" Berry instantly realized his fuck up. "We followed him in from the other end of the block."

Nizzy and 'em watched closely as Young Danny walked backwards, talking shit for a moment to some fine ass chocolate bitch waving from her doorway. "Get on him now, Cuzzo!" Lor'Homie spat.

Nizzy flipped the hood up over his head and pulled the draw-string to conceal most of his face. Then he removed the Calico M950 from the front hoodie pocket, eased out of the car and started across the street.

"You better call me, Danny! I ain't playing either!" Nizzy heard the female yell to Young Danny before he laughed and said something about her good pussy. "Boy, don't be saying that in front of my neighbors!" the female cautioned.

Young Danny turned around, laughing to hit the button on the alarm system on his car as Nizzy limped out from between the cars, instantly opening fire.

Young Danny froze up. But only for a split second. Then he attempted to run back to the house. However, hot rocks from Nizzy's Calico ate his side and back up. It wouldn't have done him any good because the bitch had already slammed her door shut, anyway.

"Ahhhhh!" Young Danny cried out in pain and began to pull himself across the pavement towards the tone that had fallen off his waist, as Nizzy walked up and stood right over top of him as he rolled onto his back.

Nizzy yanked the hood off to reveal his face. He wanted to look right into Young Danny's eyes before he said good night. "Any final words, nigga?"

"Yeah, you better not miss!" Young Danny threatened as Nizzy aimed the Calico at his head.

"I won't." Nizzy lightly tapped the trigger twice, and watched as a couple of rounds smashed into Young Danny's face and skull. Then he limped back out into the middle of the street, as Lor'Homie came to pick him up. "Go, go, go!"

Lor'Homie didn't waste another second before burning rubber down Dallas. He knew that they had to get the hell out of East Baltimore quick.

"Oh shit yo, look!" Berry hollered, spotting Murdock coming towards them on a dirt bike as they turned the corner. "That's Murdock."

"Man, run that bitch over, Cuz!" Nizzy ordered, and Lor'Homie complied without a moment's hesitation. ,

Murdock saw the approaching car swerve in his direction, and tried to slow down so that he could cut in between two parked cars. His calculation was off, though. So, he ended up crashing into the front bumper of one of the cars to avoid being hit. Murdock was going so fast that the impact knocked all the wind out of him.

"Back up, Cuz! Back up!" Nizzy urged, impatiently turning around to look back after his cousin ran into a parked car. After barely having avoided Lor'Homie, Murdock was now trapped between two cars, penned halfway under his dirtbike. "His dumb ass stuck!"

Lor'Homie threw the car in reverse and backed up as the sound of untangling, twisted metal and broken glass became evident.

Murdock heard Nizzy's familiar voice, and saw the car backing up. So, he quickly used what little strength the parked car hadn't knocked out of him to push the dirtbike up off of his leg, so that he was able to crawl as far underneath the car as possible.

"Shit!" Nizzy barked, frantically ramming his right shoulder into the passenger's seat door frame. "The fucking door's jammed," he added, knowing that they didn't have much time.

"Mine too!" Berry exclaimed, trying his door.

After leaning sideways to try and kick the door open, Nizzy stuck his arm out of the window, aimed the Calico in Murdock's direction and emptied the rest of the extended clip, and Berry followed suit.

"Shoot the tires out, Cuzzo!" Lor'Homie encouraged, as bullets ricocheted off the dirtbike and car Murdock was hiding underneath.

"That bitch shielding himself with the bike." Nizzy aimed at the tires, but the clip was empty.

"Hold on," Lor'Homie said, noticing that his cousin was out of bullets and Berry wasn't killing nothing but some car tags. Lor'Homie backed the car up, turned the wheel, and stepped on the gas. The car went forward and rammed into the car that Murdock was hiding underneath. Lor'Homie backed up and repeated the same move until the car was smashed up against the curve, and he was sure that Murdock was crushed beneath it. Then he backed up, steered the bent up car straight and took off as fast as he could.

"That was some straight movie shit!" Berry said, looking out the back window for any sign of life as Lor'Homie drove off to put some distance between themselves and the crime scenes.

"You haven't seen nothing yet," Nizzy assured, knowing that they were about to really fuck the city up. "Run the next five lights!" Nizzy added, looking into the rearview mirror. He could hear the sounds of sirens in the distance.

Chapter 4

"Trust in the Lord with all your heart, and lean not on your own understanding. Who knows why God does what he does? Nobody! But, I'll tell you this. God will continue to guide, strengthen, and comfort us all in these troubling times. Yes, Daniel was a good child. Yes, Daniel was a good son. Yes, Daniel—"

"Damn!" I snapped, walking out in the middle of Young Danny's eulogy, sick to my stomach. I could not believe that Nizzy and Lor'Homie had the balls to attend my nigga's funeral service. I swear I wanted to get up right then and there, inside the New Antioch Baptist Church, and straight punish them niggas. Push their wigs back for the death of my man. But, no matter how livid I was, disrespecting Young Danny's family or Bishop Orlando Wilson's church wasn't an option. Especially since when I'd been locked up, we use to clown dudes for involving civilians in street business. To me, it was some bitch shit. You couldn't fade your man. So, you go get at one of his innocent family members.

I took a few deep breaths and looked up and down St.Paul Street. The game was about to get so cold that niggas were going to feel the hurt to their fingertips! "Damn!" I fired again, feeling guilty. I mean honestly, I knew that I wasn't totally to blame for Young Danny's death. That was just how the game we were playing went. Nevertheless, I knew that had I not botched the hit on Nizzy, my nigga would still be here.

"What's up, Dummie?" JuJu came out of the church, interrupting my thoughts.

"You already know." I eyed him. "I'm fighting like shit with myself right now," I confessed. "I'm thinking about reaching out to the nigga Big Al and his man E-Don real quick, so that they can come grab these niggas as soon as the funeral is over without making a scene," I added, knowing that them niggas wouldn't have a problem getting their hands dirty, especially if the price was right.

"Nah, Dummy," JuJu shook his head. "You know you can't do no shit like that with Young Danny's family around."

"Especially his mother," I agreed, smiling for a moment, remembering how crazy Young Danny was about Mom Dukes. "She deserves some peace after losing her baby to the streets."

"Yeah, plus that nigga Young Danny might haunt a nigga for doing something stupid at his funeral."

"Facts," I agreed. "But I can't lie, Dummie—When I saw that nigga Nizzy and that bitch Lor'Homie squeezing into the row across the aisle from us, I almost jumped up and wore them niggas out."

"Me too," JuJu admitted.

"I just wished I'd listened to my gut back in the day when it kept telling me that this nigga was a snake." I shook my head. "But, I was like, nah! I thought I was tripping. I mean, we all know how egotistical Nizzy is, and how bad that nigga wanted to be on top. But I never thought that it would come down to this. Even after all the bullshit, I never thought that we'd actually have to clip Dummie's nuts."

"I told you, Dummie," JuJu reminded.

"Yeah, you did, but I wasn't trying to put no bread on Dummie's head. He was still my brother. And I'd honestly thought that we could co-exist.

"Yeah, I'm hip," JuJu continued. "But, once that nigga starting to hang with niggas you use to hang with, and fucking bitches you use to hit, I knew that it was only going to be so long before he came for the thorn. Dummie always wanted the crown."

I stood there with JuJu and drifted back off into deep thought. I knew that war was unpredictable. I knew that each man conducted it according to his own laws. But, for Nizzy and Lor'Homie to show up at Young Danny's funeral after they were responsible for his demise was going too far. Even hood politics—as I liked to call them—stipulated that.

After the funeral service was over, everybody began to spill out of New Antioch to get ready for the burial. Deli, O, JuJu and I stood on the church steps and watched as Young Danny's brother,

Murdock and four other male family members carried his black and gold trimmed casket towards the hearse. For a second, I wondered if I would've been happier to see my nigga get judged by *twelve*.

"If there's really a heaven for a 'G', I can guarantee you that that young nigga going to be there," Deli said, making everybody laugh. It was so true. Young Danny was in a class all by himself.

"What's good, Charm?" I turned around and came face to face with Nizzy as he walked up followed by Lor'Homie and their latest two followers, Berry and Cock-eyed Willie. JuJu instantly began to move, but I waved him off.

"Be cool, Dummie," I instructed, putting my hand on JuJu's chest. "Now's not the time," I added, knowing just how bad he wanted to get at Nizzy.'

"Yeah, JuJu, be cool, listen to your Father," Lor'Homie taunted.

"Father!" JuJu repeated, laughing. "Y'all niggas the only ones getting *soned* out here. It's big difference between a Dummie and a follower."

"Yeah, just like it's a big difference between an apostle and a disciple," Nizzy retorted with a dumb ass, silly grin on his face. "But look, like Charm said, this isn't the time nor the place to be giving out lessons. We're here to lay our men to rest."

"Man, fuck you niggas!" JuJu spat through clenched teeth, like he was trying to control himself.

"Why the fuck y'all niggas even here?" I questioned, glad that Murdock hadn't noticed Nizzy and them yet because between Young Danny's death and the attempt that they'd made on him, I wasn't so sure that he'd be able to maintain his composure.

"It's still honor over everything, Dummie. And I'm still more than my brother's keeper. So, we just came to pay our last respects." Nizzy smiled and continued. "You see, unlike you, when I kill a nigga I love, I always pay for the coffin and wake. Which reminds me—Who do you want me to give the money for your funeral to? Miss Peaches or our baby mother?"

I stared Nizzy right in the eyes as I stepped into his personal space and spoke with pure venom. "Your days are numbered, bitch, believe that. And I promise you that I won't miss the next time."

"Man, Dummie, come on. Fuck this hoe ass nigga." JuJu grabbed my arm.

"All this over a bitch who was dying to give me the pussy." Nizzy threw his hands up and stepped back, smiling.

Deli must've sensed my next move because he whispered, "Calm down" into my ear before correcting Nizzy. "Nigga, you know this shit is about a lot more than some pussy."

"Well, I guess now it is," Nizzy admitted, backing down the church steps slowly with Lor'Homie and them in tow. "But whose fault is that? I mean, after all, you can't display your wealth and then cry when niggas come to get it. You taught me that."

"What?" I took a step forward and reached for my tone. But Deli grabbed my wrist and reminded me of exactly where we were, as Nizzy and them continued to make their way down the church stairs. "You better count your blessing, nigga! You too, Lor'Homie—bitch!"

"Likewise!" Nizzy replied, as Lor'Homie grabbed his crotch and shook it at me.

"You still got the same number, Nizzy?" I questioned.

"Why?" Nizzy appeared curious.

"As a matter of fact, don't worry about it," I smiled. "Just keep an eye on your Instagram and Facebook page, nigga!"

"Yeah, whatever, nigga!" Nizzy retorted before turning around and disappearing into the crowd of well-wishers.

"I swear I wanted to let them niggas have it right here!" JuJu fired with his eyes still on the crowd.

"You're not the only one," Deli seconded. "Disrespecting my nigga's funeral with their presence. And did you see Berry and Willie fat, cross-eyed ass?" Deli twisted his face up in disbelief. "Like, when these niggas get crazy? All of a sudden they're tough guys."

"Yeah, overnight tough guys," O assured.

"I'm telling you, Dummie," Deli added, shaking his head. "It's only so much fuckery that a young nigga can take."

"I know, don't even worry about it though—We're gonna see them niggas again," I said, feeling Deli's pain. "Right now, let's just worry about laying Young Danny to rest."

We followed the caravan through the city streets until we reached the cemetery located on North Avenue, near Greenmount. That nigga Young Danny was East Baltimore to the end. By the time they lowered Dummie's casket into the earth, the whole squad was in tears. It hurt like shit to know that my nigga was gone forever. *I'ma paint the city red*, I thought before silently vowing to seek revenge against all those responsible for my nigga's death, as one last soldier tear rolled from my right eye down my cheek.

After the burial, we hit the road, posted some 'rest in peace' shit on Faceoook and Instagram, and headed on over to Murdock's mother's house near Old York and Cater to turn up. Before long the Henny, Hydro, and Heineken had us all lit and bent out of shape, talking shit and selling death to each other.

"Fuck that shit, Dummie! Let's just go over there and run down on everything moving," JuJu spoke with a drunken slur, waving his tone around in the air. "Nizzy, Lor'Homie, everybody 'cause you niggas playing!"

"Man, somebody get that gun from that silly nigga before he fuck around and hurt somebody!" I said.

"I'm good, Dummie," JuJu assured, and nobody else moved. "I know exactly what I'm doing," he added, aiming the tone at the basement door.

"I don't care if you know what you're doing or not," Murdock spoke up. "If that tone go off in my mother's house, I'm fucking you up."

"And I'ma jump in it," O added his two cents.

I looked around and shook my head. It was hard to point fingers when you lived a life of sin. I'd ride for any one of my niggas, lose or win. "Ohhhh Dummie, these niggas want some smoke," I encouraged.

"They don't want that smoke, Dummie," JuJu retorted, making everybody laugh, and I knew it was going to be a long night.

***

Nizzy and them tailed Murdock, Deli, O, JuJu and Charm to an East Baltimore row home. The plan was to wait until night completely fell, and then run up in the spot with guns blazing. Nizzy had Berry followed Charm and them to two bars and a weed-strip. So, he knew that they'd be wasted before the night was out. The only problem seemed to be the fact that the streets were still live as shit. People were everywhere. To make matters worse, a gang of lil'niggas had already walked up on the car, asking twenty-one questions.

"Man, you see these lil'niggas?" Berry questioned, looking across the streets as two of the lil'niggas patiently observed their every move. "We're gonna fuck around and have to do these lil' niggas too."

"Yo, I don't think this shit is such a good idea," Cock-eyed Willie confessed from the passenger's seat. "Did you see the way them lil' niggas were looking all around inside the car?"

"What you think, Cuz?" Nizzy looked to his cousin. He wasn't paying Berry or Cock-eyed Willie's jumpy ass any attention. He was only concerned about what his cousin thought.

Lor'Homie thought for a moment. He knew that his cousin didn't trust East Baltimore dudes anyway. As far as he was concerned, they were all a bunch of snakes trapped in an internecine struggle. That's why they were constantly losing. Because a house divided against itself could not stand.

"Fuck them lil' niggas, Cuzzo!" Lor'Homie looked at him with his face all twisted up. "We been sitting out here all day waiting to spank something."

"Already," Nizzy agreed. "But I ain't feeling these niggas moving all up and down the block, clocking the car and shit."

"Cuzzo, you sweating them lil' niggas?" Lor'Homie questioned, concerned. "I bet you any amount of money that if I jump out with this tone, them lil'whores break. They don't want no work for real. They're doing the same thing we use to do when somebody we didn't know pulled up on our block."

"Yeah, but still, there's no telling who these fools are," Berry interjected. "What if they try to warn Charm and 'em?"

"Then, they're getting it too!" Lor'Homie said. "Just like you or anybody else who try to get in my way is getting it!"

"Come on, Cuz. Chill, cut yo some slack," Nizzy pleaded honestly, knowing how reckless his cousin could be at times. "He's just a lil' concerned."

"So what you wanna do, Cuzzo?" Lor'Homie questioned, staring at Nizzy impatiently. He didn't give a damn about Berry's concerns. "You wanna bounce?"

"I don't know." Nizzy took a deep breath and tried to think of something that would make everybody happy. "I mean, niggas gotta do something."

"Yeah, because when Charm and 'em sober up, it's going to be business as usual. And them niggas aren't going to miss a beat.

Nizzy knew his cousin was right. Charm and 'em were definitely going to be out for blood. But, that didn't mean that they should act without precaution. However, before he could explain, Deli's childhood girlfriend—Bucky Love—pulled up and Deli came out of the house and jogged over to her car, opened the passenger side door, and climbed in before leaning over to kiss her.

"Oh, I'm getting this nigga now!" Nizzy bragged excitedly.

"Nah, Cuzzo, sit tight," Lor'Homie appealed. If anybody was putting in some work, it was going to be him. Nizzy had dropped his nuts the last time when they hit Young Danny. "They're pulling off anyway."

"Fuck is you doing?" Lor'Homie questioned, slapping the back of Berry's seat aggressively to get his attention. "Follow them dumbass!"

***

"Didn't I just tell your crazy ass not to come over here?" Deli argued as Bucky Love slowed down for a stop sign. "It's too much shit going on right now!"

"Delvon, please," Bucky Love rolled her eyes. "I'm not trying to hear that."

"Man, you geeking." Deli shook his head. He knew Bucky Love was upset with him for ducking her calls. But, it was for her own good. He'd go crazy if something ever happened to her, especially on account of him.

"No, negro! You the one geeking!" Bucky Love fired, making a left. "I been worried sick about your dumb ass. But do I get a call? Noooooo," Bucky Love emphasized. "Do I get a text? No. Shiddd, if I hadn't call your mother, I'd have not even known if your ass was alive or not." Bucky Love reached over and mushed Deli. "Ooooo, I can't stand you sometimes!"

Deli loved Bucky Love to death, but he wasn't in the mood for her shit today. She did the same thing every time somebody she knew got shot or killed. Started texting his phone all day. Posting on his page. Sending him all types of positive quotes from the Honorable Minister Louis Farrakhan her Nation of Islam father loved to mail to her from prison. Going on and on about knowledge, wisdom and understanding.

"Why don't you just get out of the streets, Delvon?" Bucky Love looked over at Deli seriously. "You really need to wake up and get your act together. You're out here throwing bricks at the penitentiary for what? Some crumbs? Some Negroes who don't respect the game no more? I remember when we were young and my father and your brothers were in the streets. There were rules and codes. And guys honored them. But now, these Negroes out here today—I don't even know what to say about them."

Deli remained silent. He knew that Bucky Love was right. They both knew first-hand just how wicked and evil the streets could be. They'd watched it destroy the lives of so many people they loved. Still, Deli understood that regardless of how hip Bucky

Love was to the game; regardless of how gangster she was at heart, she would never truly understand that he was cut from a different cloth. So, even when all the conditions of the game began to change the outcome or dudes' actions, he remained true to who he was and everything he knew.

"Boy, are you listening to me?" Bucky Love questioned, taking her eyes off the road again.

"I'm listening, man, damn!" Deli lied, hoping that would shut her up. The truth was, Nizzy and 'em had murked one of his men. And there was no way that he wasn't going to settle the score.

"I hope so because your mother ain't got no money to bury your black ass. And I damn sure am not paying for it!" Bucky Love said. "You hear me?" she asked, popping Deli upside the head.

"Yeah," Deli eyed Bucky Love in frustration. He was about to tell her to stop putting her hands on him. But, he knew that she suffered from a bipolar disorder and wasn't trying to get into it with her, especially while she was already on one hundred. "I said, I'm listening."

"I don't care nothing about your shitty attitude, Negro." Bucky Love exclaimed. "A lot of shit going on in the world. Police killing us! The system destroying families and shit. And you Negroes wanna be out here helping the enemy!"

Deli opened Bucky Love's glove compartment and started looking inside, as she continued to sound like a life coach.

"Don't be going through my shit like you pay no car notes!" Bucky Love fired, reaching over to slap Deli's hand before closing the glove compartment after stopping at the red light. Deli shook his head and took a quick look into the rearview mirror. He just couldn't win with her. Now, he understood why his family loved her crazy ass so much. She was the only one who could honestly handle him. "I know this motherfucker see that the light done changed." Deli cursed at the driver of the white Ford LTD in front of them. "Hit the horn!" Deli leaned over and laid on the car horn. "What the fuck are they doing? The light is green."

"I think that's the police," Bucky Love confessed.

"What?" Deli said. "The police?"

"Yeah, the police," Bucky Love confirmed. "This the third time I done saw the car. It was across the street from Murdock's when I picked you up. Then I saw it follow us. But it cut off near Saratoga and Howard Street. So, I figured they were done. Now, they're in front of us."

"Why the fuck you didn't tell me that?" Deli inquired, wondering who'd put the police on him.

"You the gangster, Negro," Bucky Love laughed. "You suppose to be on point."

Deli was about to hit the horn again when the LTD began to drift forward. Then, the reverse tail lights lit up and the LTD came slamming into Bucky Love's front bumper.

What the fuck! Deli thought, unbuckling his seatbelt, ready to whip somebody's ass. "You see that shit?" Deli asked in shock, about to tell Bucky Love to pull out her iPhone and record, when the back doors of the Ford LTD opened up and he saw two masked men exited with large weapons.

"Oh shit! Get down!" Deli warned, pushing Bucky Love's body down as he dove across her body, simultaneously going for his tone. The two shooters ran up from both sides of Bucky Love's car and opened fire. All Deli was focused on was Bucky Love's safety, as bullets tore through the frame of the car and sent pieces of debris everywhere. Deli knew whoever it was wasn't playing. He couldn't believe he'd allowed himself to get caught down so bad slipping.

Deli heard the familiar clicking sound of an empty gun outside the car and came up firing. He wasn't about to go out like no bitch balled up in Bucky Love's car.

One of the shooters jumped up on the hood of the car and began firing through the windshield with no regard, hitting Deli in the legs, chest and stomach, tearing his flesh up as he continued to scream for Bucky Love to stay down, and he bust back blindly, praying that she didn't get hit.

What seemed like minutes passed before the passenger's side door came open and Deli felt himself being yanked from the car.

"Ahhhh," Deli cried out in pain from the burning sensation of the fire-balls now inside his body as blood poured from his wounds.

"Nah, bitch. Don't cry now." Deli could barely make out Lor'Homie's voice, as he dragged him out onto the street and used the collar of his shirt to lift his dangling head up off of the ground and issued two life-ending head shots.

***

By the time we got to the hospital, it was in an uproar. There were police and news reporters everywhere. Everybody wanted to be the first one to get the exclusive story as to what had actually gone down. But, of course, we already knew what was what, and who was who. We were just trying to show some respect to Deli's family before we rushed out into the streets and murdered everything moving. Because there was no way that Nizzy and them were going to trash Deli like that and live to talk about it.

"They killed my baby!" Deli's mother was going off as tears poured down her face. Everybody in the waiting room was trying to console her to no avail. I didn't know what to do because it was obvious that she didn't want us there. I really just needed to holler at Bucky Love to get the full spill.

Social media was saying all kinds of dumb shit. Talking about how Deli had just left a funeral and how lucky the female in the car was, and so on.

"Why is he still here?" Deli's mother questioned, looking around before eyeing me across the waiting room. "Why are any of them even still here?" she asked no one in particular, looking around the waiting room again. "Get the hell out!" she ordered, storming across the room towards us. "Get out!" she screamed. "Please just leave us alone." Deli's mother began to break down again as family members grabbed her and pulled her into a loving hug.

"Calm down, Ma," Deli's older brother walked her over near the soda and snack machines. "Yo, I think it'll be best if y'all bounced, homie," Deli's eldest brother suggested.

"That's what's up," I said, understandably.

"They shouldn't be here!" Deli's mother barked, attempting to get at us again.

"I know, Ma," Deli's brother squeezed her tight, and began to gently rock her back and forward and rub her back.

Bucky Love saw what was going on, and offered to walk us out. In the hallway, near the elevators, she told us what happened and exactly what Deli's last words were before he closed his eyes forever.

"Oh, it's on with these niggas!" Murdock was ready to drop his nuts once he learned that Nizzy and them had been camped outside his mom's house.

"Look," Bucky Love said, "I know y'all going to do what y'all gotta do. And I ain't about to try and stop y'all because y'all know Delvon was my life." Bucky Love paused. "But, don't do what them Negroes did." Bucky Love shook her head. "That was some real sucker shit! Shooting at him while I was in the car! Had Delvon not been thinking so quick or didn't love me so much, I probably wouldn't be here right now."

"What are you saying, Bucky Love?" I asked, confused. "Are you asking us not to see niggas behind Dummie?" I stared at her curiously.

"Of course not!" Bucky Love retorted. "I want them suckers dead for what they did to my baby," she admitted. "All I'm saying is, individual responsibility leads to collective accountability. So, when y'all handle that shit, handle it like men."

"I hear you, Bucky Love." I turned to leave. It was getting hard to remain moral when the game you were playing was growing increasingly immoral everyday. "I hear you."

Chapter 5

Over the next couple of weeks, Charm and 'em had Nizzy and Lor'Homie under constant attack. They were coming from so many angles that Nizzy began to wonder if they'd called in some reinforcement because his soldiers were falling left and right. But Nizzy wasn't losing no sleep. After all, Baltimore had more than enough Dummies willing to die for his cause. So, just as quickly as they fell, Nizzy and Lor'Homie recruited more to replace them.

Lor'Homie and O ran into each other near O's babymama's house and ended up in a Wild West style shoot-out. JuJu used some 'Squeegee Boys' to ambush who he believed was Nizzy at a red light after he'd slapped his female cousin—Jaxkey—and tried to run down on him up Whitelock. However, it wasn't until Charm released the video footage of himself and Murdock blowing Butta's back out on Facebook and Instagram that shit got crazy.

"I just ain't feeling it, Cuzzo," Lor'Homie eyed Nizzy like he was soft. "You're going to have niggas looking like bitches."

"So?" Nizzy said. Sometimes his cousin just got on his last nerve with all the super thug shit. "Let them niggas think whatever they want to think. It's too hot to be fucking with them niggas right now. We aren't even getting any money. What if niggas go to jail?"

"Mannnn, Cuzzo, all that shit a part of the game." Lor'Homie replied. "So what are you going to do? Kiss this nigga Charm's ring? Ask Safe Streets to set up a cease fire?" Lor'Homie couldn't help but laugh. "This wild nigga drugged your girl and posted video of himself and Murdock gutting her. And you out here trying to call it quits. I can't even believe you're considering that shit. You're out of your fucking mind, Cuzzo."

"You always talking, but you rarely listen, Cuz!" Nizzy challenged. "Ain't nobody say shit about talking to Charm's bitch ass!" Nizzy fired. Only the nigga who couldn't stomach the beef asked for a sit-down. "The only thing I want from Charm is his life—Especially because of that hoe shit he did to Butta." Every time Nizzy thought about Nizzy drugging Butta and sexually assaulting her, he wanted to kill him. But, the constant back and forth just wasn't good right now.

"Them niggas' luck eventually gonna run out. And that's when it's game over. But for now, we need to let the dust settle."

"What about shop?" Lor'Homie questioned. "Fast money done already started slowing up."

"Berry and Cock-eyed Willie can hold shit down while we get out of town." Nizzy saw Lor'Homie considering his words and knew what he was thinking. "We're not ducking nothing, Cuz. We're just taking precautions," Nizzy eased his mind, knowing how stubborn he could be when his pride got in the way. "That way, we don't make no costly mistakes."

"And when we get back, we can give these niggas the blues?"

"I wouldn't have it no other way," Nizzy replied.

Lor'Homie nodded. What his cousin was saying was beginning to make a lot of sense. "Let's go party then, Cuzzo."

"So, where do you want to go?" Nizzy questioned.

"I don't even know," Lor'Homie paused. "But, we damn sure aren't going nowhere near New York or D.C. I done had enough of this cold weather. I'm trying to go somewhere where I can enjoy myself."

"Miami, nigga," Nizzy smiled, shaking his head. "Ain't nothing down there but sunshine, beautiful beaches and bad bitches."

"I like the sound of that," Lor'Homie admitted honestly.

"Miami, here we come then." Nizzy made a quick U-turn and headed straight for the BWI Airport to book a flight. He wanted them to be on the next thing smoking out of the city.

"Hold up, Cuzzo, we got to hit the outlet so we can get fresh," Lor'Homie said, rubbing his hands together. He was ready to travel. He'd get back to all the Bodymore Murderland foolishness when they got back.

"We can get fresh when we land."

"Shiddd," Lor'Homie balled his face up. "They aren't gonna to have nothing but Baltimore Ravens shit down there. I'm trying to represent the city to the fullest. I'm talking Baltimore Orioles, Maryland Terps, and Ravens Jersey's Charm City hats, all that!"

Nizzy just nodded. His cousin was right. If they were going out of town. They had to do it big, Baltimore-style. "A'ight," Nizzy agreed. "But, after we get fresh, we're gone," Nizzy said. He was ready to do him. Especially after all the shit with Butta.

"Already." Lor'Homie fell back, thinking about all the fun they were about to have. He planned on fucking everything moving down south.

***

"Wohh, what's up, Dummie?" JuJu's voice echoed through the speaker of my phone when he finally picked up.

"Yo, where you at, Dummie?" I checked the rearview mirror before tossing my phone up on the dashboard.

"Why? What's up?" JuJu sounded concerned.

"I'm being followed!" I turned left and checked the side mirrors to see if the dark color Sedan stayed on me.

"Man, don't start tripping again." JuJu laughed. He'd been fucking with me lately about my paranoia.

"I'm telling you, Dummie. I'm fucking being followed!" I declared. I knew I wasn't tripping. The car had been on me for the last thirty minutes. "I think it's Lor'Homie and 'em. I'ma bring them right to you."

"Nah, chill." JuJu got quiet for a moment. "Listen, let them niggas follow you for a minute. I'ma call Murdock and text you when we're in position. That way you can bring them bitches right to us."

"Bet." I ended the call and continued to drive around on all main streets, never allowing the car to get too close or box me in. "Game time, bitch," I said to myself, checking the rearview mirror to make sure Lor'Homie and them were still on me when JuJu texted me a picture of the gas station on North Avenue near Eutaw. I smiled and headed in that direction.

Spotting Murdock and JuJu sitting in the back of the gas station, I pulled in slowly and quickly hopped out. Then, I dipped inside the service station before Lor'Homie and them could pull up and get out.

"Where y'all ice cream at?" I questioned the store clerk, keeping my eyes on the huge circular mirror hanging above the counter.

"Check the last freezer." He pointed, watching me like a hawk.

I grabbed more ice cream than I realized and walked back over to the counter. "How much?" I questioned, using the mirror to watch my back as I pulled out a knot and gave the store clerk too much money.

Just when I was beginning to wonder what the fuck was taking Murdock and JuJu so long to go berserk on Lor'Homie and them, I saw the reflection of the car pull up right outside the service station door before two plain- clothes white boys climbed out with badges around their necks. *Fuck!* I thought. *Police!*

"I'ma grab a soda too," I said, quickly dipping over to the cooler machine. Carefully removing my tone, I stuck my hand inside the freezer as if I was reaching for a soda, dropped the tone behind a row of sodas and came out with a Pepsi before walking back to the counter, nervous as shit.

"Will that be all?" the store clerk questioned.

"Yeah, that'll be all for him," one of the white boys said, flashing his badge to the store clerk before addressing me. "You mind coming with us, Mister Johnson?"

"'What?" I played dumb. "Man, I ain't going nowhere."

"You don't have a choice," the second white boy said, pushing me up against the counter to pat me down before placing me in handcuffs.

"This is harrassment!" I complained, looking at the store clerk. "You see this man! I didn't do shit!"

"I don't see nothing," the clerk said, picking up a magazine off the shelf to bury his face in.

"Yeah, I heard that!" I mean-mugged him as the white boys marched me out of the service station to the waiting car. "This some bullshit!" I yelled, looking across the gas station parking lot at Murdock and JuJu before being forced into the back seat and driven off. At least now, them niggas knew that I wasn't tripping about being followed.

"You wouldn't want your friends to know that you work for us now would you?"

"Work for who?" I laughed because it was actually funny. "What would make you think that I'd ever work for or even with the police?"

"Well, for starters, the nine hundred grams of Fentanyl, fourteen-thousand in cash, and four unlicensed firearms we confiscated inside one of your drug houses," the federal agent said, trying to scare me for the umpteenth time in about two hours.

"That's definitely not enough." I looked around the new interrogation room without a care in the world because I knew for certain that they had absolutely nothing on me. First of all, the so-called house she was referring to was one of Nizzy's. And secondly, there was no way for them to place me in the house.

"Are you sure about that?" the cute little Indian-looking agent asked. "We got our ways, you know!"

I was already up on the new Federal 'Strike Force'. It was composed of local, state and federal prosecutors. The Baltimore City Police Department Gang Task Force, Maryland State Police, DEA, FBI, Homeland Security, the Bureau of Alcohol, Tobacco, Firearms and Explosives, and the U.S. Marshal Service. I also knew about their new 75,000 square feet of office space in Southwest Baltimore, and their little 'snatch and grab' tactic program that targeted so called high intensity drug-trafficking areas and dealers under Carilyn Cosby's direction.

The problem was when they grabbed me, and I finally realized who they actually were. I didn't know whether to take it as a warning or a wake-up call. Sure, they were talking about a bullshit ass house raid. But, honestly, they weren't saying nothing. So, I just kept my mouth shut and listened because I knew the game and played it well.

The agents went on and on about Mexican and Dominican drug suppliers I had no idea existed. And some upper echelon of Baltimore's so-called gang leaders who they believe 'exert near-complete control' over the supply and distribution of heroin, Fentanyl, cocaine, and marijuana in the Baltimore region. I wanted to laugh at that. Maybe that was true for some jail shit. But most of the gang members I knew in the streets were fucked up, broke or crumb-snatching. They weren't eating in the streets unless you were talking about how they were eating each other.

"Like I said, that ain't enough."

"'Oh, it better be. Otherwise, you're looking at an easy twenty years." The cute little agent continued.

"You got me fucked up if you think you can flip me, shorty," I exclaimed. "I mean, I'll admit. You're sexy as fuck! But not that sexy, baby. And although I've never had the pleasure of sleeping with an FBI agent, I can assure you that nothing you've got beneath that skirt is that good."

"I may make your friends think otherwise." She smiled, and I couldn't do nothing but smile also. This bitch was treacherous.

"I doubt it. My squad more loyal than the Griffin Twins [Shaquila and Shaqeem]. And they know that even if I had a hand tied behind my back, I would never have a problem carrying my own weight—Win, lose or draw."

"I can make the local paper read differently!" she threatened.

"Yeah, but how safe you think you're gonna be once they find out what you did while I'm doing my time?"

"Are you threatening a federal agent, asshole?" Her partner shot to his feet.

"Let me tell you something, young boy," she waved her partner off, "if you think your guys are loyal, take a shot at the FBI and see how that turns out for you. I dare you. Not only are we backed by the biggest gangs, we're also the definition of loyalty."

"Yeah, well, I don't give a fuck how big and loyal the Feds are. You'll never turn me into a rat, shorty." I stared at her sternly.

"Is that so?"

"Ain't no question!" I declared wholeheartedly.

"Yeah, well, I got to tell you, Mister Johnson, there have been many gangsters that sat exactly where you are sitting and said the same thing. How else do you suppose we got on to you? You name them. I've broken them."

"I don't care!" I yelled, tired of all the games. "As a matter of fact, either call my lawyer—Elizabeth Franzoso—or arrest me. Because, I'm done talking." I sat back in my chair. There was nothing else to talk about. I knew that they couldn't link me to Nizzy's trap-house, unless it was for a robbery. I also knew exactly what they were doing. But the little psychological warfare tactics didn't work on a vet like me. So, I knew that no matter what happened, in the next few hours, I'd either be booked on a bullshit ass charge, or I'd be back out on the streets telling the squad about the games these bitches were beginning to play. One thing was for sure though: I now had the blessing of knowing that we had the feds' attention.

Chapter 6

I am doing this for us, I thought, looking at the photograph of my daughter as I sat outside of the El Pie del Caballo (The Foot of the Horse) House of Ink. It was time to go sink my claws deeper into Roofy's mind, body and soul. Of course, I'd never been with a woman before. And no woman worth her weight wanted to honestly exchange her flesh regardless of the reason. But I was on a mission. And Roofy was a major piece in the game I was playing. And play I would.

I took one last look at my daughter's photo, swallowed my pride, climbed out of my car, smoothed my blouse out before making my way into the shop. The same little, shade-throwing bitch from the previous visit was behind the mirror-covered counter, giving me the evil eye. But I just ignored her and requested to see her so-called sister. Roofy had already confessed about their little fling after I allowed her to eat my pussy the last time I was at the shop.

When Roofy appeared, she couldn't do anything except bite the corner of her glossy lips and stare. I knew I was killing 'em softly. In a loose fitting orange blouse, black hip-huggers, and some open-toe sandals. I wasn't rocking much jewelry. Just some small gold hoops earrings, a few diamond rings, and a blue diamond ankle bracelet that my mother had given to me for my eighteenth birthday.

"You gonna invite me back or stand there gawking all day?" I questioned, cutting my eye at the counter girl.

"We don't allow animals in the shop." The jealous little Mexican bitch behind the counter let her true thoughts slip out before covering her mouth.

I couldn't help but laugh. However, honestly, if I wasn't on a greater mission at the moment, I'd have drugged the bitch up in there. Because one thing I didn't tolerate was basic, bum bitches coming for me.

Roofy said something in Spanish that sounded like 'Shut the fuck up'. But I wasn't sure. The only word that I did know was *Puta*.

"Right this way, sexy." Roofy held the black-beaded curtain to the side, as I smiled and slowly made my way around the counter.

"You gotta learn how to train your lil' sister better." I snapped my claws at the little Hispanic bitch and made her jump as I switched past. "Messy bitches always cost you customers."

This time Roofy led me down the dimly-lit, photo- plastered hallway past all the tattoo rooms to some secret stairs. "What's this? Your lil' pussy palace?" I questioned, after we ascended the back stairs that led upstairs and spilt out into a brightly lit, colorful checker style room that instantly reminded me of a Rubik's Cube.

"Something like that," Roofy smirked, making her way over to sit on the arm of a couch. "I do love pussy," she added, gesturing towards my skirt.

Envisioning future success against all those responsible for the death of my one true love, and all those who benefited from his fall, I carefully began to unbutton my blouse. Once that was done, I stared into Roofy's eyes and lowered the blouse off of my shoulders, revealing my hard nipples. Then, I took off my sandals and slowly slid the hip-huggers over my hips and let it fall to my feet before stepping out of it.

Roofy took me in for a moment as I stood before her in nothing except a pair of snow-white, Victoria's Secret lace panties and matching red bottoms. "Turn around for me," she instructed, and I quickly complied. "Slowly," she ordered, and I obeyed. I guess she liked to be in control.

"Black women have the most beautiful bodies on the planet earth."

I twirled around slowly, letting Roofy get a real good look at the meal she was about to have the privilege of eating. "Come over here," Roofy pointed to the space between her legs and waited. I smiled at her seductively before confidently making my way towards her.

"I love the way your hips move, Mami," she disclosed, almost in a whisper, reaching her hand up to gently touch my cheek. "I wish I had a body like this."

I stood there, in between Roofy's legs, and allowed her to slowly run her soft hands up and down my body, pausing to caress me in certain areas.

"Open your legs!" she commanded, and I felt a chill go down my spine as she hooked her fingers underneath the waistline of my panties and ripped them off. "Wider!" she added, tossing my panties to the floor before running her warm hands over my hips, down around my legs, and up the inside of my thighs as I complied.

I could feel my pussy juices beginning to leak as it throbbed, opening and closing with a mind of its own. "Ooooooh baby!" I sighed, placing the heel of one of my red bottoms up on the edge of Roofy's couch to give her more access to my now hot, wet pussy.

"Damn Mami, that pussy dripping." Roofy appeared to be impressed by the juices flowing over her fingers as she teased my clitoris. "It taste good too," she confessed after licking the palm of her hand and sucking the juices off of her fingers. "Almost as good as it looks."

I grabbed Roofy by the back of her head, pulled her mouth to my breasts, and told her to tease my nipples. Then, I watched carefully as her long, pretty tongue shot out and rolled back and forth across my nipples as she continued to gently play with my clitoris and finger-fuck me.

"A tongue-ring, huh?" I said when Roofy pushed my breasts together and I saw the silver horseshoe on the tip of her tongue as she left a trail of saliva from my nipples, down to the middle of my belly button. "That's new."

"I only wear it on special occasions," Roofy said, smiling up at me. Now, keep your leg just like that, okay," Roofy requested, using three fingers to stretch my pussy wide open. I just bit my bottom lip and nodded. "I don't want you to move."

When Roofy made contact with my pussy and started eating or more like devouring it, it was over. I was no more good. And I mean, I'd had my pussy eaten by some serious plate-cleaners. But it was obvious that this bitch knew all the secrets to eating pussy. I especially loved the way she used her tongue to make it feel like she was tying my clitoris into a knot. No nigga had ever eaten my pussy that good. By the time I pried Roofy's head from between my thighs, she had eaten me into a convulsion.

"Hold up!" I pleaded, pushing Roofy completely onto the couch. "Give me a second," I requested, standing in front of her on shaky legs, breathing like I'd just finished racing Allyson Felix, with streams of cum and pussy juice trickling down my inner thighs.

"Uh, I gotta fuck you," Roofy suggested, standing up to remove her clothes. "But first, you're gonna show me if that pretty little mouth of yours is good for more than manipulation."

Roofy wasn't the baddest bitch I'd seen naked. But she was far from the worst. She had long, pierced nipples and one of those phat, puffy looking pussies that I'd always secretly admired.

Roofy sat back down on the couch, leaned back boss- style and threw one of her legs over the armrest. "You know what's next, right, baby?" Roofy reached between her legs and teased her own clitoris. "It's time to put that pretty little mouth of yours where the real money is at."

I licked my lips and stared at Roofy's pussy for a moment. I'd never tasted any pussy besides my own. But honestly speaking, deep down inside, I'd always wanted to. Most women did. I took one of the cushions off the couch, carefully placed it on the floor between Roofy's leg, and slowly sank to my knees, finally about to see just exactly where her large back tattoo ended at.

First, I did a smell test. Shiddd, revenge mission or not, I wasn't about to eat no funky pussy. Then I just enjoyed the sight, taking in all the details. Roofy's pussy lips sat out like a pair of pouty lips. And her clit kind of reminded me of the tip of a chilli pepper, though not as red. I had never seen a pussy up so close.

Not even my own. Honestly, it was turning me on. I mean, shiddd, I might as well enjoy myself!

I thought about all the things I'd loved done to my pussy when I was being eaten, and went in head first like a soccer star. Yeah, I'm not going to even lie. I went to work on Roofy's pussy. I wanted to eat all the fight out of her, and suck all of the sense out of her head. I wanted to have the bitch so wrapped around my finger that she wouldn't question nothing I said or did.

I took my time eating Roofy's pussy because there was only one thing that could truly control both men and women alike— Bomb ass sex! In other words, world-class head and premium pussy. Intentionally making smacking nosies as I slowly licked up and down in between Roofy's pussy lips, I paused to blow on her clit before using my tongue to slowly trace the yellow dragon tail tattoo that was literally covering her pussy. I could tell that Roofy was enjoying herself because her head kept falling back with her eyes closed the way mine did when a nigga was eating my pussy or ass right. Plus, she kept pulling my hair, locking her legs around my head, and twisting and curling all kinds of ways as she came right in my mouth.

"Mmmmhhhh," I moaned, tasting Roofy's essence for the umpteenth time, as she arched her back and came in my mouth again.

"Hold up, shit! Hold on. Si, Mami, right there! Right fucking there," Roofy cried out, as her eyes rolled back into her head. "You gonna make me—" Roofy just started groaning, threatening to fuck the shit out of me.

After Roofy came, we fell into what Roofy referred to as the '72'—An old variation of the '69' wherein she inserted three fingers into my ass to loosen me up as she began to eat my pussy again. "I got you, Mami," Roofy gasped, slapping me on the ass before going back to work, finger-fucking and tongue-fucking me out of my mind.

"You ready to see if I can make you tap out, Mami?" Roofy questioned, holding my ass cheeks apart so that she could easily lick me from my pussy to my asshole as I continued to eat her pussy.

"Yes," I managed, ready to get fucked. Roofy's head was good. But, a bitch like me needed to be dug out.

Roofy directed me to the bed and walked over to what looked like a treasure chest. I crawled up on the bed and got comfortable. If Roofy honestly thought that she could tap me out, it was going to be a long night. If I wasn't good at nothing else, I was good at going the distance. They didn't call me 'Sweet Pea' for nothing.

"Now, it's time to see if you can take some dick." Roofy turned back around and—I swear to God—this bitch had a snake between her legs. But I refused to let her see me sweat. Instead, I just threw my legs back, rubbed my clit to open my pussy up and told that bitch to come to 'Momma'. Besides, it had been a minute since I had the bottom knocked out of my pussy anyway. When Roofy crawled across the bed and began stuffing me like a turkey with what appeared to be about twelve inches of plastic dick, I had to look down in disbelief as it slid in.

"Sssssss," I could feel my pussy stretching open and I loved it. "Get it, baby," I encouraged, knowing that by the time Roofy finished with me, I'd probaby be walking funny—If I was walking at all.

***

Billy Lo was loving general population. He was finally able to move around and stretch his legs a little bit. Billy Lo had ended up on C-section. This wasn't actually a bad thing at all, especially for well-known gangsters and jailhouse celebrities. Niggas with clout or status like Billy Lo usually ended up on A-section. Right across from the City Jail's Intake Center where they housed the most dangerous inmates in one of two cells. Motherfuckers like Marcus 'Moon' Alexander, Calvin 'Disco' Leigh, Robert 'Ceed' Crowder and Little Clyde Burrell. Billy Lo had Shaneeka greasing the palm of the young, clown ass guard who ran the tier on the 7 to 3 shift. So, he didn't want for absolutely anything. Cellphones, weed, food, information, and so on! From what the clown told Billy Lo, he was 'affiliated'. How and why, Billy Lo wouldn't ever understand. Whatever the reason, all the clown loved to do was: stand at Billy Lo's cell door, name-dropping and telling everybody and their mother's business. Including that of his so-called homies.

Billy Lo had thought the game was fucked up when he first went home. But the jail was even worse. You had young boys running around like straight up, old dope-fiends. Guards claiming to be 'bullet-proof'. Females knowing too damn much. And old heads doing too little. Yeah, they spoke highly of the old laws. But none of them had the heart to enforce them. It was crazy. Everything was watered down. Gangsters wanted to be rappers. Everybody was walking around with their pants hanging off their asses. Rats were gang-banging and some more shit. Billy Lo remembered when the jail wasn't nothing to be played with. When only certain types of dudes wore their pants off their asses. When certain sounds was the sound of battle. Now, it was just niggas playing. Billy Lo knew that all it took was the right nigga to get shit back in order.

Billy Lo was sitting on his bunk, listening to his cell mate gossip about the latest stabbing. Although he hated niggas 'that weren't ever there' when shit went down but somehow always 'managed to know everything', he sat there and listened as if it mattered. It was the price he was willing to pay since the sucker agreed to not only hold and hide his cellphone and knife, but also swore he'd take the charge if either one of them were found during a shakedown. Honestly, Billy Lo wanted to tell him to shut the fuck up and stop dick-riding. But he knew that most lames were like ladders. They could take you up or down. It all just depended upon how you used them. "Billy Lo!"

"Yeah," Billy Lo looked up to see the clown who ran the tier. "What's up?"

"You got a visit, homie," the clown said, trying to sound cool.

"Bet." Billy Lo stood up and stretched.

"You ready now?" the clown asked, standing around.

"Nah, give me a minute to get myself together."

"Already, I know you about to do you." He smiled. "I'ma hit the door anyway." He continued, "Your pass will be on the desk 'cause I'ma bout to go run back over to S-section and finish fucking with this lil' rookie bitch."

Billy Lo brushed his teeth, double checked his appearance, threw on some sandalwood cologne and hauled ass out of the cell, happy as shit to be saved by the visit.

When Billy Lo got to the visiting room and saw Shaneeka stepping through the threshold killing it in some leggins' and 6-inch heels, all he could do was smile. It was days like this that made him miss the hospital ward.

"Hey, baby," Shaneeka smiled. "How you doing?"

"Fine now," Billy Lo replied, licking his lips as Shaneeka blushed. "Hold up! Let me take a look at you." Billy Lo requested before Shaneeka could sit down. "Turn around," Billy Lo smiled. "Damn!" Billy Lo said, shaking his head. Shaneeka was the definition of 'Bad'.

"I didn't know that you were coming up here today. I thought you had to work." Billy Lo spoke as they took their seats.

"So what? You want me to leave?" Shaneeka questioned, standing up as if she would leave.

"I wouldn't mind seeing all that ass again. I mean, don't go." Billy Lo smiled and slowly looked Shaneeka up and down. Her pussy was so phat that it didn't make any sense.

"Muh-unh," Shaneeka smirked, sitting back down.

Billy Lo shook his head and started updating Shaneeka on everything. He couldn't lie, though. He loved Shaneeka's sassy side. He could still remember when they first met. She was still dealing with some East Baltimore lame from Zone 18 at the time. But once he laid that Park Heights word and dick game on her, it was curtains.

". . . So that means that your March court date will stay the same, right?" Shaneeka questioned, trying to understand exactly what Billy Lo was saying.

"More than likely," Billy Lo replied. "I mean, the state has the right to appeal it to the Administrative Judge. But the speedy trial shit is hard to get around. So, I'll be surprised if they overturn the trial judge's decision."

"Well, I just hope that they don't push the court date back."

"You and me both," Billy Lo seconded sincerely. "Because I'm ready to get this shit over with, one way or the other."

Chapter 7

I entered the room as silent as the wind and stood still for a second to be sure that I hadn't been seen. Then I eased across the room to the hospital bed where Billy Lo was laying, and removed the revolver before firing four shots, after which I snatched the sheet back to survey my work. Lo and behold, the person lying in the hospital bed was actually me—Myself! I found it eerily scary as though it was an out-of-body experience.

"What the fuck!" I stumbled backwards into a small table next to the window and busted my ass. It took me a second to recover and stand up. The endless beep brought my attention to the flat-lined heart monitor.

I stepped back up to the bed and shook myself. "Get up!" I shouted. "Get up!" I repeated, but it was no use. The entire left side of my face was missing, and my chest was caved in.

"Nooooooo!" I shot up in the bed frantically, feeling my face and chest. For a moment I didn't realize where I was until I heard my phone vibrating. *Shit!* I thought, taking a deep breath, running my hand over my face again to double check if it was there.

"Wohh!" I said after reaching over to pick up the phone.

"Wohh shit!" A voice cracked in my ear. "Where the fuck you at, fam?" '

"Huh?" I looked at the phone, lost for words.

"*Huh* shit, man! You can hear, nigga!" the voice fired. "Where the fuck you at?"

"Who the fuck is this?" My mind was still trying to catch up with my body.

"*Who is this?*" the voice repeated. "It's your cousin, nigga!"

"Oh shit!" I jumped up out of my bed with my mind working over. "Slate?"

"Yeah, nigga, Slate! Your big cousin. You remember now? You were suppose to have your little ass down here to scoop me up today.

"Damn!" I looked at the clock on the nightstand. "You downtown already?"

"Where the fuck you think I'm calling you from?"

"My bad, fam, I was sleeping," I admitted, sliding my leg into a pair of balled up, wrinkled True Religion Jeans. "Where you at right now?"

"'Mmmmh, hold on for a second," Slate requested before I heard him talking to somebody, asking for the name of the establishment he was in as I continued to put my clothes on. "I'm at the Black Starbucks on Uath Street," Slate revealed.

"I'm on my way," I declared, hung up and quickly finished getting dressed. I wondered why my mother hadn't woke me up before she left. Then I remembered that she actually had. My dumb ass had somehow fallen back to sleep. I washed my face, gargled some mouthwash, hit the safe for some cash, slipped the tone into my pocket, picked up my car keys off the dresser, and was gone in 60 seconds.

When I pulled up in front of the *Seven Stars* on Uath Street, Slate was standing outside in front of the store, brushing his hair, shooting his game at a fine ass, heavy-set chick who seemed to be loving it. *Look at this bluffing nigga*, I thought, shaking my head. *He thinks he still got it*. I double parked and jumped out of the car.

"Nigga, if you don't come on," I fired, bringing an end to Slate's old-school ass game, "I'ma leave your dumb ass." I walked up behind my cousin.

It had been damn near three years since Slate had left the streets and ended up with juvenile life for the shit with Shawn Stanfield's bitch ass behind his sister. "My bad, shorty, but everybody's waiting on him." I turned to the female and apologized. "Plus, I know you aren't feeling his old ass rap game anyway. So, look, just put your number in my phone and—"

"Excuse me for a second, baby," Slate held up a finger, grabbed me by the arm, and pulled me off to the side. "What the fuck is you doing, fam?" Slate questioned with muscles and veins popping out all over his body. "I'ma bout to slide to shorty's spot and beat that pussy up."

"Man, that fresh outta juvy game not that strong." I laughed.

"What you wanna put on it?" Slate challenged.

"Man, your mother and everybody waiting on you." I waved him off.

"I know," Slate admitted. "But I just seen them last weekend. Right now, I'm trying to get some pussy." Slate stole another look at the thick female.

"Come on, man, you know I'ma get you some pussy," I argued, thinking about how much he use to be on Butta back in the day. "I got something nice for you too."

"Yeah, well, you can get me some more pussy later," Slate exclaimed, smiling as he brushed the deep waves all over his head with the brush in his hand. "I'ma fuck shorty now."

"You don't even know that bitch!" I fired, peeping over his shoulder at big girl again. I couldn't lie: the thick bitch was super bad. One of those fly big girl type. Still, there were too many diseases floating around. "She's not about to just give you no pussy."

"Shiddd, she's gonna give me more than that!" Slate assured. "And for your information, nigga, I been knowing shorty for a minute now."

"Yeah, right," I shook my head. "Where you know her from, nigga? You been locked up over two years."

"Juvy, nigga", Slate smiled. "Yeah, she was out there soldiering like me. Getting ready to touch down and cause hell."

"Yeah, well, all that Bonnie and Clyde shit gonna have to wait. 'Cause I done already told Aunt Joyce that I'll be dropping you off. And I'm damn sure not about to wait around like a lame for you to get your dick wet." I walked back towards the car.

"Shiddd, I haven't ever been shy, fam—I can do my thing in the back seat," Slate explained, signaling to his jailhouse jump-off to come on. "Just drive slow," Slate instructed, following me to the car.

"You better be lucky you're my cousin," I walked around to the driver's side, shaking my head as I opened the door. "And I swear to God, if her pussy stinks—"

"Oh nah, shorty shit good," Slate whispered, opening the back door for his little hot-in-the-ass gangster bitch. "I smell-checked it on the bus."

I took the long route to Slate's mother's house so that he could do his thing. And I won't lie—A few times I was forced to take a peek in the back seat. I mean, I'd hit a few big girls myself. So, I knew how wet they got. But man, I swear I couldn't tell the difference between shorty's mouth or pussy without stealing a look. Because they were both super soaked!

My dick was so hard that after I dropped Slate and his gangster bitch off, I shot around to one of my side pieces house and blew her back out real quick before texting everybody about Slate's release. After all, he was basically the founder. So, I knew that they were going to want to set him out.

"When motherfuckers start going to school this late?" Slate questioned, looking at the new yellow & black G-Shock watch on his wrist as I pulled into the Coppin State College parking lot so he could finally meet Ebony.

"This a college!" I reminded him, looking for a parking spot after spotting Ebony's black Acura Legend parked near the front entrance. It had been a couple of hours since I'd picked Slate back up from his mother's house. By now, we'd hit the mall, gotten fresh, hung out with the squad, and updated each other on everything that was going on. Especially the static Nizzy and I were having. I had even taken Slate to see Butta.

"I hope you're not planning on going in," Slate said lazily, as I continued to search for a parking space. I knew he wasn't feeling no pain after turning up with JuJu and them.

"Nah, we're good." I laughed, glancing at the clock on the dashboard. "Ebony doesn't even know we're here. But she should be on her way out soon. She texted me and told me that all of her classes were over at four."

"What! Are we picking her up?"

"Nah," I located an empty parking spot and quickly backed in. "She got her own wheels."

"Oh, you getting it like that, huh?" Slate teased as I threw the car in park.

"Don't worry, fam. Once your shop set up, you gonna be getting like that too." I saw Ebony coming out of the building talking to one of her professors and a couple classmates. "There go my baby right there."

"Which one?" Slate looked at me.

"The fine one with all the books," I replied proudly with my eyes locked on Ebony. I didn't know if it was the college campus, the confidence or the books. Maybe it was a combination. Whatever it was, something about seeing a sexy, educated woman stunting across campus just did it for me.

"All of 'em fine with books."

"The finest one right there with the eagle head crocodile belt and matching heels." I pointed Ebony out.

"Yeah, fam," Slate began nodding as I moved to get out. "Shorty right."

"I know," I hit the locks and opened the door. "I'll be right back."

"Yo, see what's up her girls!" Slate hollered, as I stepped from the car and began walking towards Ebony. When Ebony saw me approaching, she smiled and stopped to say something to her professor near his car.

The next I knew, shit was going down, happening so fast that I couldn't even think. I spotted two masked men emerging from behind a parked car a second before they grabbed Ebony. I moved like lightning until I was able to strike. I shot the first would-be kidnapper in the head at point blank range as Ebony's chump ass professor screamed for help. Then, I turned my attention to the second kidnapper as one of Ebony's male classmates tried to play hero with the wrong nigga.

"Nigga, move! Before I bust your dumb ass!" I barked, pushing him out of my way as Ebony continued to struggle with the second kidnapper to keep from being forced into the side door of a waiting van. "That's my girl!"

Ebony's classmate retreated just as my cousin Slate came up out of the car, dumping like he was crazy. I didn't know who else was shooting. But I grabbed Ebony and tried to maintain my balance as the second kidnapper pushed her into me and jumped inside the waiting van. I was about to shoot when I looked inside and noticed Nizzy aiming something big at me from behind the driver's seat.

"Get in the car!" I pushed Ebony out of the way just as the first few shots rung out.

Slate came around Ebony's Legend, cranking, forcing the van to burn rubber. "Who the fuck was that?" Slate stuffed the tone into his dip and ran over to help me up.

"Nizzy and 'em!" I exclaimed, already moving towards Ebony. "Take the car and get the fuck outta here!" I ordered, shoving Ebony behind the wheel of her Acura Legend. There was no doubt in my mind that all the shooting had alerted campus security.

I ran around to the passenger's side door as Slate took off for my car, opened the door and jumped in. Ebony was having a panic attack, fumbling with the keys, breathing all wild and shit. So, after attempting to calm her down a few times, I just leaned over and slapped the shit out of her.

"Motherfucker! I know you didn't just put your fucking hands on me!" Ebony stopped everything and stared straight at me like she was about to pounce. "Don't no nigga put his hands on me. My father doesn't even put his hands on me! I'll kill your stupid ass up in—"

"Hold up baby!" I put my hands up and leaned back up against the door as Ebony connected with a few crisp jabs. "I'm sorry! I was just trying to get you to calm down before I end up getting locked up out this bitch!"

"Oh nigga, you done fucked up! Believe that," Ebony snapped, jamming the car key into the ignition to start the car. "You must've lost your fucking mind." Ebony threw the car in drive and pulled off like a mad woman, still talking shit. "Wait until I call my father—"

All of a sudden, it just started getting hot as shit. And before I knew it, I was sweating like a convict in a car full of guns during a routine traffic stop. Then my heart started beating extra fast, pounding. So, I began to remove my clothes. "Baby, why is it so hot in here?"

Ebony took her eyes off the road momentarily to look at me. Then she started screaming something before reaching over.

I looked down and there it was—a monster-size hole in the center of my stomach. Instantly, I began to feel faint. Ebony placed her hand over the hole and tried to stop the bleeding as she continued to drive. But it was no use. The blood just seeped between her fingers.

I saw Ebony's lips moving but no words were coming out. I saw the string of saliva-coated blood trickle from my mouth. But, I couldn't find the strength to lift my chin off of my chest. How the fuck had Nizzy gotten one off on me? I wondered, remembering the grin on his face as he took aim at me with the big ass tone with the extended clip hanging out. I couldn't believe it. But here I was, blacking out in the passenger's seat of my girl's car. It can't end like this for me. I was supposed to go out like a fucking Dummie. Black Scarface style.

Chapter 8

"I just don't trust the move, Slim," Little Dinky confessed, looking up and down the block as he, Gooh and Zimbabwe sat outside of the row-home they'd just followed Nizzy's cousin Lor'Homie to.

"We're good, shorty, trust me." Zimbabwe checked his blicky to make sure that the safety was off. Things had been pretty quiet since all the shit with Charm up at Coppin State. So it was time to make some noise. Especially since Charm was out of the way. "This the best move."

Little Dinky stared at Zimbabwe for a second. There was no need to reply. When it came to the intricate pieces and essential components that went into playing chess, Zimbabwe was next to none. And he'd taught Little Dinky everything he knew.

"So, what do you need me to do?" Gooh questioned anxiously. Unlike Zimbabwe and Little Dinky, Gooh was dying to prove himself.

"Just follow my lead, soldier," Zimbabwe replied, and Gooh nodded.

After surveying their surroundings one more time, Zimbabwe, Gooh and Little Dinky exited the car and headed for the house Lor'Homie had entered.

Honestly, Little Dinky couldn't understand why Lor'Homie would risk his life taking a chance to get some pussy in Charm's backyard with the stakes so high. Either he had a death wish or he was just the most arrogant nigga alive. Because there was no way that the young girl's pussy he'd disappeared with was that good. Then again, Little Dinky thought maybe the pussy was good. After all, he'd seen some of the smartest hustlers he knew, make some of the dumbest and dangerous decision chasing pussy. In fact, he'd used it against them.

Zimbabwe walked up and tapped on the door as Little Dinky and Gooh hung back. A moment later, the locks rattled and another cute, little girl opened the door.

"Can I help you?"

Zimbabwe asked for the first name that popped in his head. So, the young girl quickly informed him that he had the wrong address and began to close the door. However, Zimbabwe jammed his foot in the door, pulled out the blicky, and put a finger up to his lips. Then, he slowly backed the young girl up inside the house and signaled for Little Dinky and Gooh to come on.

"Where's the little kid that just came in here with the lightskin girl with the dreads at?" Zimbabwe asked calmly, as Little Dinky and Gooh slipped inside and locked the door.

"Upstairs," she admitted, instantly beginning to cry. "Please, that's my sister."

"Look, we're just here for the little dude, that's it," Zimbabwe assured. "But, if you scream or do something stupid to alert him, I'ma kill you and your sister, understand?"

The pretty little girl nodded, her head going up and down rapidly as if she overstood.

"Good," Zimbabwe said before going on to explain to her exactly how things were going to go as Gooh and Little Dinky searched the first floor. "Is there anybody else in the house."

"No," she replied without hesitation.

Zimbabwe was sure to magnify their intentions. All they wanted was Lor'Homie. He also assured her that, if she ever mentioned anything to anyone about who they were, he'd personally hunt her and her sister down and mechanically dismember their bodies.

"Now, which room are they in?" Zimbabwe asked, looking towards the stairs as Gooh returned from the basement.

"The first room at the top of the steps. You can't miss it. There a big poster of Drake on the door." She explained nervously. "Please just don't hurt my little sister."

"We still got a deal, right?" Zimbabwe questioned.

"Yes," she nodded in agreement.

"A'ight, go over there and sit on the couch," Zimbabwe pointed. "And you better not make a sound."

"Please, no, my sister," she began to plead and cry uncontrollably.

114

"Look, bitch!" Gooh grabbed the girl by her arm, marched her over the couch and pushed her down. "You got two choices. Either sit down and hush up or get your shit pushed back!" Gooh threatened impatiently.

"Chill, soldier," Little Dinky instructed, walking over to the young girl. "Nobody's going to hurt you or your sister." Little Dinky kneeled down in front of her. "We're only here for the guy she's with, okay?"

The young girl nodded again and continued to weep quietly. Little Dinky gently placed his hand on her shoulder and continued. "Just calm down and we'll be out of here in no time. I promise." Little Dinky wanted to put her at ease because he knew that they could attract more bees with honey than they could with shit.

Gooh looked at Little Dinky questionably. It seemed like every time he had the choice to hurt or help, he always chose the former.

"A'ight, Slim," Little Dinky turned his attention back to the mission at hand after the young girl appeared to calm down. "What's the hook?"

"You grab the young girl while I take care of Lor'Homie."

Zimbabwe replied before turning to Gooh. "You're on baby-sitting duty, soldier."

"What? Nah, man," Gooh shook his head and looked over at the young girl on the couch like he wanted to shoot her right then and there.

"How about this," Little Dinky spoke up. "You and soldier go handle Lor'Homie and I'll keep an eye on baby girl," Little Dinky suggested, not really trusting Gooh to baby-sit. Especially, since he still needed someone to watch over him. So that he didn't do anything stupid himself. .

"Bet," Zimbabwe nodded understandably. He already knew what time it was. No masks meant no survivors. But, they didn't need to prove that right now and end up putting Lor'Homie on point before they could grab him. "Okay, soldier, it's you and me when we get upstairs. Don't worry about nothing except securing the little girl."

"I'm all over her," Gooh exclaimed, already moving.

Zimbabwe looked over at Little Dinky and followed Gooh up the stairs with his blicky at the ready.

It was quiet except for the light sound of music leaking through the cracks of the first door at the top of the stairs. Zimbabwe grabbed Gooh's shoulder and squeezed it. When Gooh looked back, Zimbabwe pointed to the only closed door and slowly crept past him. Gooh tripped over a pair of red and gold, high-top, studded-out Versace sneakers, and Zimbabwe paused for what seemed like forever.

Once Zimbabwe was sure that Lor'Homie hadn't heard them, he slowly turned the door knob and placed his ear up against the bedroom door. That's when he heard the unmistakable sound of danger.

"Move!" Zimbabwe ducked as the bedroom door exploded from a gun blast, sending door fragment pieces everywhere.

Gooh dived to the floor and fired back through the door as Lor'Homie continued to unload blindly. Zimbabwe crawled up, placed the barrel of his blicky against the bedroom door and fired a few shots. He could hear the young girl inside screaming like crazy, and knew that their plans of snatching Lor'Homie to collect a quick ransom were now out the door.

"He's trying to reload!" Zimbabwe exclaimed, stepping forward to kick the bedroom door in just in time to see Lor'Homie sprinting across the room.

Zimbabwe instantly took aim. There was no time for bullshitting. But, before he could get a clean shot off, Lor'Homie went flying through the second floor window.

"Shit!" Zimbabwe fired as the young girl came running.

"I got him!" Gooh vowed, coming through the bedroom door as Zimbabwe snatched the young girl by her dreads before she could escape the room.

Zimbabwe blew the young girl's brains all over the bedroom and looked over just in time to realize exactly what Gooh meant before he jumped out of the bedroom window behind Lor'Homie.

"What the fuck?" Little Dinky heard something smash through the window upstairs and hit the concrete with a loud thud just outside the front window a split second before a single gunshot echoed in the distance. When he rushed over to peep outside, he saw Gooh laying on the ground next to Lor'Homie.

"Oh my God! My sister!" the young girl screamed, as Little Dinky witnessed Gooh shoot Lor'Homie in the side of the face as they rolled around on the ground tussling for the gun.

"Stop!" Little Dinky ordered as the young girl hopped up off the couch and took running for the stairs. "I said stop!" Little Dinky took aim and knocked her little frame into the stairs with a few back shots as Zimbabwe came bouncing down the stairs.

"Here!" Zimbabwe tossed Little Dinky a black t-shirt. "Cover your face up! We got to torch this motherfucker!" Zimbabwe added, stepping over the body. "Come on, Shorty, move!" Zimbabwe rushed into the kitchen and snatched the table cloth off of the kitchen table, and went over to the stove. "Burn everything!"

Little Dinky went into clean up mood, burning a hand-towel that had been hanging above the sink, before dashing into the living room to set everything on fire.

Once Zimbabwe and Little Dinky got the firer blazing, they ran from the house, threw a towel over Gooh's head, snatched his broken leg up off of the ground, and got the hell out of there.

Chapter 9

Nizzy sat outside on his back steps of house, lost in thought. Every time he read the morning newspaper article about his cousin, he got angrier. He was definitely going to be considered Baltimore's newest no.1 trigger puller after he finished fucking the city up behind his cousin's death.

Nizzy had told Lor'Homie time and time again to lay low and stay the fuck away from Gold Street chasing them thots he was fucking. Especially after the wild ass Coppin State College grab-mission that Charm interrupted and turned into a triple shooting. But no, as always, Lor'Homie had more courage then common sense. And now it had finally cost him more than he could stand to lose.

Nizzy picked up the *Baltimore Sun* again and began to read: *Authorities are still investigating links between a triple homicide during a home invasion Monday afternoon in the 600 block of Gold Street, and that of several shootings and murders in and around the West Baltimore area. Including the Coppin State University Campus shooting that left several people injured, two seniors wounded, and one suspect dead. Detectives won't say much, but insiders did confirm that they've tied the severe beating and stabbing of an FBI informant, who was forced to jump to his own death from a third floor balcony last month, to an on-going drug-turf war between rival gangs.*

"Fuck!" Nizzy slammed the paper down. The lines between freedom and jail seemed to be getting thinner each passing day. "I told this silly nigga!"

"You alright, baby?" Butta popped up in the doorway with a small bag of trash in her hand.

"Yeah," Nizzy lied. Of all the things he'd seen, all the family and friends he'd lost, the shit with his cousin hurt the most. It just did not seem right that he was gone despite all the shit they had done out in the streets. "I'm cooling." Nizzy got to his feet, brushed past Butta, and headed back inside the house. Taking out his phone, Nizzy strolled down to Berry's name. It was time to see what he'd come up with. Nizzy needed facts before he made his next move because the streets were always talking, and they were liable to say anything nowadays.

"Wohh!" Berry answered halfway into the third ring.

"Talk to me," Nizzy glanced over his shoulder at Butta's nosey ass trying to eavesdrop on his conversation. "I need to hear some good news."

"Yeah, well, I definitely got some good news," Berry said. "Charm was the only one who could be identified. The bad news though is that his bitch ass survived."

Nizzy cut his eye at Butta's nosey ass again and stepped into the other room before replying. "Did you holler at Tiph yet?"

"Yeah, I talked to her Friday. Charm hasn't even hit the bookings yet. But, he's definitely being charged already. She looked it up for me."

"A'ight, that's what it is," Nizzy pondered his next move. What if he reached out to Billy Lo and told him that Charm was now in his arena? "A'ight, look, I'll get up with you later around the way. I got a few more calls to make. Make sure you call that nigga Cock-eyed Willie too."

"Already," Berry assured. "One."

"One," Nizzy hung up, feeling a little better. The fact that nobody else had been identified was a plus. Because if he didn't know nothing else, he knew that Charm's bitch ass could hold water. He wasn't like most niggas who only applied the rules when they were beneficial.

Nizzy's phone rung again and he saw Berry's name before he answered, "What's up?"

"Nah, I forgot to tell you I confirmed that other thing you asked about too," Berry reminded him. "It was exactly who you thought it was. He got released about two weeks ago. The same day that shit jumped off up the school."

"Say no more," Nizzy cracked a smile and hung up. *So Slate's home, huh?* Nizzy thought. Now, he knew exactly who spanked his cousin. It was no doubt in his mind. Slate was the only nigga he knew crazy enough to jump out of a window behind his target.

The nigga was loyal to his family almost to a fault, which also made him predictable and vulnerable.

Nizzy knew that Slate was a soldier. He also understood why he'd let his gun go off for Charm without question. That was his blood. What he couldn't understand, however, was how Slate could kill his cousin without reason. Especially, considering their history growing up. He'd helped Slate commit murder.

"Okay, Slate, that's what's up." Nizzy shook his head in deep thought. *You want that smoke, bitch? It's open season on your hoe ass too!*

***

"Hey, Baker, I think I got something you may want to take a look at." Detective Baker looked up to see Detective Venus Malone from the Robbery/Homicide Division walking into his office with what looked like a normal organizational chart in her hand.

"What the hell is this, Venus?" Detective Baker questioned, accepting the file as Venus sat down on the corner of his desk and crossed her legs to where one was draping over the edge.

"The classified 'Dummie Squad'—the file the Captain just received from intelligence."

"What?" Detective Baker repeated, opening the file. The only thing that got the attention of the Intelligence Unit was high-level FBI material. "Like federal intelligence?"

"Yup," Detective Malone smiled. Everybody at the office knew that she had a sweet-tooth for Baker's attention. "Now, why don't you go to the second page and have a look at the pyramid."

Detective Baker turned the page to see at exactly what it was that Malone was so excited about. He saw a couple of old photos of a few former pains in the side. "You know most of these assholes are dead, right?"

"Keep reading," Detective Malone gestured towards the folder. "And don't speak negatively about the dead."

Detective Baker began to read what was written on the label beneath the photos. *Enforcer, former suppliers, known associates,* etc. "You say this hierarchy chart came from intel?" Baker paused to look up at Detective Malone.

"Just this morning."

"Has Detective Gibson seen this?" Baker focused on a photo of an older Baltimore gangster who had a fetish for cutting up corpses.

"Absolutely not," Detective Malone rolled her eyes. She was not too fond of Baker's partner. "The Captain would have my ass. You're lucky you're seeing it. I told you it's classified," Detective Malone said, reaching for the file. "I just wanted you to get a quick look at it before it went upstairs to the captain. Maybe one of them is your babyface killer from the hospital."

"Hold up a sec," Baker pulled the folder out of Malone's reach and tapped on one of the photos. "I know this kid."

"You should—He was all over W-J-Z just a few weeks ago," Detective Malone replied. "He got charged with that Coppin State School shooting."

"Nah, I know this kid from somewhere else," Baker said, thinking hard. "Oh yeah, I got it. He was with Pair one day when Gibson and I was given him a hard time about those Blue Caribbean Park Heights murders." Baker remembered the day vividly. "He was also one of the prime suspects in those projects and skating-ring shootings," Baker's eyes locked in on another photo. "Delvon Whack. He's the one that beat you in trial, right?"

"Yeah," Detective Malone admitted. "Somehow, he got our main witness silenced while on the detection-box."

"I remember, Tyree Stewart." Baker shook his head. "The shooters roughed the grandmother up a bit also."

"Yeah, well, Whack's dead now. Ambushed at a stop light."

"Poetic justice." Detective Baker smiled.

"Maybe, who knows?" Detective Malone reached over to flip the page.

"This here," she pointed to another photo, "is Ryan McClain. Waters and I interviewed several witnesses about his death.

Nobody talked. The only thing we were about to discover was the fact that he loved to post, 'Shag B Baggin Em' on his social media after every time we believe he dropped a body." Baker continued to look over the photos, names and titles. Daniel Carter, Jason Murdock, Frank Lance, Odie Hill, James Tanner, Slatheo Bush— A lot of the names looked very familiar from various investigations, more as suspects than victims.

"Hold up," Baker requested, rereading a couple of the names. "Intel has these little misfits tied to the Crudy Muslims Brothers?" Baker questioned, almost as if he couldn't believe it. "Where is this information coming from?"

"I don't know," Detective Malone admitted. "I just know the feds have been building a Continuing Criminal Enterprise case against them for months now."

"They want to go after these little fuckers with the Rico Act?" Baker stared at the names again. "You got to be kidding. I mean, a couple shootings. Yeah. But these are no kid kingpins."

Detective Malone hunched her shoulders. "From what the file says, them little babies moving more weight and dropping more bodies then Peanut King in the eighties."

"I would love to get a crack at these little bastards before the feds show up and take over," Detective Baker exclaimed, thinking out loud.

"You and me both," Detective Malone admitted. "I just know that I can close a few cold cases."

"Why is Donald White mentioned?" Detective Baker questioned curiously. "Gibson and I nailed that bastard to the cross on a plea agreement two years ago."

"Yeah, well, that plea was tossed."

"Come again." Baker eyed Detective Malone.

"White's plea agreement was tossed." Detective Malone had been in the courtroom when White pleaded out to avoid the death penalty. "The appeals court vacated his sentence. Some shit about his attorney not clearly explaining the plea deal or something."

"You have got to let me make a copy of this," Detective Baker requested, getting to his feet. He had to know exactly what the hell was going on.

"Not so fast, detective," Detective Malone grabbed the folder, held it up against her chest and smiled. "What are you willing to give up for it?"

"What is it that you want?" Baker inquired.

"I think you know, detective." Detective Malone slowly uncrossed and recrossed her sexy legs. "But for now, I'll take your word that the next time I offer you something to eat, you'll accept it."

Detective Baker agreed with a smiled. Then, he promised not to file sexual harrassment charges because he really needed a copy of that file.

"Make it quick," Detective Malone handed Baker the file. "You got two minutes."

"Thanks, I only need one." Baker removed the papers from the file and headed towards the copy machine, wondering why people continued to play a losing game. Sure, there was the money, the women, the nice car, the life style. But, in the end, it always ended the same: With some poor pathetic woman crying over a dead or incarcerated gangster. All the big names! All the big wigs! All the big shots! They all fell victim to the game in one sense or another with few exceptions. *When will these fools learn that there is no retirement plan in the life of a gangster?* Baker thought, placing the papers inside the copier.

***

"Where were all those motherfuckers when I was marching down to that jail, waiting outside for hours, huh? Where were they when I had to run down there, be here, and you handle instructions such as *grab this*, *move that* and I did everything else you asked me to do!" Tiara screamed into the phone. "Where's the appreciation for that?"

"Bitch! You did that because you were my girl. Ain't no reward for that shit!" Wakal fired.

"*Bitch*, huh?" Tiara giggled. "That's the Donald I know. But you're a Muslim right, Ock?"

"You know I didn't mean it like that," Wakal said, knowing that the hardest part of figuring out who you are was, letting go of who you used to be. "I was just trying to say that a good woman is a good woman regardless of the situation. Plus, I took care of business when I was out there!"

"Took care of business how, Donald?" Tiara sucked her teeth. "By constantly putting your hands on me?"

"It's not how you start—It's how you finish that counts," Wakal said, not wanting to remind her of how she wasn't complaining when she was reaping all the benefits of the evil he did out in the streets. "Plus, I was lost then."

"You can miss me with all those half-slick jailhouse lines."

"Jailhouse lines?" Wakal repeated.

"Yeah, jailhouse lines," Tiara spat. "All that shit niggas get in jail and start talking. *I've changed. I'm a better man.* You know, whatever it takes to get a bitch to accept y'all damn calls."

"What about the good times, Tiara? You can't tell me it was all bad."

"It was always bad, Donald," Tiara replied softly. "Nothing about us was ever good."

"What wasn't good?" Wakal heard what he assumed to be Tiara's baby father's voice in the background. "Who you talking to?" Wakal heard him inquire.

"Huh?" Tiara appeared to be caught off guard.

"Huh shit! Don't play with me, Tiara," he warned. "Who the fuck is that you're talking to about shit being good? I know that's not that jail nigga?"

Wakal pulled the phone away from his ear and looked at it in disbelief before shaking his head. Dudes in the streets killed him with their insecurities. *Nigga must not be on his job.* Wakal thought. Otherwise, why would the nigga see him as a threat?

Especially while he was locked up! He couldn't even touch Tiara. At least not physically.

"Didn't I tell you not to accept that nigga's calls no more?"

"I didn't accept no call."

"Tiara! Tiara!" Wakal tried to get Tiara's attention. "Tell Dug I'm just trying to get you to help me with my court stuff!" Wakal pleaded honestly. He needed Tiara to be an alibi witness if he wanted any chance at seeing day light again "Tiara! Tiara!"

"Fuck!" Wakal shouted, slamming the phone when the line went dead, and he heard the dial tone. Wakal walked over to the dayroom window and tried to get the officer's attention up in the control center.

His mind was all over the place, and he wanted to get out of the dayroom before he zapped out and broke the telephone. What Tiara's baby father didn't understand was that Wakal did not want Tiara. Honestly, he still had visions of taking a play out of his next-door neighbor's playbook. Tricking Tiara up to jail so that he could jump over the visiting room counter and knock her out cold the fuck out! The truth was, he just couldn't forget how she'd written him off.

Just like he could never forgive the motherfuckers who'd turned their backs on him or let him down when he needed them the most. Even family members! Wakal knew in his heart that he was wrong, especially since he served and worshipped the most forgiving God. But he just couldn't let it go. Honestly, it just made him love white women that much more because despite all their shit, they were loyal, their intentions were pure, and their words were always followed by actions.

"Ms. Smith!" Wakal yelled out the crack of the door to get the tier officer's attention. "I'm ready!" he yelled again when Ms. Smith looked in his direction.'

"Give me a moment, White," Ms. Smith held her finger up and continued to escort another inmate towards the shower. Wakal had been on administrative lock-up since returning from the hospital a few weeks ago. The chief of security had placed him on single-man recreation. But, it was all good. Wakal wasn't tripping.

His mind was on freedom. Allah had blessed him with another chance to plead out or go to trial. Turns out, his public defender hadn't properly advised him on his plea agreement. Which violated the requirements set forth in Maryland Rule 4-242 (c). Furthermore, the Court of Appeals, in Daughtry v. Maryland explained why and how a judge must or should explain exactly what is taking place in open court on the record during a 'guilty plea' that a defendant is knowingly and intelligently waving their Constitutional Rights to a fair and impartial trial.

"Hi, how're you doing today, Ms. Smith?" Wakal questioned, coming out of the dayroom after she'd handcuffed him in the front because of his wounds and radioed for the dayroom door.

"Fine, and yourself?" she replied, gently cupping the back of his arm.

"Trying to get home," Wakal confessed sincerely.

"That's good," she encouraged, carefully guiding Wakal down the stairs. "A lot of these guys act like they love it in here."

Ms. Smith reminded Wakal of a sexier version of Miss Clause. She was what he liked to call a 'gilf'. Besides Ofc. Coke, Ms. Smith was the only other officer he'd love to get behind closed doors. And there was no doubt in his mind that she'd probably still turn a nigga out though. It was in her eyes. The way she looked at him, if Ofc. Coke was his kryptonite, then Ms. Smith was his Achilles heel.

"I bet you were something else when you were young, Ms. Smith," Wakal teased.

"You would lose your money." Ms. Smith grinned devilishly.

"Yeah, a'ight," Wakal mumbled. Ms. Smith was an old freak, and he could tell by the way she carried herself, whether she admitted it or not.

"As salaam alaikum, Ock!" Wakal saw Shabazz standing in the door, waiting for recreation as he walked him down the bottom tier pass his cell and greeted him.

"Walaikum asalaam," Shabazz returned his greeting. He and Latif had tripped out when they first brought Wakal on the tier and moved him in the cell across the tier. Latif had wanted to just try and hit him. But Shabazz wanted to feel him out first to see what he did or did not suspect.

Wakal stepped inside the cell just before the door closed, and got un-cuffed. He knew Shabazz was still leery of him, especially since he could expose him. But, he'd given Shabazz his word that he'd not inform the community about his part in the situation with the white boys. And he planned to keep his promise because he did not want to cause any more trouble amongst the brotherhood.

Shabazz had tried to deny his involvement at first. He'd called Wakal crazy and even paranoid. But, once Wakal explained to him how one of the silly white boys had slipped up during the hit, Shabazz couldn't do nothing but accept it and come clean. Still, Wakal wasn't tripping. His attorney was using the situation to get him transferred back over the city jail. He just prayed that Allah would have mercy on Shabazz's soul. He loved his Muslim brothers, all of them. Even the ones like Shabazz, Latif and Shaheed, all of whom did not practice the true principles of Islam.

"Have a nice one, Ms. Smith."

"You too, White." Ms. Smith replied, locking the slot.

Wakal walked over to the sink and began making Wudu, washing his hands, mouth, nose, face, and so on. Then, he grabbed his prayer rug off of the bed, carefully laid it on the floor near the window facing the east, and began reciting *Salat* in Arabic.

Chapter 10

"A'ight, but what are they saying about the fact that them niggas were trying to snatch your baby's mother?" JuJu questioned, as we all sat inside the Baltimore City Detection Center visiting room.

"Not much right now," I admitted, shaking my head. "And I probably won't really know too much until the preliminary hearing."

"That's crazy," JuJu fired. "What Franzoso talking about?"

"That a nigga might have to fight this shit," I confessed.

"Franzoso? Who the fuck is Franzoso?" Slate questioned curiously.

"That's the lawyer the whole squad basically use," JuJu offered. "Elizabeth Franzoso."

"Yeah, well, why would she feel like that when it was self-defense?" Slate seemed concerned.

"Cause they wanna know who the other shooters were," I said, looking at my cousin. "Plus, some stiff ass, bitch nigga name Tavon Shuley, who got hit in the leg, been all over the news and internet going viral him put a fucking gun in my hand."

"Fam," Slate looked at me, and I knew what he was thinking.

"Don't even trip, I'm good," I assured, calming his nerves. "If it gets to that point, then you already know what it is."

"The news said Miss Coppin State University got hit too." Murdock spoke up, I assumed, to change the subject.

"Yeah, Katrina Griffin," I said. "Shorty refused to cooperate though. She's about that black lives matter shit." I respected how Miss Coppin State had carried it. "Ebony's gay ass professor even held up. And here it is you got this fuck nigga Tavon Shuley, who got the nerve to call himself 'Bullet', singing like he's on 'The Voice'."

"Did you hear about Lor'Homie?" JuJu questioned with an evil smile.

"Ain't no question," I smiled back. I didn't know which one of them Dummie's had spanked Lor'Homie, but I was happy either way. "I been hearing about a lot of other shit too though." I looked at JuJu in disgust because that meant somebody was talking. And there wasn't anything worst in my eyes than a nigga who couldn't carry his own weight. "The type of shit I don't have no business hearing about over here."

"What? Like the type of shit that can get a nigga jammed up?" JuJu inquired.

"Yeah, that type of business."

"Yeah, well, you must not be hearing too much," Murdock said, knowing that we always kept 'Dummie Squad' business on the 'need to know' tip.

"It's still more than they need to know," I retorted, knowing how dirty the police could get when they really wanted a nigga. "So niggas need to play their hands more close to their chest."

"We're on it, Dummie." JuJu nodded but I knew it was more easier said than done.

"Ayo, let me see that shit real quick," Slate gestured towards my stomach.

"See what?" I played dumb because I wasn't dying to show them another nigga's handy work.

"Your stomach, nigga!" Slate fired. "What? You got a shit-bag or something?"

"Fuck no!" I retorted, carefully lifting my Polo shirt up. It had been three weeks since Nizzy had tried to have Ebony snatched and almost ended up taking me out of stock, and my stomach was still torn up.

"Oh them niggas gonna answer for that!" Slate threatened, leaning forward to slowly eye the staples running down the center of my stomach to where my belly-button used to be.

"Why it look like you got on a brown butter-soft leather?" Murdock joked with a grin, and we all started laughing.

"Fuck you, nigga!" I held my stomach, forced to laugh through the sharp pain. "You play too much." I eased my shirt down. It felt good to be around the squad.

"Seriously though, Dummie," Murdock continued to laugh. "You got the zipper and everything."

"I'm not paying your funny looking ass no mind," I retorted.

"You think you can get a bail?" JuJu questioned on a more serious note after the moment passed.

"Ain't no telling. I talked to Franzoso the other day about it. But, you know I'm already out on bail for that gun beef. So, she felt like if she could get me a bail, it would be a fucking ransom. And you know how tight shit been with all the bullshit going on. Nigga barely seeing re-up."

"Don't even worry about all that, Dummie. You get a bail. We're grabbing you, period!" JuJu assured, making me smile. There was nothing in the game more valuable than real niggas. Especially when you were staring down football numbers.

"Already," Murdock seconded. "He's starting to piss me off. Like he don't know we'll hit everything in the city to pull him"

"Oh, I ain't never doubted that, Dummie."

"Did you see any of them bitch ass Park Heights niggas that pulled that shit over here?" Slate looked around the visiting room, gently running a hand over his waves.

"Nah, most of them niggas on the bricks," I said. "I think one of 'em on lock-up though. So you already know what it is if this bitch come off. His homies know too. They done already told me that they ain't got nothing to do with it."

"Yeah, that's 'cause they know niggas out here making house calls!" Murdock suggested.

"Oh yeah, Dummie," JuJu cut in as if he'd just remembered something important. "Guess who pulled up on me the other day?"

"Who?"

"The old head you were chasing from Sandtown," JuJu replied and continued when I gave him the clueless look. "The one you said use to come up on the hopper tier checking for you."

"You better not be talking about none of my old heads." Slate stood up and started shadow-boxing. "I'll go to that body."

"Man, if you don't sit your silly ass down," I ordered as other visitors began to take notice of him. "Don't nobody even know your dumb ass. You were over here so long ago."

"And I left a mean impression too," Slate retorted, sitting back down. Honestly, his name was still ringing bells on the tier. But,

I'd never tell him that. The nigga was already big-headed enough. "Who you think started all that East Baltimore, West Baltimore shit?"

"Definitely not you, nigga!" Murdock interjected confidently. "The first time I got charged as an adult and hit the hopper tier, we were over here getting in. They waved me back down to the juvenile system because I was—"

"Hold up, Dummie," I requested, cutting Murdock off. "Y'all can trade war stories later. I'm trying to hear what Dummie talking about." I turned my attention back to JuJu. "Go ahead, Dummie."

"You know who I'm talking about?"

"Yeah," I nodded. "Miss Sellman, Tiph's homegirl from Sandtown."

"Right," JuJu nodded in agreement. "A'ight, well, she pulls up on me the other day asking me if you were okay and all this other shit."

"What?" I twisted my face up, wondering why Shekey would be concerned about me.

"Yeah, she said Tiph been asking her to keep an eye out for you," JuJu added.

"Oh yeah," I laughed. "That's Nizzy bitch ass."

"I was thinking the same thing, Dummie," JuJu confessed, shaking his head. "What! He trying to get you touched or something?"

"You already know," I said, considering for the first time if Nizzy had had anything to do with me getting stabbed on the section during my last stay. "But you know I stay on point."

"That's why I didn't tell her nothing. I think I told her you were still in the hospital."

"It doesn't matter. She can easily find out. That was probably her way of pulling my coat tail. See if you can fox her ass for some information the next time you see her though."

"I got her ass," JuJu assured.

"In the meantime though, we got to figure out what to do with this bitch ass nigga Bullet," I said before making myself crystal clear. "Do not spank him unless it's absolutely necessary." I cut my eyes at Murdock. "I mean, the nigga's a lemon. So, just squeeze enough juice out of his heart until he changes his mind."

"We got you, Dummie." JuJu smiled.

"I'm serious, Dummie," I looked from JuJu to Murdock to my cousin sternly. "That sucker got too many followers and likes and shit on his social media. And we can't stand that type of heat right now."

"A'ight, Dummie, we're on it," JuJu assured.

"Fam, did you take care of what I asked you to with Ebony yet?" I turned to Slate.

"Nah, I haven't been able to get up with her," Slate admitted. "You know I been chilling since all that stuff happened. So, I don't even know if she been pass Aunt Peaches house. She definitely hasn't called me back yet though."

"She's probably staying over her godmother's house," I defended, knowing how much Ebony hated being in the house alone.

"That's cool, but she still could've at least texted a nigga back or something," Slate argued.

"You right," I acknowledged, anxious to find out what the problem was. For some reason, Ebony had been half-stepping lately, and I needed to figure out what type of shit she was on. Whatever the case though, I needed to get that money up outta her house. "I'ma get on top of that shit tonight. But if I can't get y'all together by Monday, I'ma send you up in that bitch."

"Does she know where you keep the money stashed?" Slate inquired.

"Hell no!" I fired. "I'm not that stupid."

"What money?" Murdock looked at everybody, clueless.

"Nah, I got thirty bands hidden at my baby mother's crib."

"Yeah, well, we're still gonna have to pull a lick," JuJu urged. "I mean, thirty racks ain't nothing, especially if you end up getting a crazy bail."

"Yeah, Dummie's right," Murdock agreed.

I thought for a second. Thirty thousand definitely wasn't much. Still, it was better than nothing since niggas couldn't be out on the strip heavy right now. "Look, y'all niggas out there—So, y'all do whatever y'all feel like y'all gotta do to stay on top," I said, knowing they would come up with something.

"I told you I got some thorough niggas out in Eastern Shore trying to come up," Slate reminded everyone. "All we got to do is hit them niggas with some work. They're hungry."

"I like the sound of that," JuJu confessed, always ready to expand.

"Me too," Murdock nodded. "It's money out Salisbury, especially on the west side. My cousin Love'L and his man Black John used to have Collins Street on lock before they fell."

I started shaking my head before I even realized it. There was no way in the world that I was fucking with no Bloods. "I already told you I ain't fucking with no Bloods under no circumstances. Them niggas murked my sister."

"That was a different set, fam," Slate said. "My man Gunna and his crew 'All About That Money'. They're A-B-T-M."

"I don't give a fuck who they are. Rollin' Twenties, Shower Posse, L-Gang, Tree-Top Piru, Bounty, G-Shine. None of that shit! All them niggas the same."

"A-B-T-M is different, fam. They're not on no gang shit. They're all about that money. And how many times I gotta tell you the real 'Shower Posse' bang green? The bloods work for them. "

"You know eventually you're going to have to let that shit go, Dummie." JuJu stared at me. "It was an accident."

"I don't believe in accidents—That's some shit guilty motherfuckers done came up with so they don't have to take fault," I replied, starting to get mad. "And for the record, I'm not ever letting that shit go. One Blood, some Bloods, all Bloods. Dead Bloods. So, if you want to hit them niggas off, you can hit them niggas off by yourself."

"A'ight, what about my man I was telling you about out D.C.?

"Do whatever you want to do, yo," I said, finished with it.

"I heard that, fam." Slate fell silent.

"There's always another option," Murdock suggested with a smile. "We get back on our day one shit and start snatching all these niggas. Friend and foe alike. I mean, what you think about that?"

"Shiddd, it's already on anyway," JuJu added. "Plus, I can't think of a more profitable way of conducting war."

Nodding in agreement, I said, "Let's show these niggas that we still know how to get it from the mud. They done got too comfortable anyway."

"I guess it's sort of like solving two problems with one answer, get it?" Slate said, losing everybody.

"Yeah, something like that," I replied, trying to save face. "Ayo, Nizzy still hasn't reponded to that Instagram shit?"

"Nah, you know he think that bitch Butta a saint," JuJu said.

"Oh yeah," I smiled. "Let's see how much of a saint he thinks she is after he sees me and Slate wearing her ass out the day he was released!" I exclaimed, thinking about the new video footage I had of Butta asking Slate what the caked up white stuff was all over his dick and nuts as she ate him up, oblivious to the fact that Slate had just finished fucking his lil' jailhouse jump off. "You still got my cellphone, fam?"

"Yeah, it's outside in the glove compartment of the car. I don't even touch it, why?" Slate said.

"Outside in the glove compartment?" I was confused. "What! You drove my whip down here?"

"Dummie ain't stop pushing your shit since you got grabbed," JuJu laughed. He of all people knew how I was about my wheels. "He be having dummies and everything up in that bitch."

"Fuck outta here," I fired before checking myself. How could I honestly tell a nigga who'd basically taught me everything that he couldn't stunt out and dropped his nuts in the streets! "Nah, all is well. Anyway, when y'all bounce, give JuJu the phone. That way, after y'all lick that nigga, Dummie can post all that shit with us and Butta."

"Some more video? That nigga gonna go donkey this time," Murdock said. "That's how you touch a nigga anywhere, anyhow."

"Yeah, well, that will teach him to worry more about his bitch and less about mines!" I said, realizing at that moment that the day Slate and I had 'DP-ed' Butta was the exact same day Nizzy tried to grab Ebony. "As a matter of fact, when you post the video, tell that nigga, *That's what happens when you stalk another nigga's bitch instead of worrying about your own.*"

"That's what it is then," JuJu spoke up. "You know we're going to need some help hitting Nizzy. They're running both of their shops on Braddish now. So, we're gonna have to probably hit them bitches at the same time. And then you're talking about getting other niggas too."

"What about Shanell's lil daughters, Muffin and 'em?" Slate suggested. "I know they're still getting it in. What's the name of the lil click they run with?"

"Tabu," I revealed. But honestly, there was no way in hell we were recruiting them crazy bitches.

"Yeah, Tabu," Slate nodded. "You know they'll carry that mail."

"True, but them lil hookers too thirsty," I said, thinking about a few niggas they'd taken down. "Plus, Butta and her lil posse be beefing with them. So Nizzy knows exactly who they are. But, we can definitely put them on some of them other niggas."

"Yeah, we gonna need some real robbery experts for this," Murdock explained. "Some niggas who don't give a fuck. Niggas about that action either way."

My mind started racing. Certified gangsters were hard to find. Old-school gangster Shorty Boyd was on the run. Dominick and Little Jarod's crazy ass hadn't been around since they decided to stick up the entire South Baltimore Reunion down Carroll Park on Washington Boulevard. And North Avenue Brock hadn't been seen since he'd given his life sentence back on appeal, retired from the game and left the city. I was about to say *fuck it* and tell them to go with the Tabu bitches when the names of two goons we'd gotten into it with in the past popped in my mind. "I got it, Dummie," I snapped my fingers. "Go around Crisco's and get up with White Boy and his man Fredro."

"White Boy and Fredro?" JuJu looked at me strangely.

"Just hear me out," I requested, ready to justify my idea. "Despite our history, we all know that them niggas get down. They're Dummie Squad material."

"I'm not riding with them niggas on no level," JuJu retorted. "I don't care how gutta they're."

I knew his emotional response had a lot to do with White Boy and Fredro running around talking shit about the Dummie Squad after they'd refused to fall under our umbrella. That, and of course the fact that White Boy and JuJu had threatened each other's lives some time ago.

"You ain't got to ride with 'em Dummie," I exclaimed honestly. "All you got to do is not ride against them. At least until after y'all take care of business, you feel me?"

JuJu's evil ass smile said it all. I knew he hadn't thought about it that way. "That way, we get the help we need, and you get to settle an old score."

"Now that's how you kill two foes with one tone." JuJu looked at Slate.

"Yeah, whatever," Slate waved him off. "So, you say these niggas be around by Crisco's?"

"Yeah, on Bloomdale," I confirmed.

"Don't worry about it," JuJu interjected. "I'ma send O around there to get up with them niggas today."

"Enough said," I laughed. There was nothing else to talk about. I mean, we all knew that White Boy and Fredro would get busy under pressure. I saw the guard passing out the visiting time slips, and knew that our time was just about up.

I waited until after the guard handed Slate the visiting slip, and continued on before expressing my final thought because I knew that the last thing said on a visit was the most memorable. "Look yo, if this shit with the school get drawn out, I'ma need you niggas to hold it down out there. Especially, if I end up having to do some time."

"I'ma keep these niggas in line, fam, believe that!" Slate said, but I wasn't so sure because he tend to be crazy at times himself.

"Wrap it up, gentlemen," the guard ordered with an attitude, walking back past like it was our fault that his fat, sloppy, big belly ass was on fuckboy duty.

"Yeah, a'ight," I eyed the chump. "Listen, make sure y'all stay on top of Nizzy too. Y'all think he went nuts about Shaggy. He's gonna really go ham about his cousin."

"Man, fuck that nigga, Dummie," Murdock waved his hand nonchalantly.

"Listen, Dummie," I said, seeing the fat guard making his way back towards us again. "When y'all do what y'all do, if that nigga Nizzy up in there, y'all already know what time it is. Leave 'em. And don't give the rest of them niggas no cushion."

"Already." JuJu stared at me understandably.

"Let's go, Johnson! Your visit is over!" The fat guard walked up next to Slate. "You're not the only inmate with family."

"Damn Fatboy, chill out," JuJu teased. "Go eat a case of Little Debbies or something."

"Love y'all niggas, man," I said, getting to my feet before Fatboy ended up barring my niggas out of the jail. Wasn't nothing more dangerous then a fuckboy with authority.

"Love you too, Dummie." Murdock pounded a fist on his chest. "One."

"Already," I replied, watching the fat guard follow them out of the visiting room.

Chapter 11

"Stop playing, Slim," Billy Lo stopped bushing his teeth to look back at his Park Heights homeboy Phillip 'Lil' Phil' Cook. "He said what?"

"That if I plan to keep playing the game, I had to either tell on these niggas or kill them," Lil' Phil reiterated.

"You serious?" Billy Lo spat some toothpaste into the toilet. He knew that Lil' Phil was as real as they came up Park Heights. He'd put the dirt on a lot of niggas. He was currently over the jail for dirting a Gilmore Homes heavy hitter for some major players. So, for his cellmate to say some stupid shit out of his mouth about snitching was crazy. It was equivalent to confusing a Blood with a Crip. Just straight disrespect.

"If I'm lying, I'm dying," Lil' Phil ran a hand over his bald head. "That's why I slapped his brains out and made him check in."

"He's lucky you didn't put that knife in him for real." Billy Lo knew that such offense could warrant death, especially over the city jail.

"Cold blooded," Lil' Phil agreed. "If I really thought he had a clue who he was talking to, I would've knocked sparks off his ass. But, that's the game these niggas playing nowadays, Slim. It's not like it use to be back in the day when we had real gangster lacing our boots."

Lil' Phil was right, and Billy Lo knew it. Not only were dudes being miseducated by so-called gangsters. They were also following them.

"And I don't say that to make no excuses for these suckers," Lil' Phil assured with a touch of disappointment in his voice. "But, it's them niggas that got this shit so fucked up. Fucking wannabes gangsters!" Lil' Phil added. "How the fuck you gonna even fix your mouth to tell a man it's okay to tell on a nigga if you can't kill 'em? That's why you got so many niggas in court fighting bodies now 'cause their enemies couldn't kill 'em. "They're getting that shit from all these wild TV shows. '*Power*', '*Snowfall*', and all those other gangster shows."

"You ain't never lied." Billy Lo couldn't count how many good men he personally knew doing life sentences behind some weak, wannabe gangster. "That's why a head-shot is the only solution for stopping these rat niggas from moving."

"You're still crazy like glue, Slim," Lil' Phil smiled. He and Billy Lo went back some ways. All the way to the training school days when they had niggas scared to say that they were from anywhere but Park Heights. "But construction definitely starts with destruction."

The young C.O. chump who usually had the section walked up and excused himself. "When you get a chance, come holler at me," he said.

"A'ight." Billy Lo sat his toothbrush in the cup on the sink, flushed the toilet, grabbed his cane, told Lil' Phil that he would be right back, and headed on down the tier to talk to the young guard.

"What's up?" Billy Lo strolled up the desk cautiously. No matter how many conversations he had with the young C.O. or how cool he acted, Billy Lo just always felt out of place being in his company. After all, at the end of the day he was still a pig.

"You were right," the young chump admitted, looking around like only he and Billy Lo were in on a secret. "They changed your little cousin as an adult. He's on the juvenile tier."

"You sure?" Billy Lo questioned, trying hard to hide his excitement. "Because I don't want to give my folks no bad information."

"He's over there, trust me," he declared. "I recognize him from the news. Plus, y'all look just alike for real."

"Yeah, a lot of people say that," Billy Lo lied with a smile.

"I can get a kite to him if you need me to," the chump volunteered.

"Nah, but thanks, I owe you one." Billy Lo nodded to him and used his cane to limp back to the cell.

"What's the word?" Lil' Phil questioned anxiously.

"That little bitch on the hopper tier again," Billy Lo said.

"It's on then," Lil' Phil didn't know exactly what Billy Lo had in mind. But, he knew murder was a part of it.

"You motherfucking right it is." Billy Lo rubbed his hands together. He wouldn't miss his second time around. This time, instead of sending rabbits, he'd go after the fox himself.

***

"Come on now. Talk to me. Somebody knows something, right?" Nizzy stopped talking long enough to look around the table at all the sad faces, then continued. "I mean there's no way that two of my traps get hit and not one body drops."

Everybody remained silent, not really knowing what to say or do. The big ass chrome .357 lying in front of Nizzy had everybody on edge. Especially after he slid one round into the cylinder and began aiming it at them and pulling the trigger every time they gave an answer he refused to accept.

"Okay, I got five bands for anybody who can tell me how they got the drop on us." Nizzy looked around again.

"I think they had inside help," Cock-eyed Willie spoke up.

"You know what your problem is, Willie?" Nizzy picked up the .357 and aimed it at Cock-eyed Willie before pulling the trigger a third time, as Cock-eyed Willie jumped back. Luckily for him though, the hammer only fell on an empty chamber of solid steel. "You think too much," Nizzy continued before laying the .357 back down on the table. "I need facts, not thoughts. Now, where are our eyes?"

"Right here, big homie," a tall goofy, bushy head nigga with some crazy shit tattooed on the side of his face raised his hand.

"What have you done about getting my money back?" Nizzy couldn't remember the knotty head nigga's name.

"I put the word out," the nigga said, standing up.

"Oh," Nizzy looked around and laughed. "He put the word out. The word is out, huh?"

The tatted face kid looked around nervously. Nizzy snatched the .357 up off the table, extended his arm across the table and pulled the trigger until the .357 exploded and the bullet smashed into the center of the tattooed face nigga's forehead.

"There's nothing worst than a nigga that can be bought," Nizzy spat as the nigga's body crumbled to the wooden floor. There was no doubt that the goofy nigga was in JuJu's pocket. "Because he's only loyal to the money and can't be trust."

"Now listen, when one of us fall, all of us hurt. So everybody's taken a pay cut until we make up for the eighty grand lost," Nizzy declared over the sounds of murmurs. "I mean, unless one of you niggas got a problem with that?"

Nizzy surveyed the room and waited. He liked what he saw or what he felt. The love his team once had for him was quickly turning into fear because they didn't know what to expect next. "Good. Now get the fuck out of my sight!"

Niggas couldn't move quickly enough. They were stumbling over each other, trying to get away from the threat of death and the smell of blood.

"Berry," Nizzy called out, pulling out a flip knife. "Cut that clown's eyes out and give them to the next nigga you assign as a lookout." Nizzy tossed Berry the knife. "Hopefully, four eyes are better than two. If not, the one after him will have six."

Berry caught the knife and looked at Nizzy like he was mad. But that didn't stop him from moving towards the dead body to execute Nizzy's order. Berry didn't know what the fuck had gotten into Nizzy. But the shit he was on made Berry uneasy.

"You knew that chamber was empty, Dug?" Cock-eyed Willie asked, noticeably concerned as Berry walked over to the dead body, kneeled down, turned his head and slowly began trying to cut the dude's eyes out.

"Actually no," Nizzy replied, dismissing him. "Man, get your silly ass up! I was playing, nigga." He laughed at Berry, stuffing the .357 into his pocket.

"Oh," Berry stood up happy as shit. "So what now?"

"First, we clean up this mess," Nizzy gestured towards the dead body. "Then, we hit these niggas with everything we got. And I mean everything."

"Yo!" Cock-eyed Willie stumbled backwards into the wall, trying to keep Berry from touching him with his bloody hands. "Stop playing, nigga!" Cock-eyed Willie scrabbled from the room.

"Scared nigga!" Berry exclaimed, as he and Nizzy laughed uncontrollably. Berry enjoyed the moment because he knew that shit was about to get very serious. Not because of Lor'Homie's murder. Not even because of the money and drugs JuJu and 'em had taken. They were insured, and the Muslims had already assured Nizzy that the robbery wouldn't go unpunished. The reason why shit was about to get turned up a notch was because somebody had had the nerve to post some more video footage of Charm slutting Nizzy's bitch out.

Chapter 12

When Tariq brought word about the new robbery and internet stupidity, Adnan immediately got on the phone to reach out behind the prison walls to a few brothers who had control on the inside. Once he found out exactly where Charm was located, he had a cellphone delivered directly to him so that he could express his distaste concerning the recent chain of events.

"How can I be held accountable for some shit I didn't even know was insured?" Charm rationalized, after Adnan explained that the drugs and cash taken from Nizzy's spots needed to be given back as a sign of respect.

"Sometimes we've to pay for the mistakes we didn't realize we made," Adnan reasoned. Despite how much he liked Charm, rules were rules. And Adnan never broke the rules under no circumstances. That was how he'd been so successful during his climb to the top.

"Man, you the one told me Nizzy was out!" Charm argued.

"And I apologize for that. But don't look a gift horse in the mouth, Charm," Adnan warned with a hint of anger. "It could've been a lot worst. Instead I'm giving you a two week grace period to make whatever arrangements you need to make to straighten this thing out."

"Yeah, whatever, man." Charm hung up in Adnan's ear.

Adnan looked at the phone, amused for a moment. Then, he removed the chip, broke it in half and threw everything into the Chesapeake Bay. "Get Yah-Yah and Abdul Azziz to pick up one of Charm's little homeboys. It's time to send him a message."

"I told you not to deal with them *kafirs* in the first place, Ock," Tariq reminded. "Especially after all the stuff with Italians. All they do is a bunch of dumb shit!"

Adnan didn't respond. How could he? Everything Tariq said was right. He'd never dealt with so many fucked-up, back-stabbing snakes in his life. "Yeah, well, life is like business. The only thing that changes is merchandise."

"Can I pull a white shotgun?" Tariq questioned with a smile.

"Not this time, Ock. There's no need to be cruel," Adnan replied. "Plus, I didn't want the body to be found. You know the feds has been stiffing around."

"What about Charm?" Tariq inquired. "You want me to have a couple of brothers over the jail give Charm some lashes?"

"Nah, I'ma show him some mercy for now. After all, we need him to recover our losses and protect our investment." Adnan was like the walking horse who mistakenly shitted on the bird. Yet, like the cat who came along and cleaned the bird off before eating it, he wasn't an enemy because he shitted on you. But he damn sure wasn't a friend because he cleaned you up.

"Suit yourself. I'll take care of the friend immediately." Tariq assured, as they turned and headed towards the waiting car.

"And Tariq," Adnan spoke as they walked to the car. "Make sure you pay Nizzy a visit too." Adnan continued when Tariq looked at him, "Make sure he knows that our favors aren't free."

Tariq smiled. He knew that you could never rest easy on the whip with kafirs because they would get big headed and cocky. "Anything else?" Tariq questioned, opening Adnan's door for him.

"Yeah, just make sure he understands that it's a favor for a favor. And no favors are too big when they're called in."

***

"I'ma fuck Calvin up!" Ebony fired, as she stood over top of JuJu's back, looking down at the hole Charm had secretly made in the floor of her pantry beneath her washer and dryer. "How long that shit been there? How much money is that?"

Ebony was going off, firing off question after question. And all JuJu was trying to do was, take care of this business for Charm and get the fuck outta there before Ebony started swinging or something.

"What else his ass got down there? There better not be no drugs in my house!"

"Come on now, yo," JuJu stood up, and began dusting the plastic wrap off. "You know Dummie not going put you under the gun like that."

"Woooo, wait until I go see his sneaky ass Saturday!" Ebony spat.

JuJu forced his fingers into the plastic, and ripped it open before grabbing a stack of bills and handing them to Ebony. "Here, yo."

"What the fuck am I suppose to do with this?" Ebony eyed JuJu with piercing eyes.

"Get the floor fixed," JuJu suggested. "I don't know."

"I don't care about that damn floor!" Ebony snapped, holding her stomach. "My lease almost up anyway. But, I do have a problem with y'all hiding shit in my house without my knowledge. What if the damn police would've came up in here—"

"Wohh, Ebony yo!" JuJu threw his hands up in surrender when Ebony started going in again. "I don't got nothing to do with nothing in here," JuJu maintained. "You're coming at me about something you and Charm need to talk about."

"You're the one over here though," Ebony retorted sharply.

"And you know what? I'ma bout to bounce too." JuJu started moving.

"Yeah, won't you do that then!" Ebony followed behind him.

JuJu shook his head. Ebony usually was chill as fuck. So, he knew it had to be the pregnancy that had her acting like a bitch. *Fucking hormone!* JuJu thought to himself. "You're right, yo," JuJu agreed, trying to soften her up. "And I'ma holler at Dummie about that shit too—'Cause he shouldn't have nothing in here you don't know about anyway," JuJu added like he was on her side.

"Nah, don't say nothing to his dumb ass—I got him," Ebony replied like she wanted to keep the peace.

Crazy bitch! JuJu thought, smiling. "You sure, yo?" JuJu touched her stomach. "Cos you know I'll step to that nigga about my god-child."

"I'm sure," Ebony replied, as they walked into the front room.

"Oh yeah, I almost forgot," JuJu realized her guards were down and got to the second part of his mission. "How well you know the nigga Tavon Shuley?" JuJu stopped at the front door.

"Not that well." Ebony paused. "I mean, I know his girly ass is on the school basketball team."

"Well, I need to holler at yo about doing an affidavit for Charm's lawyer," JuJu revealed.

"I don't know if that's a good idea or not," Ebony cautioned.

"Why you say that?" JuJu asked curiously.

"Because about two years ago, members of the basketball team were trolling his social media page about him testifying on an innocent person in a bar robbery gone bad."

"Don't worry about all that—Just point him out to me and I'll take care of the rest," JuJu assured after a brief pause. In JuJu's eyes, Bullet wasn't any different than any other sucker or rat he had to pull up on or wipe down for snitching on a good nigga. "I just need to talk to him before Charm's preliminary hearing next week."

"Well, you're going to have to come and pick me up in the morning." Ebony opened the front door.

"Pick you up in the morning?" JuJu repeated. He wasn't really a morning person.

"Yeah," Ebony confirmed.

"Like what time?" JuJu questioned, hoping it wasn't nothing like 8 o'clock in the morning.

"I'll tell you what," Ebony said when she saw the look on JuJu's face. "Why don't I just text you when I see him? That way, we aren't seen together."

"Bet," JuJu liked the sound of that. "Hit me as soon as you see the nigga."

"I got you." Ebony nodded and pushed JuJu out the door.

"That's what it is then." JuJu mumbled before Ebony closed the door. Her idea of not being seen together made perfect sense. Because, truth be told, if Bullet didn't want to have a change of heart and shut his trap, he'd probably end up dying from lead-poisoning. And he didn't want to have to explain that to her.

***

Billy Lo followed Lil' Phil to his cell and leaned up against the grill outside the cell. He needed to be able to watch the tier as Lil' Phil did what he had to do to grab the contraband he had requested. Once Lil' Phil retrieved the goods, he signaled for Billy Lo to step inside the cell and make sure everything was everything.

"You should definitely be able to solve your problem with that," Lil' Phil assured, peeping down the tier again real quick to make sure nobody was coming, as he and Billy Lo switched positions so that he could check the contents of the bag to make sure everything he wanted was there.

"Yeah, Slim," Billy Lo nodded, satisfied, securing the bag. "I really appreciate this."

"Ain't nothing to it. You my man, Slim," Lil' Phil replied honestly, taking his eyes of the tier for a moment. "Look, I already took care of shorty who got the section. And I gave her a Dot to make sure she lets you off the tier as soon as them little hoppers on their way to the gym."

"Good looking," Billy Lo said. Billy Lo knew that Lil' Phil was burning the steam off the pretty little redbone's pussy. She was from around their way, and word had it that Lil' Phil was busting (fucking) her on the streets also.

"You sure you wanna do it like this though?" Lil' Phil questioned, concerned. "I told you I can easily get his little ass chopped up for some strips. You know a lot of them little kids over there junkies for real. And there's no telling how your case might unfold."

"Yeah, I know," Billy Lo agreed. He knew that anything could happen in trial. It really came down to who put on the best performance. But it was better to have what he wanted and not need it than to need it and not have it if the time came. "I tried *that* already. And as far as the other thing, I'd just rather be safe than sorry 'cause I'm not just letting these folks kill me." Billy Lo had a serious look.

"I understand that, but as far as Charm goes, you can just hip the Jamaican Niggas to his involvement in their big homie's murder and let them p-roll his little ass."

"Nah, Slim," Billy Lo shook his head and stepped out of the cell. He'd already thought about that. But the truth was, if he told the Jamaicans about the Townhouse Motel murders of World and Pepsi, he would've to reveal himself also. "This shit personal," Billy Lo added sincerely. His mind was already made up. He had given away all his property and mapped things out in his head one hundred times. So, there was no turning back. He was going to get Charm first and see how trial ends.

"You crazy like that glue, Slim," Lil' Phil proclaimed with admiration. "But, I respect it."

"A'ight, Slim," Lil' Phil said after a moment of silence. "Once you're off the tier, you're on your own."

Billy Lo nodded. It didn't make any difference to him either way. He didn't have any plans of making it back. "I guess this is it then?"

Lil' Phil extended his hand. "I guess so." Lil' Phil took Billy Lo's hand before embracing him brotherly. "At least until next time." Lil' Phil smiled.

"Yeah, we'll see each other again." Billy Lo agreed. "On this side or the other."

Lil' Phil exclaimed, "Take care of yourself, Slim."

"Yeah, you too." Billy Lo nodded and walked off. He had to get ready to handle his business. He wanted to separate himself from Lil' Phil so that he did not get caught up in his shit.

It was about quarter past five p.m. when the tier officer opened the grill and informed Billy Lo that the hoppers were in route to the gymnasium. Billy Lo thanked her and began to step off. But she was determined to let him know that if he got caught and mentioned her name, he'd have a lot more to worry about than some little hopper.

"Yeah, I heard that." Billy Lo smiled at her commendably.

"I'm serious, yo!" she said. "I'll fucking deny everything. And I'll tell everybody up the way!"

"I am serious too," Billy Lo assured. "I got you; I promise," Billy Lo added honestly, trying to convince her to have faith in him. It was just another sad reminder of what the game had come to. "You know how I get down."

"Yeah, that's the only reason I agreed to it. But still yo, if something goes wrong, please keep me out of it."

"Say no more." Billy Lo walked off the section and headed towards his destination. He passed medical first and as usual, the tough ass Nigerian wasn't on his post. So, Billy Lo hit the back steps and made his way up the stairs.

"Hey, my man!" There was a chubby C.O. leaning back lazily in a swivel-chair eating from a tray as soon as Billy Lo emerged from the stairwell. "Where you're going at?"

"Huh?" Billy Lo mumbled, caught off guard.

"I said where are you going at?" the C.O. repeated, stuffing a large chunk of food into his mouth. "You better not be skating!" he warned through a mouthful of food.

"Nah, I'm coming from sick-call."

"Where your pass at?" he probed, pointing his fork at Billy Lo.

"It was for chest pains," Billy Lo lied again, knowing how scared officers were about chest pain complaints due to a recent death and lawsuit over the jail.

"A'ight, man, go ahead." He waved, signaling for Billy Lo to pass by. "You better hurry up too! Don't miss that movement. And don't let me catch your cripple ass out here without your pass again!"

Billy Lo smiled and went on around the corner. He was just glad that the chubby motherfucker had chosen not to pry. He probably would've become collateral damage. *There was nothing that was going to stop Charm from paying the piper today,* he thought. *Nothing!*

Billy Lo walked until he was out of the chubby guard's sight. Then he crept over to the gym door and peeped inside. There were hoppers everywhere—Playing basketball, doing push ups, huddled up on the bleachers, etc.

Billy Lo looked around until he spotted Charm on the sideline talking. "'Hey, man! Chest pain!" the chubby C.O. had just so happened to roll his chair over and look around the corner. "I thought I told your cripple ass to get back to your section! Give me your ID!" he demanded, slowly getting up out of his chair. "You're getting a ticket for skating!"

At that, Billy Lo snatched the gym door open and rushed inside. He didn't expect to go unnoticed too long. Just long enough to reach Charm. So, he moved fast, limping along the wall towards Charm as the little hoppers whispered.

Billy Lo dropped his cane, stepping around the last group of hoppers next to Charm and eased the street-knife out, just as the chubby guard came out of nowhere and tackled the fuck out of him. The entire gym erupted into chaos as more guards stormed the gym from all directions. The little hoppers started going off, yelling all kinds of obscenities as the guards maced Billy Lo and helped the chubby guard wrestle him into a pair of handcuffs and secure his weapon.

What Billy Lo hadn't known was that the moment he ran into the gymnasium, the chubby guard had called the code for assistance. When the guards finally got Billy Lo up off the floor and walked him towards Charm, he just smirked and tried to stop his eyes from burning."

"Oh yeah," Charm mean-mugged Billy Lo knowingly.

"Yeah, nigga, you know what time it is," Billy Lo managed before having another coughing and choking fit as he limped by Charm, barely able to see.

"Yeah, nigga, strictly iron slinging," Charm whispered as the C.O.'s walked Billy Lo past. "You just better hope that you're better at hiding than seeking."

***

"I think we might've just gotten a break in the Izzard case!"

"Detective Gibson came rushing into the office with a disc in her hand.

"What've you got?" Detective Baker sat up in his recliner as Gibson inserted the disc into the DVD player and hit the power button on the flat screen television.

"When the D.A. called last week about Izzard's out-of-bounds situation over at the city lock-up, I had a friend of mine fax me a copy of the full report. Turns out that the juveniles were at the gym when he ran inside and allegedly tried to get rid of a weapon. Which got me to thinking. Maybe Izzard was up there to give Johnson the weapon. Maybe he wanted to settle something."

"Something like what?"

"I don't know yet. Your guess would be as good as mine," Detective Gibson admitted. "What I do know though is that something is off. Even from the attached matter of record claiming that Izzard and Johnson exchanged some sort of idle threats as Izzard was being led from the gymnasium."

"Why would Izzard and Johnson be at odds? That just doesn't make any sense. Maybe they misread what was said."

"Yeah, maybe," Gibson agreed sarcastically. "Or maybe Izzard's little out-of-bounds confession was just a cover up."

"But why would he be after Johnson?" Baker questioned honestly in deep thought.

"That's what I've been wondering," Gibson disclosed. "So, I went and pulled the hospital footage," Gibson added, picking up the remote control, pointing it at the DVD player and pressing the play button.

"Where this?" Baker asked as the lines running across the screen began to clear up.

"The hospital lobby," Gibson replied, looking for the fast-forward button.

"Don't tell me you're thinking that Johnson was somehow involved in the attempt on Izzard's life."

"Not only that," Gibson smiled. "I think Johnson was the triggerman," Gibson revealed, pressing the stop button. "Take a look at this." Gibson used the remote control to zoom in. "Now, I checked Johnson's profile. And he fits the shooter's build to a tee."

"That'll never hold up in court," Baker explained.

"We don't need it to. We can use it for leverage. Just tell me that it doesn't make sense. Johnson was under Pair. Pair was with Izzard. And Izzard is charged with killing the boss of the Playorente family who the Feds hit with the Rico and are now linking to both Johnson and the Muslims."

Detective Baker couldn't help but laugh. "You're kidding, right?"

Baker took his eyes off the TV screen for a moment. Although he would admit that the kid in the video did favor the hell out of Johnson, he still wasn't buying it. "Okay, for the sake of argument, let's say you're correct. Why would Johnson want Izzard dead?"

"That's what I can't figure out," Gibson confessed. "Maybe he needed him out of the way to take over. Maybe Izzard was responsible for Pair's death. Maybe it was a favor for the Mafia blessings. I don't know. But I definitely believe that they are gunning for each other."

"That would explain how the feds got onto them if they're actually hooked up with the Muslim." Baker was beginning to have a moment of clarity. "That would also explain why those Italian names were in the report Malone gave me."

"Whatever it is," Gibson said, "I don't think Johnson's an innocent bystander. Him or any of his little buddies. I think we need to run him in for questioning."

"I think I got a better idea." Baker reached for the phone, wondering if Johnson was in fact their baby-face trigger man.

"Who are you calling?"

"Malone," Baker revealed, dialing Detective Malone's extension.

"You and your little man-face office wife!" Gibson shut the DVD player off.

"How else are we going to get our hands on the governments C.I. list?" Baker queried, amused by Gibson's jealous fit. "It's either Malone or we start pulling teeth," Baker said as Detective Malone's line began to ring.

Gibson knew Baker was right. Kids like Johnson did not just roll over at the sound of trouble. They had to be broken. They had to be stripped to a dentist's chair helpless while all their teeth are being pulled out one by one until their soft spot was found. Such kids were very loyal. "Yeah, well, you do that," Gibson ejected the disc with an attitude. She knew, like everybody else in the department, that Detective Malone was after Baker, despite knowing how she felt about it.

"Do you have another way?" Baker challenged as Malone picked up the phone.

"Hey, detective! This is Detective Baker over in the Homicide Division—Ahhhh, come on now. Don't be like that," Baker let out a phony laugh and winked at Gibson.

Gibson placed the disc back into the DVD case and moved towards the door. "I'll be in the break room going over notes if you need me," Gibson announced, walking out of the office because there was no way that she could sit there and listen to Baker flirt with Malone. Even if it was for her case!

Chapter 13

"It took you long enough, nigga!" JuJu said, the moment I stepped foot outside of the JI-Building on Madison Street after being released on a $500,000.00 bond.

"No bullshit." Slate seconded.

"It's not my fault they take longer to process juvenile paperwork," I gave JuJu and my cousin some love before continuing. "Where the fuck Ebony at?" I asked, looking from my cousin to JuJu curiously. Ebony knew I was being released today. She'd been on the front row in the courtroom during my preliminary hearing.

"I don't know, Dummie," JuJu hunched his shoulders. "I haven't heard from her since we left the courthouse yesterday. She's probably still in bed somewhere. You know how that pregnancy shit be having them females."

"She's not in the house," I said. "I've been calling all morning."

"A'ight, we'll figure it out on the way," JuJu interrupted my thoughts. "Let's get the fuck away from here before these bitches find some warrants or something." JuJu laughed, getting into the car. I climbed into the back seat to change clothes as Slate made his way around to the driver's seat. "Boy, y'all niggas came through, Dummie," I acknowledged, as Slate slid behind the wheel.

"Nah, Dummie, you just got a horseshoe," JuJu declared, as Slate slowly pulled off into traffic. "I was just telling Slate how lucky your ass is."

"Ain't no question," Slate agreed, adjusting the rearview mirror.

"Don't be adjusting my mirror, nigga!" I demanded, pulling a fresh black and white, checker-board Polo shirt over my head.

"Uh, this my shit now," Slate retorted, laughing. "That's another thing we're going to have to talk about."

"Fuck outta here," I slipped into some black joggers and reached for the white-on-white Dope's (Penny Hardaway's). "Ain't nothing to talk about."

"Reach under the seat right there," JuJu directed, turning around to point. "Grab that bag."

I had to lean down to pull the bag from underneath the passenger's seat. "Fuck is this?" I questioned, sitting the bag on my lap.

"Oh yeah," I smiled, peeping inside the bag. It contained a bullet-proof vest and a Chrome .45. "This how y'all doing it, Dummie?"

"Something like that," JuJu spoke over his shoulder. "We got that up off Nizzy, though."

"Them niggas had a baby arsenal too, fam," Slate added.

"He's probably still fucking with Ugunoba," I revealed, thinking about the African gunrunner that we all dealt with.

"Yeah, well, we need to holler at him and put a stop to that," JuJu said. "In the meantime, wear that vest like your life depends on it because I'm tired of looking at you all sympathetically and shit."

"Ah nigga, fuck you!" I said, laughing. But, if the truth was to be told, JuJu couldn't have gotten me a better gift. Because I definitely needed something after that last slip up. "Slate, did you get on top of that other thing?"

"Yeah, yeah—I hollered at my man about setting something up," Slate replied, never taking his eyes off the road. "He's all for it too."

"You really gonna rock with some Maryland niggas?" JuJu glanced over his shoulder at me seriously. "P.G. County niggas?"

"D.C.," Slate corrected before I could respond.

"D.C., P.G., V.A.—They're all the same to me," JuJu retorted. "Them niggas don't have no discipline, so they can't be trusted. You're better off dealing with the Bloods."

I knew it came as a surprise when I first agreed to meet with my cousin's Washington D.C. homeboy. Especially after I'd flipped out in the visiting room. But, after great consideration, I realized that we needed a source of steady income. Plus, it wasn't like they were Bloods or nothing. From what Slate explained, his man wasn't too fond of them either. In fact, he'd been on their line since hitting the bricks.

"You must've had a Bad Boys' Village experience," Slate joked.

"Yeah, a'ight," JuJu mumbled like he had an attitude.

"Seriously though, them niggas just like us, yo—They treat suckers like suckers and men like men," Slate explained.

"Look," I interjected, "both of y'all niggas are entitled to y'all own opinions. And y'all ain't got to like the other's to respect it. But they're real and we're real. Plus, they aren't Bloods. So, I'm with it." I knew that my cousin and JuJu had different experiences when it came to Washington D.C. dudes. JuJu had been in a couple brief, but rememberable knuckle-fights out Boys' Village too, whereas Slate had met and bonded with men from both P.G. County and D.C. at the Charles Hickey Training School while doing juvenile life.

"Because with all this shit going on with Nizzy, we're going to need another outlet, Dummie," I continued. "We can't continue to keep putting all our eggs in one basket," I added, seeming to have JuJu's attention.

"Well, I still ain't trusting them back-alley ass niggas," JuJu argued.

"Already," I replied honestly, knowing that them niggas were probably going to feel the same way. "You don't have to worry about that right now anyway. First, we got to deal with this shit with Adnan."

"Man, fuck them hairy face ass niggas, Dummie." JuJu never made it a secret that when it came to beef. Anybody could get it.

"Yeah, fam, you know I ain't never been picky," Slate added. "Them bitches done basically threatened your life. So we need to hit them before they hit us. Fuck waiting."

"That's why I want to get everybody together," I explained. "Which reminds me—What the fuck is up with O? That nigga stopped answering his phone."

"He hasn't been answering my text messages or nothing," JuJu confessed without hesitation. "One of the old head around the way swear he was the dude that got cracked in the head with the two-by-four and tossed into the back of the F-150."

"What about his daughter's mother? Anybody rap to her?"

"Murdock did," JuJu shook his head. "She hasn't heard from him either."

That definitely did not sound like O. He was the main one that stay on us about always answering our cellphones. "A'ight, find out what you can about this F-150 truck," I ordered, hoping and praying that nothing bad had happened to Dummie. Especially not now with so much stuff going on. Lord knows we couldn't stand to lose another Dummie.

"I'ma holler at the old head again," JuJu said.

For reasons difficult to understand, being released was proving to be more exhilirating than being free with all the madness that had awaited me.

It did not take us long to get to Ebony's spot. I used my key to let myself in. I tossed my stuff on the sofa and told Slate and JuJu to make themselves at home as I headed on upstairs to see what was up with my girl.

"She still up there sleep, isn't she?" Slate looked up as I came bouncing down the stairs.

"Nah, she not even here," I admitted, trying to figure out where the hell Ebony could be. She hadn't said anything about no clinic appointments or nothing. "She probably thought I was going to meet her at her godmother's house," I defended, pulling out my phone. "Where the fuck you get that from?" I questioned JuJu as he came strolling out of the kitchen with a pint of strawberry ice cream and an open pack of chocolate donuts.

"The refrigerator, nigga," JuJu walked past me and sat down on the sofa.

"Don't be touching shit, Dummie," I warned.

"Nigga, I'm hungry! I been sitting outside that jail all fucking morning," JuJu argued.

"So what! I'm not trying to hear Ebony's mouth."

"And I'm not trying to hear yours!" JuJu exclaimed, eating a big scoop of ice cream.

I just shook my head and dialed Ebony's cellphone number. *This nigga play too much*, I thought.

"Hello!" a soft voice echoed into my ear on the end.

"Hello?" I repeated, taking a look at my screen to be sure I'd dialed the right number. "Ebony?"

"I was wondering when you were going to call."

"Who is this?" I questioned, curious, figuring it was probably one of Ebony's little fresh ass, grown-acting god-sisters playing on her phone. "Put Ebony on the phone."

"Ebony can't talk right now."

"Look, I'm not really in a playing mood right now."

"Oh, you think this is a joke huh?" The sexy voice purred in my ear. "Take the gag outta that bitch's mouth and bring her over here!"

There was a brief pause and then I heard what sounded like struggling. "Talk, bitch!" I picked up a male voice a split second before what sounded like a heavy-handed slap echoed on the other end of the phone. "Talk!"

"Calvin! Calvin!" My heart stopped the instant I heard the fear in Ebony's voice.

"Ebony! Ebony, baby!" I called out. "Ebony!"

"Now that I have your attention, we can talk business," The sexy voice vibrated in my ear with assurance this time.

"Bitch," I fired, full of rage. "I swear on everything I love. If something happen to my girl I'm—"

"Yeah, yeah, yeah, I know," she interrupted sarcastically. "Right now though, you need to shut up and listen carefully because I'm only going to say this once. You with me?"

I took a deep breath. I felt like a chess player who'd just lost his most value piece in a grown man's game of chess.

"I said are you with me?"

"'My bad, yeah," I submitted, swallowing my pride. I'd zoned out for a moment.

"Good, that's better," the sexy voice taunted. "Now listen very carefully because, like I said, I'ma only going to say this once."

"I'm with you!" I vowed, clenching my teeth. By now, Slate and JuJu were both on their feet, standing next to me, trying to figure out exactly what the fuck was going on. I kept waving them off, though, signaling for them to fall back. I had to focus precisely on what was being said, and I couldn't afford to miss anything. Especially since the lives of my girl and unborn child depended on it.

"Hold on, you're gonna have to give me a few days," I pleaded, probably sounding more emotionally frantic than Ebony. "I don't just have that kind of bread laying around."

"Well, I suggest you use what you do have to start making funeral arrangements. Because in twenty-four hours. I'ma gut this bitch like a pig and scatter her body parts all over the city!" the sexy voice declared before hanging up.

"Fuck!" I squeezed my phone so hard that I cracked the screen. I was too mad to cry and too angry to panic. But my thoughts were all over the place. I knew I had to stay level-headed, especially if I planned on getting Ebony back alive.

"What the fuck is going on, Dummie?" JuJu stared at me, concerned.

"Somebody snatched my baby mother," I finally revealed, as what felt like a sword ripped through my heart.

"What? Who?" Slate questioned.

"I don't know. Some bitch answer the phone. She said that if I don't have two hundred bands when she calls back tomorrow then it's game over."

"You think it's Nizzy again?" Slate inquired.

"I don't know," I admitted, disappointed in myself. "Probably so, he's the only one who knows we're sitting on that kind of bread around the first of the month to cover Adnan. Plus, the bitch said something to the fact of gutting Ebony."

"Them niggas probably done got some information out of Ebony," JuJu observed "You know she caught me pulling that money outta the floor?"

"Damn!" I flipped the little living room coffee table over, wishing Ebony had never been pulled into my street business. Then, I began to feel sick to my stomach as thoughts of some wannabe gangsters torturing my baby played out in my head. She was liable to tell them any and everything they wanted to know to survive.

"So how these motherfuckers plan on getting the money?" JuJu asked, probably thinking something dumb.

"I don't know. The bitch just said that she'd call me with all the details tomorrow. I should've never even had Ebony around this shit. I knew better too. Only a dumb nigga has street shit around those he loves. Why the fuck did—"

"Look, fam," Slate cut me off, "there's no sense in crying over spilt milk. Niggas gotta think this shit through."

"He's right, Dummie," JuJu seconded. "You can't go walking into something you can't walk out of."

"That's my baby mother, Dummie!" I argued, looking from one to the other. "I don't give a fuck. I'll murder everything moving about her."

"Yeah, and you're my family!" Slate retorted. "So, I'm not going to just sit back and let you do some reckless shit!"

I ignored Slate because I already knew his motto. He didn't trust nothing that could squeeze the sense out of a nigga in seconds, get beat up for hours, bleed for days, spit out babies every nine months and survive.

"A'ight, what about the money?" JuJu looked at me. "I mean, you know we just really scrapped that fifty bands together for your bail."

"Yeah, I'm hip." I paused for a second to think. I knew what I was thinking could potentially cause us a lot of trouble. But it was trouble I was willing to accept for the life of my girl and unborn child. I just needed to know that the squad was behind me. "I'ma use the bread I got for Adnan," I stated.

"You sure you wanna do that?" JuJu stared at me.

"You motherfucking right," I said, not really believing he had the audacity to question that.

"Then let's go get this bread—So when these motherfuckers call, we can box them in and make some toast," JuJu said. "I mean, after all, it was probably going to come to that anyway once yo and 'em didn't get that other bread back."

"What about you, fam?" I turned to my cousin Slate.

"What about me *what*?"

"I mean look, you just really came home and I'm not trying to get you jammed up in all this bullshit," I admitted honestly.

"What? Fam, stop playing. You family over everything. I just hope Ebony didn't see these motherfuckers' faces because we all know what that means."

Chapter 14

"Peanut? What are you doing around here?" Charm questioned with a touch of curiosity in his voice, looking around the carry-out cautiously. He hadn't seen me since Black and Mumbles' funerals.

I gave Charm a wicked grin as two of Roofy's henchmen walked in and posted up. "We'll save that for another time. Right now, I just want the two hundred grand I came for so you can get your bitch back."

"What?" Charm seemed surprised. Maybe even amazed. "You got my girl?" he asked, slowly reaching for what I assumed was his gun.

"You sure you want to do that, Charm?" I opened my arms wide as Trini and Charco drew their weapons. "Because you know what happens to your little girlfriend after that, right."

"Si," Trini slowly licked his lips a moment before anger flashed in Charm's eyes.

"How—how could you?" Charm's words came out slow as he realized exactly what it was. "You suppose to be family," he added, and I sensed more pain than anger.

"You too," I reminded. "Yet, here we are." I confirmed that I was the reason for his current dilemma.

"I don't get it. You fucking with Nizzy?" Charm was still confused. "Why you snatch my girl?" Charm questioned, finally realizing that it had been my voice on the other end of the phone.

"You started this game, Charm," I said. My pain wouldn't allow me to feel sorry for him. "Mumbles took you in and laced your boots. And how did you repay him, huh?"

"I never crossed Mumbles. That's my brother!" Charm argued.

I couldn't help but laugh. "What did you think you were doing when you decided to join forces with the motherfuckers who had him killed? Honoring him? Better yet, what did you think you were doing when you went and accepted a contract on Billy Lo?" I questioned, knowing for a fact that Mumbles had taught him how true honor was measured by the things a man did and didn't do in the dark. The things he never thought would be discovered.

"Billy Lo got my sister murked!" Charm defended. "Mumbles was the one who use to always say it was all fair in love and war as long as you didn't snitch on a nigga. So, I just got paid for doing what he talked me out of doing twice."

"And look what it has cost you. Look at the position you're in."

"You aren't any better than me, Peanut! You violated my family." Charm's hand twitched as if he was having a hard time not going for his gun.

I wished there had been a better way. But war had always been about deception. "You made your bed, Charm. Now you got to choose if you want to lay with your baby's mother or the Muslims," I challenged with a smile. "Now, where's my money?"

"Under the driver's seat of my truck," Charm confessed. "Where's my girl? I wanna talk to her."

"First, you need to hand me your keys." I gestured towards Charm's front pocket and waited for him to reluctantly comply.

"Good." I accepted the keys before pulling out my cell phone. I strolled down to Zimbabwe's burner number and hit the call button.

"Hello. Yeah—we're handling it now—Put the girl on the phone," I ordered, tossing Charm's keys over to Charco. "Go get the money."

I heard Charm's bitch voice, and switched the speaker phone on. "Say hi," I held the phone and stood there listening as Charm went through a series of questions. Asking his girl if she and the baby were alright. If anyone had touched her and so on.

"Okay, show's over. You talked to her," I ended the call. "Once my guy verifies that the money is good, I'll give you the address to a vacant house out in Dundulk where you will find her tied up and blindfolded."

Charm just stared at me as Charco came in and whispered into my ear. If thoughts could kill, I'd probably be dead. Nodding for Trini to hand Charm the folded up piece of paper with the location of his girl scribbled on it, I spoke, moving towards the exit. "Well, I guess that concludes our business. You should find your property intact at that location."

Charm quickly unfolded the paper and followed me out of the carry-out. "If a curl is out of place on her head, I swear to—"

"Unlike you, Charm," I stopped to turn around, "I always honor my word."

"Oh, this isn't over, bitch, believe that!" Charm threatened. "You think you're just going to walk away from this. You think I'ma let you kidnap my baby's mother and get away with it?"

"The way I see it, you're in the same boat Mumbles was in when he was killed. So, you know what's coming."

"You think I give a fuck? I'ma fucking gangster!" Charm spat. "Fuck you! Fuck them Muslims! And fuck Billy Lo! I got a squad of goons behind me!"

"Good luck." I smiled, walking towards Charco's car.

"You're the one who's going to need the luck, bitch," Charm warned. "Because if I don't know nothing else, I know how to get money. So, I'ma definitely see you again."

"Yeah, well, you know Mumbles was Black's brother. And Black's strength in the city outweighs any wealth you can ever obtain. Don't ever forget that."

"We'll see," Charm shook his head and stared at me as I opened the car door, climbed inside, and left him standing there in his own thoughts.

I knew Charm would probably come looking for me. Honestly, I didn't expect nothing less. I was actually anticipating it. Because I knew his pride would blind him. However, I knew that Charm didn't know just how gangster I was. He couldn't fathom how well Black had trained me. If he could, he would've known that I'd inevitable lead him to his own death. Because my next trap was a one-way ticket to hell.

***

Shabazz got up earlier than usual to make *salat* and workout while Latif slept. The plan was to play today like it was any other day, although it wasn't. They say that the hardest part of your bid was the beginning and the end. The beginning because you were trying to get back what you'd lost, and the end because you were dying to apply what you'd learned.

"Tryna get that early money, huh?" Latif rolled over half asleep, rubbing his eyes. "You want me to go with you?"

"Nah, get your rest, fat boy," Shabazz joked. "You know we gotta go out in the cages and break Masood and them tonight anyway." Shabazz reminded Latif of their weekly workout session with a few Muslim brothers.

"Today's babygirl birthday, right?" Latif questioned, readjusting the covers.

"Yeah," Shabazz smiled at the thought of his daughter. He was so proud of her. She was a mother, beautiful wife, strong black queen, successful business woman, and so on. Everything he did was for her and his only grandchild. People could say what they wanted. But his mother had always told him that if he hadn't done anything else right in life, he'd nailed that part. "Do me a favor though, Ock."

"What's that?" Latif turned over.

"The next time you got something to say, put that toothbrush in your mouth first and kill those motherfuckin' germs," Shabazz teased as Latif snickered, rolled back over and pulled the cover over his head. "You almost ruin the day with your mouth."

"I know you're not talking," Latif secretly smelled his own breath before continuing to talk trash. "Your breath got your hair so scared you can't even grow a beard. And—"

Shabazz and Latif traded jokes until Latif eventually dozed back off. Then Shabazz went ahead and got to work. He did a hundred squats straight. Then he did a series of sit-ups followed by two hundred bends and reaches. Next, he did a hundred push-ups and finished up with thirty minutes of shadow-boxing. After that he took a quick birdbath and made *dua*—the prayer of invocation, supplication or request to Allah.

"Allah doesn't change the conditions of a people until they change their own conditions," Shabazz quoted one of his favorite surahs from the Holy Qur'an to himself as he came out of prayer. It was proof that Allah required man to put in work when and if he wanted to change the conditions of his life.

Shabazz ate an orange for breakfast and sat down to read his Qur'an for a moment. It was time to get his life together. He thought about how much Kaamil and Ameen had been on him before they were let back into general population. But honestly, it was the way Wakal had forgiven him that had the most impact. Shabazz remembered looking out the cell door window as Wakal was being packed up for transfer back over to Steelside, wondering if he could ever get to that point in Islam. The point where forgiveness came easy.

Once Shabazz read surah 75, 'Al-Qiyamah' [The Resurrection], he wrote a quick letter and slid it into the back of his Qur'an. Proper food for the mind was just as important as proper food for the body. It was just before 8:09 a.m. when the cell light was flicked on from outside, and a loud knock repeatedly rattled the door. The knock made both Latif and Shabazz look up.

"Yeah," Latif barked, kicking his leg out. "I know you see me moving!" Latif added, knowing it wasn't nothing but one of the asshole officers who liked to use the, 'I gotta make sure you're still alive' excuse to wake a nigga up for no reason. "Turn the fucking light off!" Latif ordered, snatching the cover from over his head.

"Bulovan!" The big face redneck who normally worked the compound pressed his face against the cell window glass. "Bulovan!"

"Yeah," Shabazz shook his head. It wasn't no way in the world the cracker didn't see him sitting there on his bunk reading.

"Cuff up!" the redneck ordered before sticking his key into the lock to open the tray-slot.

"Cuff up for what?" Shabazz sat his Qur'an on the bed.

"What's up, Ock?" Latif sat up and quickly jumped off the top bunk. If something was about to go down with Shabazz, he wasn't about get caught sleeping.

"I don't know," Shabazz replied, standing up.

"Bulovan," the redneck called, pulling the slot open. "Come to the door and cuff up now!"

"What am I cuffing up for?" Shabazz walked over to the door.

"Y'all bitches always fucking with a nigga!" Latif shouted in the background, ready to go all the way about Shabazz. "Just tell him what he's cuffing up for!" Latif reasoned, knowing that chaos was these crackers' order. They enjoyed making an easy situation difficult.

"Just turn around and cuff up!" the red neck commanded again, tapping his handcuffs on the feed-up slot. "I don't got all day."

"Man, I'm trying to see the Sergeant then!" Shabazz declared, walking back over to sit down on the bunk.

Latif walked over to the door, peeped out and saw a Sheriff standing off to the side. "Ayo, Ock, it's a Sheriff out here."

"What?" Latif stepped out of the way as Shabazz went back to the door. "Oh, y'all playing games," Shabazz mumbled, slowly backing up, shaking his head. "I'm definitely not cuffing up until I see somebody."

"Are you sure you want to go down that road, Bulovan?" the big redneck questioned in a threatening tone.

"Let me speak with him," the Sheriff requested, stepping forward. "You're being charged with the attempted murder of Lamarr Harris on April first, nineteen seventy two and I'm here to escort you to intake for booking."

Shabazz nodded, turned around, and put his hands out through the slot behind his back. "I just wanted to know what was going on."

"Come and cuff up too, Stanton," the red neck requested, carefully placing the first pair of handcuffs around Shabazz's wrist.

"You good, Ock?" Latif looked at Shabazz and didn't move. When it came to riding against the police, Latif was always all in.

"I'm good, Ock," Shabazz replied, moving out of the way so that Latif could comply.

"Who the hell is Kevin Richardson?" Latif tried to remember the names of all the Jokers who'd gotten hit, as he turned around to get cuffed.

"I'm not sure, Ock," Shabazz lied. He knew exactly who Kevin Richardson was. It was his cousin—Disco Kev. "It must be one of them Joker's names."

"What nigga's telling?" Latif asked, surprised. It took a certain caliber of 'bitch nigga' to tell in the joint when everybody was already locked up.

"I don't know. But listen," Shabazz whispered as the red neck reached in and secured the handcuffs around Latif's wrist. "If I ain't back by tonight, there's a letter in the back of my Qur'an. Mail it out for me."

"I got you," Latif assured as the big redneck radioed for the cell door to be opened.

"Step out, Mister Bulovan!" the Sheriff ordered.

"As-alaam-alaikum, Ock!" Shabazz greeted Latif before stepping out of the cell backwards as the Sheriff held onto the cuffs. "Don't forget the letter, Ock."

"Walaikum salaam," Latif replied. "I'm on it."

"So how does this work?" Shabazz questioned, making small talk as the redneck hillbilly secured Latif back inside the cell.

"It's pretty A-B-C, buddy. You'll be transported over to the local station house. Finger-printed, photographed and booked on new charges." The Sheriff explained. "I am sure you know the routine, Mister Bulovan."

"How long does that take?" Shabazz continued, as they began to walk down the tier.

"Not long," the Sheriff replied.

"You okay, Ock?" a Muslim brother named Masood—aka Cedric the Entertainer—yelled from the cell, concerned.

"Yeah, they're rebooking me on some new charges!" Shabazz hollered back before being led off the tier.

Shabazz didn't smile until he passed through the Western Correctional Institution gates, cleared the vehicle search area, drove across the parking lot, and turned onto the expressway. He couldn't believe that he'd actually pulled it off. Who'd thought that after over three decades in prison, he'd escape by walking straight out of the front door? All praise be to Allah.

"Here," the phony Sheriff that his mother had hired to come get him tossed the handcuff keys into the back seat. "Get dressed!" he ordered. "There's a bag underneath the seat," he added, leaning over to open the glove-compartment to remove something. "That's ten thousand dollars in cash, two plane tickets and an entire new identity. Your flight leaves in twenty minutes."

"Where am I going?" Shabazz accepted the sealed package.

"Don't know, don't care!" the phony Sheriff retorted. "My job was to get you out and take you to the airport. The rest is on you." The phony Sheriff fell silent.

Shabazz didn't ask anymore questions. He didn't need to. He was a free man and he didn't have any plans of ever going back. He thought about Latif and Shaheed for a moment and smiled. Those were his little brothers, and he regretted having to leave them behind. But hey, once Latif read the letter that he'd stuffed in the back of his Qur'an for him, he'd be okay.

Shabazz looked over his shoulder just in time to see the Western Correctional Institution compound fade into the distance as they went around the bend. He didn't know where or how far his son-in-law's computer hacking skills would take him. But he was willing to go.

***

Billy Lo was laying across the bunk writing his lawyer about possibly waving the coming motion hearing. Billy Lo was ready to start trial. He couldn't ever remember being around so many lames, cowards, rats, and swine-dogs at one time. Especially on lock-up. A place where men used to find solace. A place where men like Billy Lo had created the entire 'swine-dog' concept back in the mid 90's to keep suckers in line. Now that was fucked up. Invaded by a bunch of off-brand niggas who didn't want to do nothing but bang, yell, throw feces, get high and sell death out of the cell doors all day. Real live cell-gangsters.

Billy Lo wondered what had happened to the days when men controlled spots like lock-up and admin. Days when motherfuckers wouldn't just say anything out of the door. More importantly, Billy Lo wondered what had happened to the men. Now, everybody wanted the fame without the pain. Dudes wanted credit they didn't earn nor deserve. Credit they weren't due.

Dickhead Detective Baker and his pussy-ass partner Gibson kept pulling Billy Lo out for questioning. Fishing as if they'd really get something out of him. But Billy Lo was as solid as they came. He was the last of a dying breed. He always got a good laugh, though. Especially when they'd try to threaten him with more time like anything could be worse than the death penalty.

"I wouldn't snitch to bring my family back!" Billy Lo always assured before promising to slump them both if he ever got the chance again.

The only good thing that had happened since Billy Lo had gotten placed on lock-up was the fact that Charm now knew that he could reach out and touch his little ass from beyond the prison walls. After Billy Lo finished writing, he tapped on the cell wall in code and waited for his next-door neighbor to pass his cellphone over. He needed to make a few calls.

"How long you gonna be?" Billy Lo's neighbor inquired, sticking his hand out, holding the camouflaged phone after tapping back on the wall a few times.

"What?" Billy Lo reached out and snatched the phone out of his hand. "As long as I want to be, nigga! Fuck is you hollering bout? You better fall back!"

"Nah, I didn't mean it like that." The sucker quickly attempted to humble himself. "I was just talking to my girl."

"I don't give a fuck who you were talking to, nigga!" Billy Lo looked at the wall crazy as if his neighbor could see his face. "Watch the fucking tier!" Billy Lo added, yanking his make-shift curtain closed so that he could make his phone calls in private.

Billy Lo shook his head as he began dialing Shaneeka's number. It never failed. Every time a man tried to treat a sucker like a man, the sucker turned around and tried to treat a man like a sucker.

Chapter 15

Over the next few weeks things really went from bad to worst. First, Adnan informed me that O was dead and that I supposely had a $50,000 'dead or alive' price tag on my head. So, I had everybody from crudy Muslims to known hitters gunning for me. Then, word got out that we were up to our old tricks. Jacking connects and customers alike. On top of that, I now knew that the cops were looking for me. That was only half of it. Whatever the case, I wasn't laying down for nobody. If the police wanted my freedom, they had to catch me. If the streets wanted to collect on my head, they'd better make funeral arrangements because they'd die trying to take me alive. It was just as simple as that.

I couldn't help but sit back and think of how good shit was when it was just all about stolen cars and neighborhood reps. There was so much love, honor and respect amongst us. We were so loyal, but broke. Then, we all got rich and everybody began to change.

"You think them nigga will go for that?" JuJu questioned, referring to the Muslims, as we sat in a stolen Honda Accord down the street from one of Peanut's henchmen's house on Pratt Street, waiting for my cousin Slate to give the signal.

It turns out that Slate knew Charco from doing time in Training School. So, when he'd saw him exit the carry-out to retrieve the money out of the truck, he tapped Murdock and told him that there was no reason for them to try and follow the kidnappers because he knew exactly who Charco was. And he knew exactly where to find him at. In fact, Slate said he still had the contact information Charco had given him before they had departed.

Charco was somewhat of a Training School legend. Not only had he and another crazy ass Holland Town white boy shot their way up out of Training School. But, Charco was the only juvenile in Training School history who'd actually been transferred over to adult custody after turning twenty-one.

"Shiddd, if I tell em' I got the money and drugs, they'll go for anything," I replied, knowing that all Adnan's greedy ass ever cared about was the profit. "I really just want to get Adnan out of the shadows," I admitted honestly. I wanted Adnan's coward ass more than anything. But he'd fled the oil shop after admitting to ordering O's murder.

"After that, it's whatever!" I added. Because there was no way that I was going to allow Adnan to sit back, relax, and call shots like it was business as usual, or like he was untouchable. This wasn't Pakistan. It was Charm City, and my squad went harder than ISIS.

"You see this, Dummie?" JuJu asked as a red low-rider pulled up in front of Charco's spot and double parked.

"Text Slate!" I exclaimed anxiously, recognizing Peanut's other henchman the moment he climbed out of the passenger's side. "Ayo, I think I know that truck from somewhere." I added as JuJu removed his phone.

"What the fuck!" JuJu and I fired in unison, realizing the car was surrounded by a gang of Mexicans at the same time. For a second, everybody seemed to pause. Not really sure what to do next. Then, Charco's front door came open and my cousin Slate stepped outside on the porch and signaled for us to come in. That was all I needed to see to know that something was wrong.

"Something's wrong, Dummie," I whispered to JuJu under my breath. "Get ready to do your thing. 'Cause I ain't going out like no bitch."

There was a tap on the window, and I looked up to see the business-end of a big ass gold-plated Desert Eagle pointing at me.

"Whatever you're thinking, I suggest you think again, homes," the Mexican warned, opening my door.

Where the fuck is Murdock? was my only thought as JuJu's door was snatched opened and I slowly climbed out of the car.

"Don't worry about your other homeboy, homes," the Mexican seemed to read my mind. "He's already inside."

"Say what?" I played dumb. Hopefully, he wasn't referring to Murdock.

"Your amigo, homes," he gestured towards the top of the block. "Up the block. The one who thought he was in covert."

Once I got completely out of the car, the Mexican pushed me up against the driver's side door and aggressively searched me as two other Mexicans searched JuJu. "This is our turf, homes. Us see everything," the Mexican searching me said.

After our weapons were confiscated, JuJu and I were marched down the street to Charco's crib as I tried to get a look at the driver of the low-rider before he pulled off.

Inside, Murdock and Slate were sitting on the living room sofa at gunpoint. "Glad you could join us, Charco smiled. "Allow me to properly introduce myself," he added, extending his hand. "Charco."

"Charm," I shook Charco's hand nervously.

"Have a seat, Charm," Charco ordered, walking back across the room. "Now that we're all friends, maybe you can explain to me why you were sitting outside my home."

"I was waiting for my cousin." I lied.

"That's funny because this guy here," Charco pointed to Murdock, "says the same thing, which leads me to believe that Slate is not as honorable a friend as I once thought."

"Come on, Charco man. You know I'm solid," Slate said.

"Hold up," I interjected. "Ain't no sense of playing games. Y'all niggas grabbed my baby's mother. What the fuck you thought was going to happen if I ever found out who you were?"

"I like you, Charm," Charco stared at me and smiled. "That's why I'm going to offer you a way out of this. You see, I'm a businessman first. And business is never personal. But it's going to cost you."

"Cost me what?' My mind was going crazy, but I was willing to pay whatever to get me and my niggas out alive.

"I'm not sure yet. I'll have to make a few calls to figure it out." He pulled out his phone.

"Can I ask you something?" I questioned, really curiously about something.

"What's that, homes?" Charco pressed his phone to his ear.

"Whose red low-rider was that outside?"

Chapter 16

Wakal gazed out the rain-drop covered window of the prison bus on the way to court as flashes of lightning flickered in the distance. It seemed like a lifetime since Wakal had seen the city, and he was amazed at all the new changes. There were new stores and construction sites everywhere. Wakal saw a 'Black Lives Matters' banner and smiled. The city was definitely changing. It made him wonder where he'd have fit in had they never got into bed with Mumbles' hot ass cousin, Fat Card. As the Bluebird entered the underground tunnel, Wakal began to say a silent prayer. He now understood that sometimes in life's darkest moments, that was the only certain thing you had. Because whenever things seemed uncertain, Allah always knew best.

"Come on, let's go, let's go, let's go!" the C.O. with the irritating voice ordered, stepping up on the Bluebird with an attitude after the door opened. "Everybody, don't move at once!"

Wakal sighed in frustration. His mind was on Tiara's chump ass baby's father, and how he was refusing to allow her to come to court and help him out. Wakal didn't know niggas like Tiara's baby father still existed. Niggas who didn't want to see a man free. Wakal was starting to accept the fact that there were just no more real dudes in the streets. Everybody was dead or in prison.

Wakal stepped off the bus carefully and stretched his legs when it was his turn. He took his time, slowly following the guy in front of him through the basement of the courthouse. The leg-irons, three-piece, and long chain-gang-like line prevented him from moving too fast. This made him more frustrated because they still had to be strip-searched again before they could be escorted upstairs to the bullpens.

Once Wakal made it upstairs to the bullpen, he sat down in the corner and tried to gather his thoughts as everyone busied themselves revealing too much information about their cases or unsolved cases. Wakal was even forced to cover his nose when a couple of idiots wearing 'Black Lives Matter' t-shirts decided to smoke some of that crazy shit. The same shit that had guys up in

Cumberland, Maryland jumping off tiers, barking like dogs, fighting themselves, and being rushed out to the emergency room. He tried not to judge them though. It was just a serious reminder of how fucked up the game was. A reminder that snakes, rats and cowards still lurked in the darkness. A reminder why he'd chosen to live his life in the light. Wakal did wonder what the hell they were putting in the drugs nowadays, and thanked Allah that he'd stopped getting high.

"Donald White?" A nerdy looking white boy with large bifocals appeared at the gate near the door. "Donald White!" he repeated, looking around the bullpen as Wakal stood up and approached.

"Yeah, what's up?" Wakal looked around cautiously. He hadn't forgotten about all the dirt he'd done during his reign. He knew that there were still sins he'd yet to answer for.

"My name is Thaddus Clemons. And I am from the Public Defenders Office. I'll be representing you today in court." The nerd used his index finger to push his huge glasses back up over the bridge of his nose.

"Oh, okay," Wakal acknowledged, trying to size him up. The motherfucker looked like he was fresh out of law school. "So what do you think?"

"Honestly, I haven't had a chance to read the transcripts yet," he admitted, pushing on the rim of his glasses again as he almost dropped all his folders. "I just wanted to introduce myself."

"So what are you going to ask for today?" Wakal questioned, concerned.

"Oh, I am going to request a postponement," he assured, readjusting his folders as his glasses slid down to the tip of his nose.

Wakal just stared at him. *Where did they find this clown at?* Wakal thought, taking a deep breath. "So that's it? You're just going to ask for a postponement?"

"As I explained, Mister White, I haven't had a chance to view your case. You wouldn't want me to go in there blind now, would you?" He joked with a smile.

Wakal wasn't amused. In fact, his anger started to build. It always did when someone mistreated him, blamed him or gossiped about him. "Did you at least read my letter about possible witnesses?"

"Your letter?" He seemed puzzled, as he pushed his glasses back up and began to flip through the folders in search of something. "Oh, yes." He smiled, appearing to remember. "The letter you sent before the new year," he added. "Yep, I did in fact receive it. Picked it up from the office yesterday when I got in from my holiday vacation.

"That's the problem. *You bitches out there just living life while we're in here fighting for ours*, Wakal thought. He knew that only a few niggas got lucky with P.D.'s who wanted to work. Most of the time, it was literally a simple draw of the hat. Wakal just wished that somebody else had pulled his name.

"A'ight, after you go over everything, can you schedule a visit so we can sit down and discuss strategy?"

"Will do," he joked. "Noted!" he added, touching his dumb ass glasses again before ruffling through his folders to call the next nigga whose life he was playing with.

"D.W.?" Someone called as Wakal was making his way back across the bullpen to his seat. Without acknowledging if he was D.W. or not, Wakal looked over to see Billy Lo's egg head ass sitting on the bench near the bathroom. "Man, I thought that was you," Billy Lo said.

"Yeah," Wakal replied, kind of nonchalant. He hadn't forgotten how Billy Lo had carried it when his twenty-page statement first hit the hood. '

"I almost didn't recognize you with all that shit on your face," Billy Lo gestured towards D.W.'s beard and forehead with his finger.

"I heard that." Wakal wasn't sure if Billy Lo was pointing at his large beard or at the massive prostration mark covering the entire center of his forehead that came from making salat. Either way, it was insulting. "That shit on my face is my religion!"

"Fuck is you doing down here?" Billy Lo inquired curiously, ignoring D.W.'s attitude. "They said you got killed by the Aryan Brotherhood in Hagerstown."

"Don't ever believe nothing *they* say. Because *they* will say anything." Wakal put emphasis on the word 'they'. "That's why if I can't verify it, I don't even believe it."

"I feel that." Billy Lo nodded. "So what? You got a new charge or something?"

"Nah," Wakal considered not telling Billy Lo the truth, then decided against it. "I give my time back on the Daughtry issue."

"Oh yeah," Billy Lo smiled for the first time all morning. It was always good when a nigga beat the system. Even if it was a nigga who he didn't feel deserve it. "That's a blessing."

"All praise be to Allah," Wakal said. "What's up with you though? I heard about your situation."

"Yeah, I'm down here for another motion hearing now," Billy Lo sounded exhausted. Honestly, he was. Mentally, physically and spiritually. It was not only lonely being one of the last real niggas in a phony game. It was draining being a pawn in somebody else's game. Especially when you were used to being a king. "How long you been back in town?"

"A couple weeks."

"Where they got you at?" Billy Lo scanned the entrance of the bullpen as a few more prisoners were ushered inside.

"J-section." Wakal sat down next to Billy Lo on the bench. "You?"

"I'm on Admin," Billy Lo said, knowing he shouldn't be in the bullpen. "I got hemmed up trying to get Charm's little bitch ass. You know he was just over the jail?"

"Yeah, I saw shorty on the news. I didn't know his little ass was getting to it like that. His little ass in everything but a hearse."

"Yeah, he just act to be after setting all of us up." Billy Lo lied, knowing that D.W. didn't know all the details.

"Setting all of who up?" Wakal eyed Billy Lo.

"You, me, Mumbles, everybody," Billy Lo clarified. "How the fuck you think you got grabbed by the Muslims?"

"I always thought Diamond gave us up," Wakal admitted. "I mean, he was the one fucking with them."

"Him and Charm." Billy Lo decided to go in for the kill. After all he didn't care who or how he got to Charm as long as he did. "Shorty was the one running around calling you a rat and everything."

"You serious, Dug?" Wakal began thinking back to how Charm stopped accepting his collect calls.

"Yeah, he's the one that called us all over Peaches house to read the *Baltimore Sun*. The whole time though, he had the Muslims limped up outside. That's how they got Lil' Dray and his cousins." Billy Lo was laying it on thick. But he didn't give a fuck. He wanted Charm got by any means necessary. Be it now or later.

Wakal sat there hurt. Billy Lo was clearing a lot of things up for him. He'd always wondered how Lil'Dray, Clyde and Pierre had gotten swallowed up by the authorities. Especially when they were usually the ones holding the hammers instead of taking the nails when it came to crucifixes.

"What about Black?"

Billy Lo just looked at him knowingly. "Everybody," Billy Lo confirmed. "I wasn't sure at first when shit first went down. I was torn. I was, like, nah, that's lil' bruh. But when that little nigga came up in that hospital and put that pistol in my mouth, I regretted not putting him down when I had the chance." Billy Lo still wished he'd gone after Charm instead of heading for the bus station.

"Allah knows best though, Ock." Wakal was ready to change the subject because he could feel his old self beginning to surface. "Insha Allah, I can get a good deal and see daylight."

"Are you gonna cop out again?" Billy Lo questioned. "Shid, you might as well fight. You're going to get the same amount of time."

"I may not have a choice," Wakal declared. "They gave me a bullshit ass P.D. and Tiara's baby father won't let her be my alibi."

"That's crazy." Billy Lo shook his head at a loss for words. Not because D.W. had a fucked up public defender or Tiara's boy friend was acting crazy. He was tripping off how any nigga could cop out to the same sentence they'd receive for going to trial.

"I thought about forcing her ass to come to court with a subpoena. But I don't want her to show up and say some crazy shit because of this punk ass nigga."

"Forcing her, huh?" Billy Lo teased with a grin as D.W. gave him an idea. *Bitch ass nigga!* Billy Lo thought, eyeing D.W. *Why the fuck would Tiara help you? You're a fucking rapist.* "You're ain't got enough yet?" Billy Lo laughed.

"Come on with the bullshit, Dug." Wakal looked around, embarrassed, hoping nobody picked up on what Billy Lo was laying down.

"You were up in them mountains, huh?"

"Yeah, I was in North Branch for a minute. Then they moved me over W.C.I."

"Oh, I know you were giving them white girls the blues." Billy Lo laughed. "They love the black man up there."

"I ain't have no complaints." Wakal played along, putting on for the bullpen.

"Ahhh nigga, you're bluffing," Billy Lo waved him off. "Nah, seriously though. How they carrying up there?" Billy Lo really wanted to know what he had to look forward to if he got found guilty.

"Oh, they sweet," Wakal replied, wanting to seem slicker then he actually was. "You got some lookers too. A couple case managers and shit. Mostly all the nurses bad though. Beyond that, the rest of them bitches look like penitentiary boys." Wakal joked, making half of the bullpen laugh.

"Young blood, do they be wearing them thumbs up there?" Some old senile cat interjecting, and nobody knew what the hell he was talking about.

"What?" A young boy with a nappy fade entertained him with a laugh. "What the fuck is a thumb?"

"Them string draws that go up the butt cracks."

"Mannnn, that's a *thong*!" everybody said in unison, dying of laughter.

"Whatever, y'all know what I'm talking about," he challenged. "Do they be wearing them, young blood? There's nothing like a woman with that thumb running up between her butt cheeks."

"Pops, I'm not even paying your crazy ass no mind." Wakal waved him off, laughing to the point of tears.

"I'm not talking about on that tip anyway," Billy Lo argued. He wasn't into snow bunnies, snow-bears, pink toes, or whatever niggas were calling them white bitches nowadays. He loved chocolate too much. "I'm talking about horsing, breaking law. Are them bitches about that money up there?"

"Come on now, Ock. What you think?" Wakal answered his question with a rhetorical question.

"Is my man Egar Davis still out there?"

"Egar Davis?" Wakal thought for a second. "I heard that name before. Is he in the Nation of Islam?"

"Not likely, them F.O.I.'s aren't going for none of that shit he be into," Billy Lo assured. Every member of the Nation of Islam was cut from a different kind of cloth. Everything about them was solid. And they didn't play no games about their walk. At least not the ones he knew anyway. "Every jail I ever been in. Them boys take that restrictive law shit serious."

"Nah, Dug, I know who you're talking about. Yo got sent out of state as one of Maryland's most disruptive prisoners last year. I think he got caught up in the indictment with a dude named Poochie."

"Figures. I can see that. Egar and Poochie go way back. All of us were over the jail together when Fat Card first starting telling on the Murphy Homes dude." Billy Lo paused to smile for a moment. He could still remember the scared look on Fat Card's face when he realized that his past had finally caught up to him. "What about my man Ameen? He still the Imam up there?

"Yeah," Wakal nodded. "That's a smart brother."

"Slim one of the only Sunni Muslims I respect for real. When he say something, he means that shit," Billy Lo said. "So, you never made it to Jessup?"

"I was out back for a minute," Wakal chose to say as less as possible because of his Annex history. "I never made it to the Cut though. I got shipped up Cumberland after all that stuff went down with the police."

"You ain't run across that nigga Big Paul yet? Diamond's man?" Billy Lo knew that it wasn't going to be nothing nice if he and Big Paul ever ended up on the same compound again. He knew Shabazz was more than likely responsible for Diamond's death. And he really appreciated that. But that still would not stop him from getting at him if they ever crossed paths again. Because he wasn't going to let Shabazz trick him out of his life the same way.

"Yeah," Wakal admitted. "I just left him on the tier. You know he's a Muslim now."

"Oh yeah," Billy Lo smiled. He was curious to know about that.

Billy Lo continued picking Wakal about Big Paul or Shabazz as Wakal called him until his name was called for court. "A'ight, Slim, take care of yourself." Billy Lo slowly got to his feet.

"Yeah, you too, Ock." Wakal stood up to give Billy Lo some love. "Walk slow, think fast."

"Ain't no question." Billy Lo broke the embrace. "I need you to promise me something though."

"What's that?" Wakal stared at Billy Lo curiously.

"Promise me that if you ever run across Charm's little ass again, you'll make him pay for what he did to us."

"I swear by Allah." Wakal gave his word. It didn't matter where he saw Charm at. In prison or on the streets. He'd make him pay for his sins. Especially the ones he had committed against his brothers

***

"Walaikum salaam," Tariq climbed out of the back seat of the late-model Rolls Royce and gently closed the door. Adnan had spoken, and there was nothing else to be said. Charm had to be dealt with. Not punished, not tortured, but finished. Snatched up, murdered and buried in a make-shift grave somewhere. Because he had become too much of a liability.

Tariq made his way back into the shop, and headed for the office. There was no need to summons the brothers. They were already inside the office waiting.

"What's the word, Ock?" Yah-Yah questioned anxiously, getting to his feet as Tariq entered the office.

"Extermination," Tariq replied honestly. "No more warnings. No more taxes. Adnan wants Charm dealt with." Tariq walked around the desk and took a seat. "So, the next time he sticks his head up, I want that motherfucker taken off!" Tariq added, pouring himself a drink.

"What about the rest of them little kafirs?" Rashid Salih spoke up. "The Stupid Squad or whatever they're called."

"Every last one of them has to go, Ock. No discrimination." Tariq made himself very clear.

"That's all I needed to hear," Yah-Yah moved towards the doors as everybody else got to their feet. "As salaam alaikum."

"Walaikum salaam," Tariq replied, as everybody exited the office. Then he poured himself another drink and drifted off into his own thoughts.

Chapter 17

I must've run the first ten red lights on my way over East Baltimore to holler at Big Al—One of Adnan's main shooters. I had not seen Big Al since he'd made headlines for running up in the 'Horseshoe' Casino Downtown and literally nailing a dude to the Poker table with nail-guns over a fifteen-thousand-dollar gambling debt behind a Baltimore Ravens game. But I knew the bear-size hitter wouldn't be hard to find.

Lafayette Projects had been one of the four major high-rises that the governor had decided to have torn down—or rather blown up—thinking that it would curb the violence. But it didn't work. In fact, the shootings in and around the destroyed projects had actually increased. Especially in recent months after all the Freddie Gray rioting. The city's murder rate became historic. Police corruption exploded, and Black Lives Matter unrest had all the politicians in fear.

I circled the block near where the #125 project building used to stand, drove past the post office, and parked before getting out of the car to make my way over to the playground where I figured Big Al would be.

"What's up, big boy?" I spoke, walking up on Big Al hugging and kissing all over a bad, Remy-Ma looking bitch in some black leggings, and off-white Coogi-looking coat with fur around the hood with the matching hat and boots.

"Oh shit! I'm seeing dollar signs," Big Al looked up with his signature grimy East Baltimore thug smile. "You're a long way from home, sporty."

"For good reasons though," I replied, giving Big Al some love before looking around. East Baltimore was not the place to get caught slipping. Especially not by police who were known to beat the fuck out of a nigga for running, plant evidence, and kill their own to cover their tracks.

"I'm surprised you're over here," Big Al said. "You know it's a healthy bag on your head, right?"

"Yeah, I'm hip," I admitted, as Big Al's bitch shifted from one foot to the other and looked at me with dollar signs in her eyes. "That's why I came to holler at you."

"Baby, let me holler at my man real quick," Big Al urged, slapping shorty on her phat butt. At which point she immediately unzippened her fur hooded coat and removed a pink, female sized Beretta and passed it to him before walking off. "That's why gangsters aren't made to be fucked with and bitches aren't meant to be trusted." Big Al licked his lips and smiled as he watched her strut over to the swings. "You never know what to expect."

"I hear you," I said but in my mind I was thinking that there wasn't nothing like a thorough bitch who had your back.

"So what's good?" Big Al focused his attention back on me. "Why shouldn't I hit you now and just go collect?"

"First of all, you're going to need something bigger than that," I gestured towards the pink Beretta Remy-Ma had just handed him.

Big Al shook his head and smiled. He knew that I wasn't nothing nice either. Especially when it came to drama.

"Secondly, I'ma make it worth your while."

"I like your style, sporty. There aren't too many West Baltimore dudes that I can bump with."

"Likewise," I assured.

"So what's on your mind?" Big Al brought his huge fist up to his mouth to blow hot-air into them before rubbing his hands together.

"How much you know about them Mexicans over on Boardway?"

"Enough to get the drop on 'em if the price is right." Big Al's lips curved into that infamous East Baltimore thug smile again.

"I'm trying to get a line on one of them that drives this red low-rider."

"You say you're going to make it worth my while?" Big Al questioned.

"So you know him?" I questioned, wanting to be sure.

"What are we talking about?" Big Al ignored me. "Because it's fifty on your head."

"We're talking six figures easy," I said, knowing that six figures sounded a hell of a lot better than five.

"Where are you parked at?"

Using my thumb to point back down the block towards Fayette Street, I said, "Around the corner", knowing I now had Big Al's attention.

"A'ight, let's take a ride," Big Al and I drove across town as I explained to him what had happened with the Mexicans. I also told him why I wanted to locate the driver of the red low-rider and gave him the entire rundown on the whole Adnan situation. We talked about the beef with me and Nizzy for control of West Baltimore. Then, I hipped him to how Adnan had gone behind my back and started giving Nizzy work. I even shared the details about a few moves we'd recently pulled on Adnan to send him a message.

"Yeah, Adnan's a fucked up dude for real," Big Al admitted. "Dangerous too—But, like I said, I don't have no skin in the game—I'm just trying to get mine," Big Al revealed as we parked in front of his man's spot on Greenmount Avenue.

I nodded understandably. I knew exactly what Big Al was saying. Whoever was willing to feed him the biggest plate was safe. In other words, if you couldn't cover his bill, your lights were going out.

"I'm just surprised shit escalated with you and your man," Big Al continued with a strange look on his face as we climbed out of the car. "I mean, y'all niggas seemed like brothers to me."

"Yeah, you wouldn't think it though."

"Shiiddd, sporty, if you shot at me and then turned around and posted a video of my bitch getting gutted on Facebook—"

"That nigga violated me first," I argued.

"Still, if that was me, I'd be haunting your ass too."

I kept my thoughts to myself and followed Big Al towards a beat-up row-house with a green paint-chipped door. Because truth be told, I was the one who had West Baltimore looking like a ghost town. Yeah, Nizzy was a little vicious. But I was big dangerous.

"E-Don!" Big Al called out over the loud music, opening the unlocked door. "E-Don!" Big Al waved me along and continued on inside. "I done told the silly nigga a hundred times to keep the door locked and turn that dumb ass music down," Big Al added, shaking his head as we neared the living room. "He ain't gonna be satisfied till a nigga creep up in this bitch and catch him slipping, watch."

After entering the living room and seeing no signs of life, Big Al made his way over to the X-Box One that was hooked up to the extremely large flat-screen with an NBA game on pause and turned the music down. "E-Don!" Big Al yelled again, looking towards the stairs.

"Wohh!" I jumped, caught off guard as E-Don slowly emerged from the shadows holding a 'Call of Duty' looking machine gun.

"Who's slipping now?" E-Don questioned, holding the ratchet Scarface-style. "Yeah, nigga," E-Don added, slowly moving his head up and down to emphasize the fact that he had the upper hand. "What?"

"Nothing, nigga!" Big Al retorted, picking up the Xbox One controller, flopping down on the couch. "If it was your time, you wouldn't have felt my presence until it was too late, believe that." Big Al unpaused the game.

"Fuck outta here, nigga. I stay on point." E-Don smirked before laying what I now recognized as a Springfield XD 9MM on the coffee table beside the game. "What's good though?"

"Nothing concerning that," Big Al replied, matter-of-factly, toying with the controller as he used Draymond Green to toss Kevin Durant an alley-oop to dunk on Lebron James. I wasn't sure if he knew that I'd seen E-Don secretly cut his eyes at me or not. "Sporty got something nice for us though."

"Is that right?" E-Don looked at me, instantly appearing serious. I guess he was weighing his options.

"Yeah, that's right," I volunteered honestly. I had a nice sting set up for them down in Black Pigtown. Two T.T.F. niggas named Bullet-Eye Ty and Little Dana who'd gotten too big for their own good. "But, I'ma need something from you first."

"And what's that?" E-Don gave Big Al a weird look. I swear it was just something about E-Don that always made me leery. It had been that way from the first time I met his lazy-eye, Lil' Wayne looking ass.

"I need you to introduce me to Goku."

"Who the fuck is Goku?" E-Don countered, twisting one of his dreads, and I couldn't tell if he was serious or not.

"That's the Mexican you always get the weed from up on Boardway with the red low-rider."

"Oh," E-Don continued to twist his dreads. "I never knew Shorty's name. I just call him Amigo."

"Well, I need you to introduce us."

"Why?" E-Don picked up a half of blunt out of the ashtray and lit it up.

I gave him the short version of what I'd given Big Al. I explained how the Mexicans had kidnapped my girl and caught me slipping. Then, I told him how they refused to tell me who the low-rider belonged to, before going on to explain how they'd forced me to pay for my life, so to speak.

"I hear all that—But I'm still not introducing you to that crazy motherfucker—He might think I set him up or something if shit goes bad," E-Don declared.

"A'ight, just point him out to me," I suggested.

"Nah yo, hold up." Big Al sat the controller down and stood up. "What about the South Baltimore lick?"

"I'ma deliver on that regardless," I assured, knowing what Big Al was thinking. "I just need to lay eyes on this low-rider cat."

"Yo, you're not just going up on Boardway pointing niggas out and shit. Them Mexican niggas like bloodhounds." E-Don warned.

"That's why I said just introduce me."

"How about this?" Big Al caressed his chin and pulled on his short beard. "You roll with E-Don to cop some weed from Goku and go back on your own accord. That way, everybody's protected:"

"That sounds fair," I admitted.

"Let's do it then." E-Don smiled just as my phone rang.

"Hello—yeah—in a minute—I'm good, sit tight," I ended the call.

"Who was that?" Big Al questioned curiously.

"My bloodhounds," I smiled. "They wanted to know what was taking us so long."

"The Ford Explorer, right?" Big Al laughed, shutting the game system off.

I hunched my shoulders and smiled, impressed that Big Al had noticed JuJu and Murdock tailing us. "That's why I like you, sporty."

"Let's go meet Goku," E-Don said, taking one last hit off his blunt before grinding it out in the ashtray.

"That's what I'm trying to hear," I said, wanting to know exactly who Goku was. Because I knew that once I gave Big Al and E-Don the goods on Bullet-Eye Ty and Little Dana, it was go-season. "Let's do this."

Chapter 18

It took a little tug-of-war. But Baker was finally able to get Detective Malone to get the name of the Feds' main C.I., and it was none other than one of Baker and Gibson's long time sources—Their friend, Don Poppa Shelton. Baker and Gibson rushed across town to pick him up from his little known hole in the wall.

After some negotiating and a promise or two concerning an upcoming state case Don Poppa was fighting with his cousin, Don Poppa positively identified Calvin Johnson from the hospital video footage on Gibson's iPad, and fingered James Tanner for a string of unsolved shootings and robberies. Then, he called his cousin— Derrick Sanders—who just so happened to be another certified West Baltimore snitch who was still making regular 'informational' payments on the last 'get out of jail' free card he'd received from Baker for turning state on his one-time friend in a Sandtown triple homicide case to get James Tanner's whereabouts.

So now, Detectives Baker and Gibson were sitting down the street from one of the Dummie Squad's safe houses in an unmarked car with Don Poppa hoping that James Tanner would walk into his cousin's rat-trap.

"Are you sure Tanner's going to show up, Shelton?" Baker glanced at his stainless steel watch before looking over his shoulder. They had been waiting for James Tanner all morning. And if it wasn't for the fact that Shelton had always been constant, they'd have called it a day. "Your cousin said twelve o'clock and it's almost one."

"Oh, he's coming," Don Poppa assured, figuring that JuJu was running a little late. "Especially since he thinks Smurf has a lick for him. That nigga don't take no days off."

"Well, for your sake, let's hope you're right!" Gibson threatened. Regardless of how reliable Don Poppa's infromation always was in the past, Gibson could not respect him. Because to her there wasn't anything worst than a low-life snitch who would sell his own mother out to save himself.

Baker cut his eyes at Gibson. It was no secret that if it was up to her, both Don Poppa and Smurf would be punished for their crimes also. But it wasn't. So, for now, they just had to wait for James Tanner to show up so that they could take him into custody and work on finding the rest of the baby-faced killers.

"Damn, Gibson, why you always giving me a hard time?" Don Poppa complained. "All a nigga do is help you out."

"More like help yourself out," Gibson corrected with a sarcastic snicker, as she continued to observe the street. "Let's get something straight, Shelton. I don't trust rats. And "I don't respect them. Especially the ones who tried to convince themselves that they are more valuable than the low lives they're selling out. You know why?" Gibson asked with no intentions of hearing his answer. "Because most of them will do anything and violate any rule to get themselves out of a jam."

"Yeah, I hear that, Gibson," Don Poppa mumbled as if he was hurt. But the truth was, he wasn't. Shid, under the right circumstances, he'd sell Gibson's ass out too.

"Remember it," Gibson suggested. "Because we're not friends. I've a job to do and you have a job to do. That's it. That's where the relationship stops. That's where it ends."

"Just worry about keeping your eyes open," Baker instructed for Shelton's own benefit. "Because if Tanner doesn't show up soon, you and your cousin are going to end up over Central Bookings with a serious resisting arrest case."

"Oh, that's fucked up." Don Poppa sat back nervously, uncertain if Baker's threat was real or not. Don Poppa thought about saying something when he spotted a Ford Explorer XSL with shadow-tints coming from the top of the block with JuJu in the passenger's seat. "Shit! There go JuJu right there," Don Poppa immediately ducked down in the back seat as the truck approached. "I think Charm's with them too," Don Poppa added excitedly, peeping over the back seat as the truck drove past and pulled over down the block. "That was close."

"You did good," Baker commended, removing his serve weapon. "Now, get out."

"Come on, Baker," Don Poppa appealed, screening the street with a worried look on his face. "You can't be serious. You expect me to get out right here? It's broad daylight!" Don Poppa argued. "That's a death wish," he added, concluding that Baker didn't have that little of a regard for his well-being.

"Get out before I arrest your ass for interfering with an officer's duty!" Gibson fired, turning around.

"That's crazy," Don Poppa pulled his red Dodgers baseball cap down, opened the unmarked car door, and slowly stepped out sweating like a glass of ice water on a hot summer day. "How the hell am I suppose to get back to the Avenue."

"Why don't you give an Uber driver some information on fair-jumpers!" Gibson joked, knowing that a rat's greatest fear was exposure.

Don Poppa mumbled something, slamming the car door. Then he flipped the collar on his coat up and headed on up the block in the opposite direction. He didn't want to be nowhere near JuJu and Charm when they were arrested. He didn't need that shit coming back to haunt him. He already had enough enemies.

***

"Ayo, you see that?"

Berry, Nizzy and Cock-eyed Willie started preparing themselves the second Murdock's Explorer turned onto the block. They'd been camped out for the past hour, waiting on Murdock and JuJu to show up for a meeting with Smurf.

"See what?" Nizzy kept his eyes glued to Murdock's truck. His focus was on carrying out the plan he had set up with Smurf to double cross Murdock and JuJu. "Don Poppa's hot ass getting out of one of them car over there," Berry spat.

"Don Poppa?" Cock-eyed Willie repeated. "Smurf's cousin Don Poppa? The nigga the Blood haunting?"

"Yeah," Berry confirmed. "That's him right there."

Nizzy glanced across the street real quick to see a nigga creeping around the corner trying to cover his face. "Man, that's not Don Poppa," Nizzy waved, disregarding the sneaking looking nigga. "He know them Bloods gonna barbecue his ass."

"Yo, I'm telling you that was Don Poppa," Berry assured, trying to figure out exactly what car Don Poppa had gotten out of. "Something not right. Maybe Smurf put them niggas on point and told them that we were laying on 'em. That could've been the signal."

"Mannnnn, that nigga not stupid," Nizzy guaranteed.

"Look!" Cock-eyed Willie snapped excitedly when the back window of Murdock's truck rolled down and he saw Charm's face. "There go Charm."

"Oh yeah," Nizzy exclaimed, readying the extended clip of his gun. He couldn't believe his eyes, let alone his luck. Murdock, JuJu and Charm together. At one time. He had to make it count.

"Get ready," Nizzy instructed, pulling his niece's 'First Lady' Halloween mask down over his face, as they watched JuJu walk over towards Smurf's car smoking a blunt. "As soon as JuJu get in the car with Smurf, we're wearing these niggas out." Nizzy adjusted his mask to make sure it was in place. "I got Charm."

* * *

Smurf nodded at me as JuJu approached his car and I smiled. I couldn't help myself. Smurf really didn't suspect that JuJu was on to him. If he did, he probably wouldn't be sitting there like he hadn't gotten some money from Nizzy to try and set JuJu up.

"Uh, this about to be funny." Murdock turned in his seat to getting a better look also. "I bet you any amount of money that nigga get outta that car."

"That boy a bad motherfucker if he get up outta that car," I said. Wasn't no way in the world Smurf was getting out of that car. "Especially if he don't get out now," I mumbled, watching JuJu from the back seat walk around to the passenger side of the car. "Here we go."

198

JuJu opened the passenger's side door and acted like he was about to get into the car with Smurf. Then, he pulled out a water bottle full of gasoline and began drenching Smurf and the inside of the car down. Smurf tried to avoid getting wet, but it was no use. Once the bottle was empty, JuJu took a puff off the blunt hanging out of his mouth and plucked it inside, the car instantly turning into a fireball.

JuJu stumbled backwards as the car burst into flames. "Come on! Let's go, nigga!" I yelled out of the back window just as Smurf smashed the driver's side window out and climbed out screaming like I'd never heard before. It was almost heartbreaking. Almost. Especially when Smurf began running in circles as Murdock yelled for him to 'Stop, drop and roll'.

JuJu must've gotten tired of the deafening wail because he pulled out his tone and shot Smurf until he collapsed in the street and continued to burn. That's when two helpful motherfuckers I instantly recognized as the detectives from around the way ran up out of nowhere and began trying to put Smurf out. "Oh shit, Dummie!" I said, alerting Murdock just as the female detective held up her badge and pulled her weapon.

"One Time! Go!"

***

"Move!" Nizzy commanded, pushing the car door open while JuJu and them's attention was on Smurf and some good samaritans. "Remember I got Charm!" Nizzy reminded, quickly walking towards Murdock's truck. He'd wanted JuJu and Murdock, but Charm's presence was a bonus. They could kill three snakes at one time.

Nizzy took one more look over his shoulder to make sure Berry and Cock-eyed Willie were ready. Then, he nodded and went running up on the truck, dumping. Nizzy caught Murdock trying to start the truck. Murdock saw him and ducked behind the dashboard, trying to open the truck's door. But Nizzy wasn't tripping. He kept coming. His rifle's bullets were made to go through everything except maybe dragon-skin. The bullet was unstoppable, penetrating shit thirty times harder than steel.

Berry and Cock-eyed Willie ran out from behind a mini-van and got the drop on JuJu as Murdock and Charm crawled from the truck and stumbled into a small crowd of screaming school kids.

Nizzy came around the truck as Charm attempted to help Murdock and carefully aimed the gun. "This for my cousin, bitch!" Nizzy smiled, slowly walking towards Charm and Murdock. He really wanted to enjoy the moment. He also wanted to allow the school kids to get out of the way.

"Police!" One of the good Samaritans appeared out of what seemed like thin air with her gun drawn. "Drop the weapon!"

Nizzy froze, but he never took his eyes off of Charm and Murdock as they continued backing up slowly. Moving out of harm's way.

"Don't you fucking move, Johnson!" The plain-clothes female officer warned with her weapon still aimed at Nizzy. "Johnson, I'm warning you. I'm going to shoot your ass. I swear it."

Nizzy was about to give up until he heard the officer call Charm's last name as a Baltimore City Police car came flying down the block. If they knew Charm, then they knew him. Nizzy thought about his next move as the female detective ordered him to drop his weapon again.

The police blocked the street off from both ends. Nizzy locked on Charm as he continued to back up, and wondered if he could finish him before going out in a blaze of glory. Or should he just live to kill another day?

"I said drop the weapon!" the female officer demanded again just as Cock-eyed Willie and Berry came around from the blind side opening fire on Charm and Murdock. The female officer was forced to take cover. Nizzy saw Charm and Murdock getting away, and let his own gun off without hesitation.

"Fuck!" Nizzy shouted, retreating behind a car to avoid being shot by police bullets, and the gun battle was on. Nizzy saw Charm and Murdock run right past the cops as they closed in to assist what he now realized were two detectives. "Fuck! Fuck! Fuck!" Nizzy repeated. It was all or nothing now. "I'm not going to jail, yo!"

"Me either!" Berry seconded, going straight at the police before they had a chance to pen them down.'

Nizzy was looking around anxiously for a way out. Because he had no intentions of holding court in the streets with a 20-round clip. Cock-eyed Willie ran over as Berry held the cops off. And that's when Nizzy saw his way out of a no-win situation.

"Go around that side so we can box these bitches in!" Nizzy ordered and watched in amazement as Cock-eyed Willie complied. *My nigga!* Nizzy thought when he saw the male detective dive between two cars to avoid being shot by Cock-eyed Willie. When the detective disappeared out of sight, Nizzy decided to make his move. It was now or never.

Nizzy fired a few times in the female detective's direction before running over to kick in the nearest front door. It was now every man for themselves. Nizzy sprinted through the house, snatched open the backdoor and hit the alley. Nizzy took a few cuts, yanked the 'Michelle Obama' mask off, hopped somebody's gate, quickly removed his sweat suit and grabbed some clothes off the clothes line in the backyard.

Back on the street in a pair of old ass, tight, faded Levi's and a small ass gray Russel hoodie, Nizzy had his gun and 'Michelle Obama' mask rolled up in a towel as he hauled a taxi.

"Where to, my man?" The taxi cab driver pulled over with a sincere smile.

"Mondawmin Mall," Nizzy replied, still thinking on his feet as he opened the back down. "I got to get over here and make it up to my daughter for fucking up Christmas," Nizzy added, pulling out a knot of bills to hand the driver. He knew that he could make it back to the block safely from the mall.

The cab driver accepted the bills with a smile, nodded and drove off as police continued to fly by every which way. Nizzy laid back, slightly slouched down and tried to figure out his next move.

***

"Jaxkey!" I screamed, stumbling through the front door of JuJu's aunt house, helping Murdock. It was the closest place in the city we could think of getting to on foot. "Jaxkey!"

"Oh my God!" Jaxkey's hand went to her mouth the moment she saw me covered in Murdock's blood. "What happened?" She rushed over to grab me.

"It's not me! It's Murdock. He got shot," I pulled Murdock's arm from around my neck. "Help me get him to the couch," I requested, knowing that Murdock had twisted his ankle trying to get away from the gunmen who ambushed him with what seemed like metal-eating bullets.

Jaxkey and I sat Murdock down on the living room sofa as he whined about his entire chest being on fire. "I'm getting weak, Dummie," Murdock mumbled. "I can feel the life being squeezed out of me every time I breathe."

"Stop breathing then, nigga!" I ordered, running to the kitchen to get a knife.

"Ahhhh," Murdock cried out in excruciating pain as Jaxkey began ripping his shirt off.

"Watch out, Jaxkey," I demanded, grabbing Murdock's shirt at the bottom so that I could cut it off with the knife.

"Hold up, Dummie." Murdock begged, clenching his jaws as I began to pull and cut.

"Man, suck that shit up, Dummie." I continued cutting.

Murdock closed his eyes and turned his head to the side. Almost as if he didn't want to see the damage.

"Lucky ass nigga!" I fired, shaking my head. "All that whining and shit for nothing," I added, analyzing the bullets that were stuck in the material of his bullet-proof vest.

"Huh?" Murdock slowly opened his eyes. My reaction convinced him to look at his chest. "Oh shit," Murdock exhaled and looked up at the ceiling. "I forgot all about the vest."

"You didn't get hit by the first shooter," I assured. "That shit sounded like it was shredding the engine."

"Yeah, I know. I think it was Nizzy too."

"At first I thought it was the police," I admitted, knowing they weren't above *shooting first, asking questions last.*

"Boy, bye," Jaxkey rolled her eyes and punched the vest. "You not even shot."

"Chill, Jaxkey!" Murdock grabbed her wrist. "That shit still hurt," Murdock said. "I think my ribs broken."

"Hold up yo," I completely removed Murdock's shirt. "Where the fuck all this blood come from?" I questioned, happy that Black Jesus had spared my nigga.

"Mannnn, you got a fucking graze on your neck." I shook my head, still grateful that we never left the house without our vests anymore.

"I'm telling you, Dummie. I got to be hit. My shit fucked up. I can feel it." Murdock argued, but I wasn't paying his ass no attention.

"Ayo," I turned my attention to Jaxkey. "Grab JuJu's spare key for me." Now that Murdock was okay, I knew it was time to get up out of there. Niggas had just shot it out with the Baltimore City Armed Thugs. So, I knew that it would not be long before doors started flying off the hinges. Especially JuJu's aunt's door once his identity was discovered.

"It's on my key-chain," Jaxkey replied, going into her pocket. "Where my cousin at anyway?" Jaxkey pulled out her key-chain and began removing the key.

"Where Dummie parked at?" Murdock sat up, moaning in pain, probably knowing what I was thinking.

"Out back," Jaxkey looked from Murdock to me curiously. "What's going on? Where is my cousin?"

I looked at the floor in defeat and tried to fix my clothes. I could not answer that. How could I tell Jaxkey that her favorite cousin—the one she looked at more like a brother than anything— was stretched out in a west Baltimore gutter with a body full of bullet holes! Some that were meant for both Murdock and I at that.

"Where's my cousin, Charm?" Jaxkey grabbed my arm. She must've felt something because her voice began to crack and I could see tears welling up in her eyes. "Where's my cousin, Murdock?"

Maybe it was my lack of eye contact. Or maybe it was my lack of response. Whatever it was, Jaxkey picked up on it. She screamed something I did not quite understand about God, and started swinging.

"I'm sorry, Jaxkey," I whispered, letting her swing. I knew how close she and JuJu were. They'd grown up together in the same house. "I'm sorry," I repeated as Jaxkey continued to wild out. I hugged her tight and eased her down to the couch as my own tears began to fall. Not only for her, but for JuJu also. How the fuck had it come to this? Why the fuck did we let some pussy, pride and power destroy the love, honor and respect that had once bonded us together. "I'm sorry."

"We gotta bounce, Dummie," Murdock said softly, looking at me knowingly before limping towards the kitchen.

"I gotta go, Jaxkey." I released Jaxkey and slowly stood up. I knew there wasn't much more that I could do for her. Her pain was internal. I squeezed her hand one more time, kissed her on the top of the head, promised to get the niggas responsible, grabbed somebody's jacket off the hook for Murdock and headed for the back door.

"What now?" Murdock broke the silence after we climbed in JuJu's Infinity.

"Get Slate on the phone." I tossed Murdock my cellphone. I knew there was no time to waste. We needed to get as far away from the city as we could. And we needed to do it fast. "It's about time we meet his man out in Washington D.C."

"What about Nizzy?" Murdock carefully rolled his pants leg up to inspect his swollen ankle as I started the car. "We got to see that nigga before we go."

"You already knew," I replied, backing up out of the yard. You'd think after catching a few bullets in his vest and damn near breaking his ankle, Murdock would be on pause. But nah, the crazy nigga was still in go mode. "Just get Slate on the phone."

Chapter 19

Detective Baker stood silently in the cold, pouring rain as Detective Gibson's United States flag-draped casket was lowered into the ground under the sounds of firing rifles. There were no words that could express the sense of loss he felt whenever he thought of Lashaun. She was the love of his life, and he had planned to ask her to make him an honest man. But now, she was gone. Shot down like some common criminal on the city streets with armor-piercing bullets.

Detective Baker stepped forward and dropped a single white rose on the top of Gibson's casket before it disappeared. He closed his eyes and vowed to chase every last one of her suspected killers to the edge of the earth. He had already convinced the city's top D.A. to issue arrest warrants on all known 'Dummie Squad' gang members in their database and talked the warrant task force into shaking down their well-known associates for information. So, Baker knew that he'd get a break sooner rather than later.

After the twenty-one gun salute, Detective Baker waited for all the officers, detectives and well-wishers to offer their condolences to the Gibson family, before walking over to Lashaun's little sister and mom as they huddled together under an umbrella near the white hearse Lashaun's body had been carried in, trying to keep the folded flag they'd been given—by the chief of police as a sign of Lashaun's patriotism—from getting wet.

"If there's anything that I can do, Missis Gibson, anything thing at all, please give me a call," Detective Baker said, sincerely handing her his card before nodding to her youngest daughter who looked just like Lashaun.

"Thank you, detective," Lashaun's mother accepted the card. She never really approved of her daughter's line of work. Especially with the things going on around the country with the police. But she always appreciated Baker's presence because she knew how much he loved her child. "Take care of yourself," she added before walking off.

Detective Baker stood there in the pouring rain as a vision of Lashaun's beautiful face flashed in his mind. Tears begin to roll down his face. He'd miss her sexy smile and contagious laugh the most. "I will get every last one of them motherfuckers, baby. I promise." Detective Baker spoke out loud as he watched Lashaun's mother and little sister climb into the hearse.

"How are you feeling?" Detective Malone walked up, interrupting Baker's thoughts.

"I'm holding it together," Detective Baker lied. He'd always hold his head high. Even in the face of defeat. "Thanks."

"Listen," Detective Malone began softly, almost as if she didn't want to say what was about to follow. "I thought a lot about what you asked me to do. And I don't think that I can be a part of that. Even under the circumstances."

"I understand," Detective Baker looked off into the distance. He knew it was easy to be a good cop when you had something to go home to. Someone who depends on you. "I honestly should've never put you in that position knowing you had a kid and all. I was just hurting." Detective Baker confessed. "I was emotional."

"I know. So was I." Detective Malone agreed. She knew Baker was a good police officer. That was the only reason that she hadn't reported him when he asked her to jeopardize her career and freedom even to help him revenge his partner's death. She also didn't want to be the cop who went against the blue code of honor and started turning cops in. Not to mention she had a thing for Baker.

"Yeah, I was just thinking that blue lives really mattered."

"They do," Malone assured. "But if we start running around killing suspects ourselves, regardless of their crimes, what does that say about us?"

"You're right," Detective Baker finally looked at Malone. "We just got to trust the system and good old-fashioned police work." Honestly, Baker knew that with or without Detective Malone's help, there was no way in hell that Gibson's killers were coming in alive. Not if he found them first. "Hopefully, a tip comes in on these assholes soon. That way we can locate them and let justice take its course."

"We'll get them. We always do." Detective Malone pulled Baker into a long hug. She knew he needed someone to keep him sane. That was the only way he'd stay out of trouble.

Baker held Detective Malone tight, but all he could think about was Lashaun's limp head in his lap as she fought to hold on until her very last breath. It was all so surreal. Even the part when the coroner grabbed Lashaun's chin, pushed her head to one side until the wound behind her ear was visible and said, "Here's the problem. She had a slow leak."

He couldn't let that go. Not after his partner had been shot three times by two different shooters, according to forensics, and died in his arms as he radioed for back up. Her blood was literally still on his hands. He'd honestly thought that Lashaun would survive because she always did.

"Any leads?" Detective Malone questioned, breaking the embrace.

"Not yet," Baker admitted. "I do believe that we'll catch Frank Lance first, though. I told you about his coming—"

"You really think he's going to stick around and basically walk himself into custody?" Detective Malone cut Baker off in disbelief.

"I sure do," Baker confirmed. "You see, Lance is different than the rest of them. He's smart. Calculated even."

"He's not going to risk going to prison," Detective Malone assured.

"He's a kid who hasn't been stopped yet," Detective Baker said. "So, he doesn't know fear. He'll risk anything because he's fearless. So, he'll be there. Trust me. Plus, he knows that we really don't know anything."

"Well, I'll be there either way," Detective Malone revealed, trying to be supportive. "I hope you're right."

"I appreciate that." Baker nodded and stared off into the distance again.

"No problem," Detective Malone rubbed Baker's back for a moment. "Well, look, I got to get out of here," Detective Malone explained when her partner pulled up. "We just caught what appears to be a drug-related double inside a Lexington Terrace abandon," Detective Malone disclosed. "Make sure you give me a call, though. You got my number."

"Sure thing." Baker contiuned to stare into the distance.

Chapter 20

The heat was on, and the news was buzzing with all kinds of fake news stories about the Muslims and the Dummie Squad's battle for control. According to the media, the alleged baby-face gangsters were wanted for questioning in connection to a Homicide Detective's fatal shooting and the attempted-murder of Billy Lo at the hospital. I had to admit, Charm and them had the city on fire. So, I knew that it was time to run my final play. Because it was no doubt in my mind that Charm would be in prison very soon.

"So, I guess this is it, huh?" Zimbabwe asked, grabbing my bags out of the trunk of the car.

"Yeah, I guess so," I replied, accepting my bags. "I've to get low before the police show up at my doorstep asking questions again. Especially since they've linked Charm to Mumbles and them."

"Well, it's been real, Peanut," Zimbabwe extended his hand. "I've to admit. In the beginning, Little Dinky and I thought Billy Lo was crazy for hooking up with you. But I gotta say. You're a soldier if there ever was one."

Smiling, I said, "It was definitely a pleasure. Make sure you tell Little Dinky's fine ass he can still get it." I giggled like a school girl.

"You're something else, Peanut," Zimbabwe and I shared a laugh. "Make sure your take care of yourself now."

"You too," I looked through the back windshield and waved to Little Dinky. "Don't forget to tell him what I said."

"I got you," Zimbabwe shook his head. I knew Little Dinky probably had daughters my age. But still, giving the chance, I'd jump right on his old ass. "Good luck! You got my number if you ever need me."

I turned and headed for the train station without another word. My plan was going better than I'd thought it would. Charm was on the ropes, and I had created enough distrust amongst his crew to make them turn against one another. I'd also basically gotten enough money to live comfortably after everything was over. The only thing left to do now was walk Charm in a checkmate.

I entered the train station and took a seat to rest my nerves. The train did not depart for two hours. So, I had some time to kill. I dug inside my handbag and removed the latest issue of the '*State vs Us*' magazine with my girl Jamila T. Davis on the cover, and began to read. Next to me, she was the baddest bitch on the East Coast.

Chapter 21

"Dummie! I can't let that nigga live. Not after that shit with JuJu!" Murdock exclaimed, looking across the table at me as we waited for Slate and his man Bucky Fields to show up. "And if it wasn't for the vest, they'd have worn me out too."

I looked around nervously. I had wanted to meet at Washington D.C.'s famous Ben's Chili Bowl on U Street for obvious reasons. But, my cousin's man chose to hook up at the 'Good Stuff Eatery' on Pennsylvania Avenue because Northeast and Southeast were always at odds. "I feel you, Dummie, but the city is too hot to be chasing after that nigga right now," I replied, knowing that patience was a virtue. Especially at a time like this. There were press conferences and everything going on behind us. The mayor was calling for our heads, and I had even read something online about the police chief requesting the alphabet boys' assistance. "We need to just focus on getting with Slate's man Bucky Fields and moving this work for a minute. That way we can run this bag up and stay away from the city for a while."

"And then what?" Murdock questioned. "We not going to see them niggas about that?"

"That's not what I'm saying," I retorted. "I'm saying we gotta let the dust settle first," I pleaded. "You know I'ma always ride for my niggas," I continued, frustrated. Murdock was geeking. "But that shit you talking about doing is suicide. You might as well turn yourself in."

"You already know my motto, Dummie," Murdock took a sip of his soda. "I'll be carried by *six* long before I'm judged by *twelve*."

"Yeah, I know you're more homicidal than suicidal. But why even put yourself in that position?"

"Because I'ma spank that nigga once and for all," Murdock retorted.

"You is crazy," I declared, shaking my head.

"Nah, I ain't crazy. I just know that this is the best time to get his ass," Murdock argued. "All I need you to do is call that African nigga with all the guns."

"And what about the rest of them lil niggas that be running behind him?" I questioned, curious as to what he would do with the little army Nizzy and Lor'Homie had built. "How are you going to get to them if you get jammed up fucking with Nizzy?"

"What about 'em? Them niggas nobodies! They're a bunch of followers. Nizzy's the leader. So once I crack him, they'll all fade away!"

"Dummie, you can't underestimate them niggas. Whether they're followers or not." I warned, thinking about something Murdock told me when we first met. "You remember why you said dudes over east would not give you no exposure?"

"Yeah," Murdock smiled. "They were scared I might expose niggas."

"Already, so don't sleep on no follower. Because if he's a good follower and he's smart, he'll be the leader one day. And what we always say?"

"An enemy of my friend is an enemy of mine," Murdock and I quoted in unison. "That's why I need you to call that African nigga with all the guns."

"Man, I'm not fucking with that nigga, Dummie!" I proclaimed, instantly twisting my face up. Murdock was acting like he didn't know we were on the run. Like the armed thugs didn't have the city under siege. Kicking in doors, threatening our family members and shit. "Why you think I tossed my phone?"

"Well, I'ma get Slate's man to give me something nice then!" Murdock countered stubbornly.

I knew how Murdock was when he had something on his mind. Nobody could stop him. So, I just let it drop. Because the strongest thing in the world was a made up mind. So, if he wanted to go on a suicide mission, that was on him. I was going to continue to stick to the script and wait for Ebony to find a low-key spot in another state where I could lay my hat down. Because I was going to be a rolling stone for a minute. And going back to Baltimore was the furthest thing from my mind right now.

It was a little after five when my cousin walked in with two dudes whom I assumed were from D.C., and gestured towards a table in the back of the eatery. "What's up, family?" I was the first one to stand up and give Slate some love as his friends continued to the back.

"All is well, fam," Slate replied. "I'm glad you got my message. My burner was acting crazy last night."

I hadn't seen Slate in a few days. He had us staying at a spot called 'Glass Monor Inn', which was located just on the other side of the Maryland line.

"That's your man, huh?" I gestured towards the D.C. dudes.

"Yeah," Slate nodded. "Come on. Let me introduce y'all."

"I hope these niggas the real deal," Murdock mumbled, getting up from the table.

"Yeah, me too." I seconded as we began following Slate towards the back.

"Fam, this is my man Buck," Slate pointed out the semi-stocky, bow-legged D.C. dude with the baldhead and full beard before pulling a chair out at the table. "Buck, this my cousin Charm I use to always talk about."

"What's up, man?" Buck stood up and stuck out his hand. "I feel like I already know you."

"Likewise," I nodded, shaking his hand. All I had been hearing about for the last few days were 'the life and times' of Bucky Fields—Washington D.C.'s, Southeast finest.

Buck then went on to introduce his partner. A slim, sneaky looking nigga named Baby-Joe. And I quickly introduced Murdock before we all sat down. Wasn't no sense in wasting time with the small talk. We all knew why we were there. So why not get straight to the business.

After Buck ordered a round of drinks, we got down to the subject at hand. We discussed exactly who could bring what to the table. Buck and Baby-Joe had a few spots throughout Southeast that sounded promising. And Murdock and I had the work they'd confiscated from Nizzy. So, we came up with a deal that we all could live with. Especially since Buck would be doing most of the heavy lifting. After all, D.C. his backyard.

Once we were all on the same page, Murdock explained to Buck that he needed some serious artillery. Buck said that it would not be a problem and promised to give Murdock something nice when we left the bar. And just like that, we were fucking with some D.C. niggas.

"To the future," Buck said, raising his shot glass.

"To the future." We all followed suit and raised our glasses. As I downed my three shot, I was trying to figure out how in the hell was I going to re-up after we ran out of work?

"There's one more problem," Murdock said, sitting his shot glass back on the table.

"What's that?" I asked, hoping Murdock wasn't about to go into our future supply problem.

"Where the fuck are we going to stay at?" he asked. "You know we can't keep staying in that little ass cheap, roach motel. Especially now."

"Oh, don't even worry about that," Bucky Fields spoke up. "I'm sure Baby-Joe got a bitch that will put y'all up."

"Yeah, man, that ain't nothing." Baby-Joe agreed with a smile. "I got y'all covered. Don't even sweat that. I know I'm from Maryland. But I got bitches all over Chocolate City."

"Good looking out." Murdock seemed to breathe a sigh of relief.

"Yeah, we appreciate that," I seconded.

"It's all good," Baby-Joe waved me off like it was nothing. "My old head a real estate agent. She got a nice spot around the corner from the Metro Club." Baby-Joe pulled out his phone. "I'll have her meet me over there in an hour."

"Any family of Slate's is family of ours," Bucky Fields affirmed.

"I heard that," I replied, nodding. There weren't too many niggas who still thought like that.

***

Tariq gave Yah-Yah the signal, and he quickly stepped from the shadows, grabbed his unsuspecting victim's head and placed a gun to his temple. Then, he fired two .22 rounds into the guy's temple before letting his body fall to the floor, where blood trickled from his temple and began to make a small pool.

"I was tired of hearing him say the same thing," Tariq confessed to the rest of the crudy Muslim brothers sitting around the thick oak table inside a 'Baby Mecca' warehouse near the Chesapeake Bay, listening to the only Muslim who'd somehow been lucky enough to escape Charm's little trap. "Wrap him up in one of those prayer rugs back there and get rid of his body."

"Are your serious, Ock?" the older Muslim brother Tariq looked at questioned, uncertain. After all, a Muslim's body had to be handled a certain way.

"Do I look like I'm joking?" Tariq stared at the older brother until he realized that he was serious. "If you don't get that body out of my face in two seconds, Ock, you'll be in the rug beside him!" Tariq threatened.

The older Muslim brother moved quickly. He stood up, walked over, slid in hands underneath the dead brother's armpits, snaked his arms across his chest and attempted to lift him up. "What the fuck are you looking at me like you're stupid for nigga? Get over here and help me!" He ordered another brother who quickly jumped up to assist him after receiving a stern look from Yah-Yah.

"Now that that's taken care of, let's get down to the real reason why we're here," Tariq spoke, commanding everybody's attention as the other Muslim picked the dead brother up by his ankles and helped carry him into the back. "It has been confirmed that a small group of our brothers have been smuggling in Arizona heroin and Fentanyl behind the brotherhood's back. Through our docks over in Fells Point the Mexicans at that. The competition!" Tariq planned to get back to the issue of dealing with both Nizzy and Charm as soon as the mess with the police blew over and they were able to smoke Charm out.

"That's a problem," Tariq paused to look around. It was widely understood that anybody who moved 'anything' through the docks of Baby Mecca had to pay a community tax. There were no exceptions. "Because first of all, they're not paying their toll fee. Second, they're allowing some Mexicans to utilize our routes to get to them Mexicans over on Boardway."

"So how do you want to play it, Ock?" a young brother questioned, ready to earn his bones.

"First, we're going to intercept their next shipment which is coming in tonight," Tariq smiled. He could see a few brothers shift in their seats uneasy. "Then, we're going to remind them why the rules of our turf should never be broken. Understood?"

"Understood." The young brother nodded.

"Good," Tariq looked around the room one more time. It was time to lay down some much needed law again. Niggas had gotten too comfortable. "Dismissed."

Chapter 22

Nizzy already knew what to expect when he got to the courthouse for the open drug and gun charges he'd gotten caught up in with Young Danny and Murdock a little more than a year ago. He knew all about the fact that the police wanted to question him about the East Baltimore police- involved shooting that left a female detective dead. He also knew that Berry was laid up in the Central Bookings Medical ward on 'no bond' status, keeping his mouth shut. Not to mention the fact that there were warrants out for Charm, Murdock and Cock-eyed Willie who was still amazingly somehow at large.

Nizzy knew all of this because he was smart enough to have retained a lawyer. He was also slick enough to have the thot whose house he was laying low at go around the way and gather all the information she could, by sitting inside the 'New Identity's' Barber Shop and Beauty Salon.

"Are you sure that you're okay, baby?" Nizzy's mother, Ms. Evon, asked as they drifted along with the downtown traffic in route to the courthouse. "It seems like there's something on your mind."

"Nah, I'm cool, Ma," Nizzy lied. There was no way that he could tell his mother about all the shit he had on his mind. The police shooting, the Facebook shit with Butta, Charm, the neighborhood rumors, everything. "I'm just hoping that the lawyer can get this case thrown out today. That's all."

Nizzy's lawyer had already assured him that he would be ready just in case the cops showed up and tried some sneaky stuff at the courthouse. But that didn't make Nizzy feel any less nervous. Especially knowing how dirty the police could play when it was one of their own that they were seeking justice for.

"Everything's going to be fine, sweety, okay?" Ms. Evon reached over to gently rub Nizzy's face.

"Yes, Ma'am." Nizzy smiled. His mother was the only woman in the world who could always put his mind at ease with a simple word or touch.

"Close your eyes," Ms. Evon took Nizzy's hands. "Let's pray."

By the time Nizzy and his mother finally arrived at the courthouse, Nizzy knew what his next move was going to be. The only thing he needed his lawyer to do was, knock down the drug and gun case before it could get in front of a jury. Then, he could get to work.

"Miss Lance," Nizzy's lawyer said, walking up, nodding to Ms. Evon, as she and Nizzy stood outside the courtroom. "Mister Lance." The lawyer extended his hand.

"Good morning," Ms. Evon replied, as Nizzy shook his lawyer's hand and went on through the courtroom doors.

"So how are we looking?" Nizzy inquired, getting straight to the point. He wanted to know what to expect.

"You're still in the clear," the lawyer assured. "As far as I can tell, there are still no witnesses. So, as long as your friend keeps his mouth close, you should be okay."

"That's what's up," Nizzy nodded, satisfied. He trusted Berry to hold water. The nigga was like a fire-hydrate when it came to holding water. He didn't even leak.

Inside the courtroom Nizzy spotted his mother sitting over near the bailiff, waving to get his attention, and made his way over.

"Everything okay?" Ms. Evon questioned, as Nizzy sat down beside her.

"Yes, Ma'am." Nizzy leaned over and kissed her softly on the cheek. He hadn't seen any signs of Murdock, and knew for a fact that Young Danny would not be making it. So he settled down and waited for his case to be called.

"I told you—That's the power of prayer," Ms. Evon said, keeping her eyes on the guy now standing arraigned before the judge. "You should've heard what this little rascal being charged with. Lord have mercy. These children today."

Nizzy looked at the orange prison jump-suit-wearing white boy with the long, dirty blond hair, and could only imagine. When it was show time, Nizzy's lawyer went straight to work. He argued the fact that nothing was ever found on Nizzy nor recovered from his person. Furthermore, he stated, "Mister Lance doesn't even reside at the residence in question. In fact, Your Honor, according to one of the arresting officer's own admission in his report, Mister Lance was observed having arrived at the location at approximately four minutes before the raid party entered the dwellings. That alone is a clear case of entrapment."

Nizzy's lawyer went on and on until the judge had no choice but to dismiss the case for lack of evidence. Afterwards he went on to issue a 'bench warrant' for Murdock's arrest and received a briefing about Young Danny's permanent absence from the court's docket.

"Call the next case," Nizzy heard the judge order as he stepped to the side to talk with his lawyer for a moment.

"The State of Maryland versus Tracy Savoy and Lamont Curtis, on two counts of felony, murder, three counts of kidnapping, one count of armed-robbery, and two counts of a deadly weapon in the commission—"

"So that's it?" Nizzy asked.

"Yeah, well, that and the paperwork," the lawyer replied. "But as far as the charges go, they never happened."

"Thanks, man," Nizzy shook his hand again. "You really came through."

"That's why you pay me the big bucks." He smiled.

"You're still gonna stay on top of everything else for me, right?"

"Of course." He nodded. "That was a part of your retainer."

"Bet." Nizzy headed towards the door, ready to get out of dodge. "Come on, Ma. Let's go."

Nizzy held the courtroom door open for his mother, oblivious as to what was about to happen.

"I don't move as fast as I use to, child." Ms. Evon said, walking past Nizzy out into the courthouse hallway.

"Yeah, I know," Nizzy teased, following her out of the courtroom a second before a pack of police officers rushed over, wrestled him to the ground, and roughly placed him under arrest.

"You like to kill cops, punk? Wait until we get you alone," one of the officers said threateningly.

"Man, you don't got to twist my arm like that!" Nizzy shouted, as the cops began clearing a path to march him out of the courthouse.

"Ma'am, you need to back up!" Another officer warned before Nizzy looked over to see his mother trying to push past the police.

"That's my child!" Ms. Evon declared. "Y'all ain't got to handle him like that! He has rights, you know?"

"Ma!" Nizzy yelled. "Go get my lawyer! Tell him that I'm being arrested!" Nizzy shouted, trying to break free. "Hold up, man!"

"Get him outta here now!" The plain-clothes detective Nizzy recognized from the East Baltimore shooting commanded as he saw his mother dash back inside the courtroom.

"You're going to need more than a lawyer this time, son," the arresting officer taunted, forcefully leading Nizzy down the hallway as people began to take out their cellphones to record what was happening. "Move!"

When they exited the courthouse, Nizzy spotted Murdock before the police did and tried to force his way back into the courthouse building as Murdock up'ed a chrome Calico.

"Stop resisting!" the officer ordered, grabbing Nizzy by the back of his neck aggressively. "I'm not going to say it again."

Everything seemed to slow down, and Nizzy literally saw the first burst of flame explode from the barrel of Murdock's tone. The officer instinctively let go of Nizzy and scattered for cover with the rest of the boys in blue as Murdock continued to advance, taking the steps two at a time, walking Nizzy down in a hail of bullets.

"Dodge this!" Murdock stepped over top of a severely wounded Nizzy with fire in his eyes, and brought the downtown streets to a dead silence before he pulled the trigger again, and again, and again until the Calico was empty.

"Freeze!" One of the officers aimed his service weapon from just inside the courthouse, behind the door, and demanded as Murdock spun on his heels and began to flee the scene.

Nizzy laid there stretched out across the courthouse steps, handcuffed behind his back—dead! Meanwhile, his one-time friend was tackled to the ground and handcuffed near the hot-dog stand that always sat outside the courthouse.

Chapter 23

It had felt strange leaving the family and everything that I knew for the first time in my life. But I had to go. Murdock had turned a simple arrest warrant into a Maryland's Most Wanted, nationwide manhunt. So, I left Slate and his man Bucky Fields with everything, and hopped on the first thing smoking under Baby-Joe's real name. Ebony was waiting for me when I landed at the San Antonio, Texas Airport. I felt out of place like a motherfucker. But I had to admit: I was also shocked. All of my life, I'd always thought that Texas was all horses, deserts and cowboys. I mean, that's what I'd been told and saw on TV. But now, I saw niggas walking around in the latest dopes, Prada, Versace and Gucci shit. It wasn't much different than the city.

Ebony had rented a small motel room on the outskirts of San Antonio, near the Mexican border, and thought it would be a good idea if I stayed out of sight until her cousin could set up a meeting with some dude who was good at creating fake identification. That was almost two weeks ago. Now, I was sitting in the passenger seat of a rental car as Ebony drove down the #10 on the way to North Star Mall.

"Tell me about this dude again," I requested. "How your folks know him?"

"Relax, baby," Ebony reached over and touched my hand. "If Erika say he's good, he's good."

"I just wanna know what I'm walking into," I said, refusing to let my guard down. There was a $30,000.00 reward out for my arrest, and I didn't trust nobody. "These Texas niggas be thinking they real cowboys."

Ebony burst out laughing, "I can't with you!" She shook her head. "I think them boys got my baby paranoid like an Indian."

"Oh, you got jokes, huh?" I couldn't help but laugh. Ebony really thought that she was a comedian. "If you say that's what it is, then, that's what it is," I accepted, falling back into my own thoughts. I had faith in my baby mother.

"That's what it is." Ebony continued to drive until we passed some huge ass cowboy boots on the side of the road and made a left into a parking lot.

"This it?" I questioned, looking around as Ebony parked in front of Macy's.

"Yep," Ebony confirmed. "That's Nate's car right there."

I admired the cocaine-white S Class as I climbed out of the rental and followed Ebony into the mall.

"We're suppose to meet him at a shoe and suit fitting store called 'Todd's'." Ebony spoke over her shoulder. "And we're stopping here to get something to eat on our way back too," Ebony added, as we passed a crowded cheesecake factory.

"Baby, you just ate," I reminded her.

"Yeah, well, I'm eating for two, remember?" Ebony touched her stomach. "Oh my God! Calvin! Give me your hand!"

"What?" I said, thinking something was wrong as Ebony snatched my hand.

"Can you feel that?" Ebony had a soft smile on her face.

"Oh shit," I mumbled, feeling a few light thumps on Ebony's stomach. "What's that? The baby?"

"The baby's kicking," Ebony confessed, as we stood there in the middle of the mall with her holding my hand to her stomach.

"Oh, baby boy ready to kick some shit off already."

"You mean, my little girl," Ebony corrected.

"Yeah, I heard that. Let's just find Todd's and take care of this business before people start thinking we're crazy." I took Ebony's hand and began walking through the mall again, looking for the shoe and suit fitting store.

"I think that's it right there." Ebony pointed to a large neon green sign hanging above the entrance of a high end looking clothing store that read 'Todd's'. We entered the shop and made our way over to an older potbelly Mexican sitting behind the counter, eating a greasy ass cheese & bean burrito. "We're here to see Nate," Ebony said as I checked out the shop. There were big buckled belts, cowboy boots, suits and ties everywhere.

The Mexican stared at us, and continued to chew his food. Then he sat his burrito down, stood up and slowly wiped his hands before picking up the phone to dial a few digits. Someone must've picked up because he began speaking into the phone in broken English. "Si, si," he said, hanging up the phone before sitting back down to grab his greasy ass burrito and began eating again.

"Yo, what's up?" I asked, but the Mexican remained quiet.

"Man, what the fuck is up with your cousin's folks?" I questioned, looking at Ebony as the dude sat there chewing with only his thick ass mustache moving.

"I don't know," Ebony confessed a second before another Mexican appeared from an employee's only door and signaled for us to follow him.

I locked eyes with the Mexican behind the counter one more time as he nodded and followed his friend into the back of the shop. I was surprised to see a young, slick, dude sitting high in a stool, having his leather boot polished by one of the baddest Hispanic bitches I'd ever seen. '

"Nate?" Ebony questioned to be sure.

"Si," he replied before saying something in Spanish that made the pretty Hispanic bitch get up and quickly exit the room with her shoe shining equipment. "You're Peanut's people, no?"

"Yeah," Ebony disclosed.

"Peanut?" I repeated as Nate got up off the stool and began shaking his legs until the pants legs of his dark slacks slid back down over his leather boots. "Who is Peanut?" I looked over at Ebony, confused. "I thought your cousin's name was Erika?"

"Yeah," Ebony gave me a wicked grin. "Erika is Peanut. You remember Peanut, right?"

Before I could reply, the door behind me opened, and I looked back to see Peanut's two muppet babies—Charco and Trini—coming through the door.

***

"You crudy ass bitch!" Charm spat, looking back at Ebony, as I entered the room behind Charco and Trini. Probably realizing he'd been played. "Checkmate," I said, smiling.

Charm lunged for Ebony, but Nate pressed the business end of a shiny ass pearl white handle Glock to the back of his head. "I'd think twice about that, amigo."

Charm froze, put his hands up and slowly backed up with his eyes glued to Ebony. "I'ma kill your snake ass, bitch!" he exclaimed.

"Ahhh, don't be upset with her, Charm," I appealed. "It was all my idea," I admitted, strolling towards him. "You see, Ebony is my girl. So, once I found out about the shit you pulled with Billy Lo, I put her on you. Honestly, I never actually thought that you'd go for it. But you actually fell in love," I shook my head kind of disappointed. "That pussy was good, wasn't it?"

"Bitch, fuck you!" Charm retorted before trying to spit into my face.

I grinned, pulled out my phone and scrolled down to Billy Lo's number. "I got somebody who wants to talk to you," I revealed, dialing Billy Lo's number.

"What's up, Peanut?" Billy Lo answered on the second ring.

"Can you face-time right now? I got somebody here you're dying to see," I said excitedly.

"Ain't no question," Billy Lo assured, knowing exactly what time it was. "Hang up and hit me right back. I got to cover this cell up."

When Billy Lo and I had first hooked up, I really didn't know what would come out of it. I just wanted to enact revenge on everybody that played any kind of part in the murder of my daughter's father. Everything else that took place was kind of like a favor for a favor.

"You ready to look death in the face?" I questioned, dialing Billy's Lo number again.

"Where that little snake at?" Billy Lo's face immediately popped up on the screen.

"Hold on," I turned the phone around so that Billy Lo could look Charm right in the eyes.

"What's up, lucky Charm?" Billy Lo taunted. "I told you this was a wise man's game. Now look at you. That little stunt you pulled hurt me, shorty. I treated you like family. I helped raise you from a puppy to a pit and look how you turned around and repaid me."

If Billy Lo was looking for some sort of explanation, Charm didn't give it to him. All he did was glare into the phone as if he wanted to kill him.

"Well, your luck has run out, Charm—This is where your game stops," Billy Lo said as the sound of Nate's hammer being cocked back echoed in the room. "Do you remember what I told you about money without honor in this line of work when we first met?" Billy Lo paused but Charm remained silent. "It's a death sentence."

"You forgot one thing though." Charm finally broke his silence and spoke up. "Both of y'all have."

Ignoring Charm, I signaled for Nate to pull the trigger. I wasn't about to let Charm draw this thing out like a bad low-budget film.

"And what's that?" Billy Lo questioned as if he was curious.

"I'm Nicole Johnson's son!" Charm declared as Nate turned his gun and aimed it at me. "So you can never count me out," he added the exact moment the door to the room opened again.

***

When Roofy and Goku walked into the meeting, Peanut's eyes got as big as golf balls. "You're not the only one with surprises, bitch." I smiled arrogantly, taking the pretty tone out of Nate's hand.

"Calvin baby," Ebony began to plead. "She made me do it baby. She said that if I—"

"Save it, bitch!" I spat, cutting Ebony off. "I know all about you," I explained, shaking my head. "Yeah," I continued.

"Imagine my surprise when I ran into my sister Cat outside of your school play and later found out that she'd tried to tell you not to go along with this bitch!" I stuck Peanut upside the head with the gun.

"Roofy," Peanut called out for some assistance.

"Nah, Peanut. You tried to play me," Roofy countered, toying with her necklace. "But, you're the one who's going to get played."

Roofy went on to explain to Peanut that after she got tired of her being her sex slave, she'd cut off her nipples and sell her off to a Mexican Cartel on the other side of the border wall who specialized in sex trafficking.

"You see, I just love dipping the nipples of whores into gold—So that I can wear them around my neck for good luck," Roofy explained, pulling the entire gold necklace out from in between her clevage to reveal two, small, golden looking raisins attached to the end. "These once belonged to my husband's mistress." She grinned, bouncing the weight of the gold-covered nipples around in the palm of her hand. "I took his and her nipples."

"Yeah, bitch, it ain't funny when the rabbit got the gun." I snatched the phone out of Peanut's hand. "You thought you had me, huh?" I looked at Billy Lo. "Yeah, well, put your 3D glasses on, nigga. Because I'm coming straight at you next. You better pray that you get the death penalty, nigga! 'Cause you're going to pay for what happen to my little sister." I dropped Peanut's phone on the floor and crushed it with my feet.

"You almost had me though," I admitted, looking at Peanut. "I mean, I didn't even believe Cat at first when she began telling me the plan. But Ebony fucked up by letting Nizzy see her in the truck with Goku who you were intentionally fucking behind Roofy's back for extra insurance. Even on her."

Peanut just stared at me. She knew, like I did, that the cat was out the bag in more ways than one and there wasn't no coming back from this. It was game over.

"Calvin baby, please," Ebony begged, grabbing her stomach, stumbling backwards like she was about to lose her balance. "I'm carrying your baby!"

"Bitch I don't care nothing about none of that shit!" I aimed the tone at Ebony head and pulled the trigger. But the chamber was empty, and the safety was still on.

"You can't kill her in my place of business, Charm," Roofy cautioned as I clicked the safety off and slid one into the chamber.

"This bitch made me kill my homeboys behind her triffling ass!" I disputed.

"Don't worry. You will have your justice as I'll have mine. Just not here." Roofy gestured towards Charco and Trini. "Take these whores over to the stable and let del Caballo (the house) break them in. He just loves pregnant puta."

"Ebony, run!" Peanut shouted, stealing the fuck out of me.

I'm not even going to lie. I saw bright stars too and it took me a second to recover. Especially since Peanut had caught me off guard. But Ebony couldn't move as quick as Peanut could. So, before she could clear the doorway, I aimed the tone and knocked the entire back out of her head.

The impact of the shot sent her crashing into the door. I spun around to knock Peanut's noodles loose next. But Charco and Trini jumped on me and started fighting me for the gun. The last thing I heard was Charco yell something about me being a dead man before the door burst open and the mall police rushed in.

Chapter 24

"You ready for your court shower, Izzard?" The administrative lock-up tier officer popped up outside the cell, toying with his handcuffs.

"Yeah, yeah," Billy Lo grabbed his shower-slippers and stuff off the bunk. He did his best thinking when he was shitting, showering or getting a serious sweat. "Did you get a chance to holler at the lieutenant for me yet about the phone?"

"Yeah, I'ma get you out after you come out of the shower," he replied, placing the handcuffs around Billy Lo's wrist through the feed-up slot after he turned around and put his hands behind his back. "You're only getting fifteen minutes. Because your ride will be here at a quarter to ten."

"Bet," Billy Lo nodded, stepping out on tier. "That's all I need," Billy Lo said. He just wanted to call Susan real quick and let her know that he wasn't taking no plea deals to avoid death row. Especially not life. If the state wanted his life, they'd have to take it. It was all or nothing. He wasn't no lying down.

"A'ight, Izzard." The tier officer locked him inside the shower and removed the handcuffs. "Call me when you're ready. The longer you take, the shorter your phone call going to be."

"Yeah, I heard that," Billy Lo shook his head. "I still don't understand why they're transporting me to court by myself."

"Come on now, Izzard. You know you're a local celebrity." The tier officer teased.

Billy Lo ignored him and jumped on in the shower. Ever since Charm's little dumb ass homeboy Murdock or whatever his name was, smashed a nigga right in front the courthouse a few weeks ago, Billy Lo's case had been pulled back into the media spotlight. The prison guards were even fucking with him. Which was why he only used his phone after midnight.

Billy Lo couldn't lie though. Killing a nigga right outside the courthouse on the front steps while he's being escorted by the police was some straight up gangster shit. Billy Lo soaped up and started rapping.

"—I'm use to thugs niggas / it's too many young niggas with too much liquid, too many drugs in em' / too many clicks, too much swag now / too many niggas wearing tight shirts with skinning jeans / walking around with their ass out—"

After Billy Lo got out of the shower and got to the phone, he reached out to his man Lil' Phil. Because he knew that Lil' Phil was probably the only motherfucker who could help him get his hands on exactly what it was that he needed if shit went south with his trial. Once he slid the kite off to the tier-runner for Lil' Phil, he got ready for court. Susan assured him that there would be no more delays. They would be starting jury selection today.

On the ride to the courthouse, Billy Lo couldn't help but think about the Charm and Peanut situation. He did not know what had taken place. But, he knew for certain that somehow Peanut and Charm had been arrested for somebody's murder down Texas. However, at the moment, Billy Lo's mind was on beating Carilyn Cosby at trial, although he respected everything that she was doing to destroy all the racial inequities that had been built into the Maryland Justice System. And he loved how she was vacating convictions that hinged on the word of corrupt cops or bad witnessing, tossing marijuana convictions, and seeking redress for wrongfully accused and convicted men. Today, inside the courtroom, she was just another prosecuting bitch trying to take his life. So, he wouldn't hesitate if he got the chance to take hers.

"—If any of you have any prior knowledge of this case or recognize any of the parties mentioned, now is your time to stand up and come forward." The Judge paused to look around the room full of potential jurors. "Okay, please come forward." The Judge instructed the two women who slowly stood up. "What are your numbers?" the Judge inquired, screening the jury pool for anyone else.

"One hundred and thirty-two," the first potential jury replied before looking to the other.

"Eighty," the second woman replied after pausing to clear her throat.

Without missing a beat, the Judge glossed over his jury list. "Miss Muhammad, I assume—" The Judge addressed the round faced, elderly woman in full garb. "That would make you Miss Octavia Bowman correct?" The Judge continued after Ms. Muhammad nodded.

"Yes, Your Honor." Octavia Bowman was a fine, little dime piece around her mid twenties.'

"I am going to need everybody to love each other up here and come closer," the Judge said, gesturing with his hands.

Billy Lo held his cane and squeezed in beside Susan next to the bench and waited for the Judge to question the potential jurors. Honestly, he was ready to skip all the preliminaries and get this show on the road.

"Good." The Judge spoke after everybody was huddled together. "Now, could you please pronounce your first name for me Miss Muhammad?"

"It's Maryam," she replied, slowly cutting her eyes at Billy Lo.

"Now, what part of the two-part question did you stand up for?"

"Oh, I know the defendant," she confessed.

"Mister Izzard?" the Judge questioned, to be sure as Billy Lo looked at the elderly woman again. She did kind of look familiar.

"Yes," she confirmed without hesitation.

"And how is it that you know Mister Izzard?"

"Well, ummm, I use to live across the alley from his parents in the late seventies, early eighties. And Anthony use to date one of my granddaughters."

"And what neighborhood was this?" The Judge continued to drill, as if he thought Miss Muhammad was just another juror trying to skip out on jury duty.

"Park Heights," she replied. "But my home was located on Belvedere to be exact."

"And what is your granddaughter's name?"

"Her name was Lotti," Miss Muhammad replied softly. "She was murdered some years back."

"I am sorry to hear that," the Judge said. "Please step to the side for a moment.

Hell no! Billy Lo thought, as Miss Muhammad stepped off to the side. He was slipping. There was no way that he shouldn't have recognized Lotti's grandmother. As much as she used to curse him out for sneaking through Lotti's bedroom window. Damn! Why the fuck she didn't keep quiet and stay on the jury?"

"I assume nobody objects to me striking this juror for cause?" The Judge looked from Susan to Cosby. "Great." He waved Lotti's grandmother back over. "Thank you for your service, Miss Muhammad. You are excused. You may return to the jury room."

"I'll pray for you, Anthony, okay?" Lotti's grandmother mumbled to Billy Lo.

"Yes, ma'am." Billy Lo nodded before she walked off. Billy Lo knew that she didn't approve of a lot of the things that had gone on between he and Lotti back in the days.

Jury number eighty—Octavia Bowman—laid her issues out next. She was a God-fearing mother of three who refused to pass judgement on another human being under any circumstances. Susan fought to keep her on the jury. But when it came out that she'd had some trouble with the law down in Florida and just didn't trust a word they said, the Judge kindly excused her and sent her back to the jury room.

After another round of questions and answers. It was time for jury selection. "Okay, ladies and gentlemen, we're going to break for today." The Judge spoke up, ready to release the jury for the day. Afterwards, they were all accounted for by number as well as name. "We'll pick up from here first thing tomorrow morning. Eight o'clock sharp! Hopefully, we can have a jury seated by noon."

Nobody had a problem with that. So that's what it was. They'd select 12 in the morning and go to war. Whatever the case, Billy Lo told Susan that he was ready—Win, lose or draw.

Chapter 25

A sealed federal indictment had come down, and the Feds started grabbing everybody. And I mean everybody. Adnan, my cousin Slate, Cock-eyed Willie, Big Al, E-Don. Everybody. They carried out several forms of home invasions across the city and told the public they were raids. Yeah, right! Them bitches even ran up in my mother's spot and search the cell I had been assigned to at the Baltimore City Jail, after being extradited. I was a Dummie. But, I hadn't ever been a fool. So, I never ate where I shitted at. So each time they came up empty-handed.

In the end forty-two people, both men and women, were arrested and charged with everything from Continuing Criminal Enterprise to murder and conspiracy. The Feds had Don Poppa's bitch ass under witness-protection and he was dreaming up all kind of things. Especially, after a couple little homies tried to walk him down and ended up hitting his son, and the state charged him with his cousin Smurf's death.

I did not agree with Don Poppa's son being shot and all. Thank God he hadn't died. But still, that didn't justify his actions. Niggas who posed as gangsters aren't suppose to make statements and violate the codes of the streets. But I wasn't surprised about Don Poppa. Niggas had been on to how he'd went out like a hoe. They were just waiting to clip his nuts.

Once it came out that Smurf had folded like a lawn chair too, I really didn't have no sympathy for his bitch ass. I guess snitching ran in the family. I was so glad JuJu had done him dirty for trying to play the fence and collect from both sides.

The Feds came and tried to get me to talk again. They had pictures and everything of me and the squad. It was crazy because some of the photos actually looked like we were posing for them bitches. I had also been questioned for my premature twins' mother's murder. As had Peanut, Charco and Trini. The Feds offered to clean that up too. But, I wasn't tripping. Nobody was talking and Roofy had already assured me that if all else failed, one of her soldiers would eat the charges. Still, even if she hadn't,

I could never cooperate with the police. I didn't give a fuck what happened. I could never testify, cop out to a plea, or surrender information about anybody to law enforcement. That just wasn't how I was made. And it damn sure wasn't how I was raised. And that would never change. Niggas would never be able to say that Nicole Johnson's son rolled on them. Never!

"I was like, okay, you know I'm guilty. If you can beat it, I'll pay you double." I joked about the murder down south with Slate and Murdock. We were all sitting in the sick call area, waiting to be called. It was the only place we got to meet up and see each other since I was still on the hopper section.

Since it was so many of us, niggas were being housed everywhere. The Supermax, D.O.C. building, City Jail and Old Penitentiary on Foster Street.

"You dumb as shit boy!" Murdock shook his head as Slate continued to laugh. "I ain't telling my lawyer no shit like that."

"Dummie, I'm telling you. If you would've seen how all this was hanging off, you'd have said the same shit." I gestured to the back of my head. "I crushed that bitch. So, I was trying to get the best bang for my buck."

"You said the Mexican bitch going to do right though?" Slate questioned.

"Yeah, this was before she got to me with her plans though," I revealed. "I was down that bitch rumbling with these county boys everyday. 'Cause you know I ain't going for nothing! Once Roofy came through though, and them niggas found out, they got their minds right. I mean, I come off the visit and they had literally laid the carpet out. That bitch got some juice down south, Fam."

"So she's not mad about the shit with Ebony any more?" Slate questioned.

"Nah," I admitted. "She was just mad about it going down in her shop. Bringing unnecessary heat."

"What they say about the twins?"

"Peaches and Keystone been dealing with that. I think my mother wants full custody so they have to go to court. She done already named the little girl Tiffany. Keystone named my lil' man Calvin Junior."

"That's what's up though," Murdock said. "Especially since niggas about to fuck around and do some major time."

"You ain't never lied," I agreed, knowing that we were definitely about to do some numbers behind the wall. "I'ma fight them bitches to the end though."

"Man, fuck all that. I'm not playing with the Feds, fam." Slate spoke up. "I'm trying to cop out to something nice. Something where I can see daylight again. I'm not trying to fuck around and get washed up like Itchy-Man."

"Heads up, Dummie!" Murdock warned, looking past me. "Here come some of them Muslim niggas."

"Huh?" I turned around to see who Murdock was referring to, and couldn't believe my eyes. There was Adnan entering the sick call waiting room with Yah-Yah and another one of their Muslim brothers.

"Yo, y'all not going to believe who that is," I whispered, knowing that Murdock or Slate had never actually laid eyes on Adnan before. "That's Adnan."

"Adnan the plug?" Slate inquired, and I nodded.

"The one who got at O?" Murdock followed.

"Yeah," I confirmed as my lips curled into a smile. "The darkskin one with the receding hairline is Yah-Yah."

Adnan spotted me and nodded before taking a seat on the other side of the waiting room. I guess he wanted me to know that he wasn't slipping. But shidddd, neither was I. How could I be? That was the leading cause of death in a place like City Jail. The Feds may have had everybody down as co-defendants. But we all knew what was going on for real.

"Fuck is yo nodding for?" Murdock challenged, knowing that we didn't fuck with, nor trust any nigga with a big beard. Especially Muslims because we can't tell which ones were crudy and which ones weren't. "Check me out, Dummie." Murdock fliped Adnan the bird.

"Man, fuck that sucker ass nigga," Slate brushed Adnan off but he kept goosing. "I'm trying to figure how we going to play this court shit."

"Hold up, fam." I turned to Murdock as Adnan smiled. "You got that hawk on you, Dummie?"

"You already know," Murdock replied. "What's up?"

"I'ma trying to see this nigga about O." I stared at Murdock.

"You tripping, fam," Slate stated.

I thought about all the shit that we were in. A lot of it was because of Adnan. Even down to the whole Dummie Squad, crudy Muslim feud. "Nah, fam, fuck that," I retorted, standing up, thinking about O. "That nigga got O cracked."

"I thought niggas said that shit was dead?" Slate reminded, and I knew he was right. He and Murdock had sat down with a few Muslims. But still, that was before I had gotten sent back to the city. "You just chill. I got this."

"Fam, you already know if you get on this nigga, I'ma be all over him!" Slate fired.

"Let's work then," I commanded, sliding my hand into my spot for the knife. Once I got a good grip on the handle, I made my way across the waiting area. It was time to see just how thorough Adnan really was.

"What on your mind, Ock?" Yah-Yah questioned, standing up as Murdock and I approached. It was time to either draw his nuts up and call for help or commit himself to death.

I looked back at my cousin Slate real quick. When he smirked I knew it was go time. "You already fucking know!" I whipped out the vicious ass knife I had with the deep ridges and rough grooves in it, and hit Adnan with the razor-blaze sharp tip before Yah-Yah could stop me.

"Hold up, Ock!" Adnan shouted, caught off guard. I guess he thought that I wouldn't bust his ass. Maybe that was why he kept sitting there like he didn't have a care in the world. Whatever he thought though, he was wrong.

"Nah, bitch, ain't no hold up now!" I stabbed Adnan again.

"Fuck is you doing, nigga!" Yah-Yah hit me with a clean right.

"Oh yeah," Murdock said, pulling out. "I was hoping you bitches wanted some work."

"Nah, Ock, y'all ain't about to do that?" The other Muslim jumped up like he was ready to get it in. But when he saw Slate coming, he knocked over a bunch of chairs escaping the room.

Adnan tried to grab my wrist. But, I pushed him over the bench and jumped on top of him as Murdock attacked Yah-Yah. I looked up for a second to see Yah-Yah squaring off with Murdock and Slate. That's when I saw the knife in Yah-Yah's hand. I hit Adnan a few more times then ran over to help Slate and Murdock. I rushed Yah-Yah and swung the knife overhead. But he blocked it and dazed the fuck out of me with another right.

"Murdock!" I called, grabbing Yah-Yah as I fell backwards. Murdock stabbed Yah-Yah in the side and it was on. We got to rocking and rolling up in that bitch. Dudes were moving, running and jumping out of our way as Murdock, Slate and I tried to kill Yah-Yah up in that bitch. I can't lie though: Yah-Yah was a goon. He went extremely hard. He hit Murdock, dazed Slate and sling my lil' ass half way across the waiting room, where I managed to slip, hit my head on the bench, and dropped my knife.

"Slate!" I yelled for assistance as I fought with Adnan for possession of the knife. "Help me yo! He got my knife!" I held on to Adnan's wrist for dear life as Slate ran over and started stabbing him again everywhere but his feet and hands.

"Get off my brother, bitch!" Yah-Yah barked, jumping on my back as Murdock continued to butcher him. "I hate all you little *kafirs*." Yah-Yah mumbled through clenched teeth, using his forearm to hold my head up and expose my throat. I didn't know if he was about to cut my throat or stab me in the neck. All the blood was making everything slippery, though I was able to squrim just enough to catch the knife in the side of my jaw. I felt the blade rip through my cheek and pierce my tongue. But, I refused to cry out in pain.

Murdock and Slate finally got Yah-Yah off of my back. But I stayed on Adnan. I locked my legs around him and grabbed the weld down bench so that he couldn't get up. Then, I went to work on his ass until the correctional officers rushed in spraying everybody with enough mace to stop an elephant. It wasn't until we were all maced out, laid across the floor that I noticed that both Murdock and Slate was wounded. Not as badly as Yah-Yah and Adnan but wounded nevertheless.

"I hope you bitches bleed to death!" Murdock fired as a fat C.O. rolled him over his stomach so that he could grab him under his armpit and help him stand up.

"Uh, I'll see you again, Ock. Believe that," Yah-Yah shook his head as they picked Slate up off the floor and escort him to medical next. I knew they were both alright. Yah-Yah and Adnan were the ones being worked on in the waiting room.

"Yeah, nigga," I smiled as the same fat C.O. came and got me off the floor. Adnan was barely able to sit up on his own. *That's for my nigga, bitch!* I thought before looking at Yah-Yah again to flip him the bird and mouth the word, 'See you around' a second before I disappeared out of the waiting room.

Chapter 26

"You got a visitor, Brown," the male turn-key informed me as I was standing in the line of Women's County Detection Center, waiting to use the prison telephone.

"Visitor?" I repeated, knowing that my brothers had not made it to Texas yet because I'd just talked to my mother last night. "You sure?" I stared at the male corrections officer.

"Yeah, visit." The male turn-key said with too much attitude for my liking before he walked off. But it was all good.

"Say, look out, kinfolk—If you don't want it, I'll take it," a nasty looking, big bitch said. Without saying a word, I just got out of the phone line and followed the male turn-key. When we got to the back steps, the turn-key pressed me up against the wall and tried to kiss me.

"Hold up, nigga!" I avoided his lips. "Did you get what I asked you for?"

Shaking his head before looking around nervously, the turn-key dug inside his pocket and pulled out a watch phone. "I'ma hold it until you come back from your visit."

"My visit?" I questioned again. Only this time more seriously. Because I didn't have anybody coming to see me. I thought it was just another one of his little tricks to try and get me alone.

"Yeah." He nodded. "You really got a visit."

"Shit," I fired. I didn't have the information for my brothers on me. "I'ma need you to escort me back to the cell real quick."

"There's no way I can do that without getting in trouble," he warned. "The camera's going to show that we've been around here too long. Because registration will call up here."

"I need something out of my cell." I took a deep breath.

"Okay," he submitted. "How about this? I'll take you to your visit and say you left your ID card. That way they can't verify who you are. Then, I'll go to your cell and get whatever it is that you need me to get."

I stared at him for a minute. I wasn't no dumb bitch. My mother had taught me about men who think with their dicks a long time ago. They couldn't be trusted. So I knew that I had to handle him with care. "Okay, cool."

"A'ight, let's go before they start calling for you," he suggested, moving towards the door.

This particular male turn-key had been sweet on me since the moment I arrived. And I didn't make it any easier for him by letting him watch me play with myself from my cell door window. Once I knew I had him hooked, it was game on. Our friendship quickly blossomed from there and before long he was wrapped around my finger. One thing I quickly leaned about Texas was that they weren't ready for that Baltimore City game. I was running circles around them county girls. At first though, I was a little lost. One bitch kept asking to 'look at me'. So that we could 'catch a cell' and she could see 'how I go from my shoulders'. But once I realized that the bitch was talking about 'hollering at me' so that we could 'find a cell to fight in' because she wanted to 'see if I was nice with my hands', it was on. I immediately stepped to the bitch and showed her just how up to date my hands were.

When we got to the visiting area, I mysteriously found my ID card and went ahead with my visit. There was no chance that I would knowingly send a guard into my cell to search for something, whether he was cool or not. I knew the game. When Roofy walked in, I almost lost it. I wanted jump the table and drag that bitch Baltimore style up in there. But of course, the thick glass prevented that.

"Hello, Peanut," Roofy spoke as I stood there contemplating whether I should walk out or not. "Come on, Peanut. Don't be like that. I came all this way to see you."

I slowly took my seat, rolling my eyes. Why wasn't this bitch locked up? How had she walked away clean as if she wasn't even present? They didn't even mention her in the charge papers at all. "You know that I am going to kill you, right?"

"I didn't come here to fight, Peanut. I came here to offer you an olive branch." Roofy paused. "Are you okay?" She continued when I ignored her again. "Did you get your watch yet?"

"What, bitch?" I looked around for the male turn-key.

"Your phone watch from my nephew?" Roofy smiled. "All he talks about is how pretty that little puta is. I told him he would never taste it." Roofy licked her lips teasingly.

"Look, bitch! I don't know what kind of game you're running. But, I'm not the one." I got to my feet, ready to leave.

"Do you want your freedom or not, Mami?"

"My freedom?" I repeated. That got my attention. When Roofy nodded, I sat back down. "I'm listening."

"I can make your charges stick or go away." Roofy spoke confidently.

"And how are you going to do that?" I questioned curiously because I really wanted to know how far this bitch could reach.

"I'm the queen of the south, baby." Roofy stared at me.

"You're still not telling me anything. Like what's it going to cost me to make these charges go away?"

"Loyalty," Roofy revealed. "I want you to be loyal to me. I want you all to myself, Peanut."

I sat there staring at Roofy. This bitch was crazy. Here it was she had me sitting in jail on some trumped up charges. And she's talking about being in a relationship with her at that! Did this bitch know how much I loved dick! But then, I thought about my daughter and how much she needed me. I thought about Ebony and how much she sacrificed. I even thought about Cat and how she crossed me. More importantly, I thought about Roofy and how she thought that she had me by the nipples.

"Loyalty in what sense?" I questioned. Because if there was a chance for me to get out of prison and paid my debts, I planned to take it because—despite popular belief—education wasn't what you put into a person. But, in fact, what you pulled out.

"Loyalty in the sense of being with me, working beside me, working with me—Us together," Roofy explained.

"Okay," I nodded, so glad that I hadn't sent her spying ass nephew to retrieve Zimbabwe's number. "I'll do it."

"Peanut," Roofy paused to toy with her necklace and stare at me intensely for a long time. "If you cross me, baby, or try to leave, I'll see to it that you live to regret it."

"I won't betray you, Roofy," I lied. "You just take care of me and I'll take care of you," I added, knowing that an enemy of mine could never be a friend. I would just bid my time. Build a strong hold from the inside, and then do what I always did the best. Rock a bitch to sleep!

***

"Wake your snake ass up, lucky Charm!" Billy Lo called out, squirting freak-ass—shit, sour-milk, and piss—all over Charm and his cell as he slept. "Ain't no sleeping around here, bitch!"

"Ahhh, you stiff ass nigga!" Charm jumped up outta bed and began to shield himself with his blanket. "What the fuck!" He threw the blanket down when the smell finally hit his nostrils.

"Yeah, nigga," Billy Lo smiled. "I'ma get at you however I can. Shit you down. Beat you up!" Billy Lo threw the empty bottle between the bars at Charm. "I'ma put that bottle on your whore ass every time I come out for the phone until I can catch you and put that knife in your little ass!" Billy Lo warned before running back down the tier to the phone, before the tier officer came.

Billy Lo could hear Charm going off. Calling him all types of bitches and whores. But, he wasn't tripping. When it came to war, there were only two things that he wouldn't do. And that was fuck a nigga or snitch on him. Beyond that, everything else was fair game.

Billy Lo slipped back into the handcuffs and dialed his lawyer's number. It was Saturday morning. So he knew that Susan would still be home. They'd been in trial all week, and had to go back at it first thing Monday morning. Billy Lo wanted to talk about strategy and go over his witness list because Lil' Phil had just gave him a serious idea. He also needed an update on the shit with the Feds. He wanted to know if they were going to pull him into Charm's indictment.

The administration assured Billy Lo that he would definitely not be seeing general population over the city jail ever again. They were upset that he'd taken off and cracked the state's 'jailhouse' snitch upside the head with his cane while he sat up on the witness stand, testifying about things he didn't even know about. Things he claimed Billy Lo had told him about when they were on the section.

The entire courtroom had erupted into chaos when Billy Lo hauled off and wracked the 'jailhouse' snitch on his way from the Judge's bench before calling him a liar, saying that they'd never even slept on the tier together. Susan fought for a mistrial. But the Judge wasn't having it. He felt like if Billy Lo was bold enough to attack a witness in his courtroom, he should be brave enough to accept the consequences. It was all good though. Billy Lo knew that the deck was stacked against him. The good news though was that Charm had got to working up medical with the Muslims and ended up right on the tier with him. So that gave Billy Lo an opportunity to be able to touch him. Until then though, Billy Lo just planned to keep wilding Charm out every time he came out for a telephone call on the weekends since he was in trial.

***

This nigga Billy Lo was a real life bitch! And I swear I couldn't wait to get my hands on his old ass. I had Slate and Murdock stalking him too. Putting in sick calls and dentist request in his name, trying to catch him slipping. It was on sight. Whoever, wherever, whenever. I'd almost had him last Sunday. I mean, I was so close that I could taste it. I waited until after his bitch ass came out for the phone and got to faking chest pains. Once the tier officer told me to get ready, I grabbed my handcuff key and knife and waited. I was going to trash his ass. But before the tier officer got me out for medical, he uncuffed Billy Lo from the phone and locked him in. It was cool though. I'd eventually get my opportunity and when I did, it was curtains.

My mother and Keystone came to see me. They'd won temporary custody of the twins and wanted me to know. Mom said they still wouldn't be out of the hospital for a few more weeks though. I really didn't know how I felt about killing Ebony. I mean, I know I talked that shit and put on for Murdock and my cousin. But honestly, deep down, it hurt that I had to kill the mother of my children for being a snake. A woman I truly loved.

I was laid back listening to the 'Love Zone' on 92Q, wishing at least one of the lil' bitty's I was hitting uptown would give me a shout out when my neighbor banged on the wall. "What's up?" I questioned, hiding the small MP3 player and earbuds before pulling the sheet I now kept hanging up back.

"I got a kite for you," he said.

"From who?" I inquired. I wasn't accepting nothing from Billy Lo. Especially not a white flag [i.e., a request for peace on paper].

"I think the older dude up the tier in cell one sent it," he said, sticking his arm out grill between the bars to pass me the kite.

"Thanks," I said, accepting the kite. I sat back down on the bed and slowly opened the kite. You had to be careful with dudes behind the door. They like to play a lot of games.

Once I got the kite open and flipped it all around to make sure wasn't nothing on it, I began to read:

Check it out, Young Blood. I just heard your man who be throwing that shit in your cell every weekend give his lawyer your name as a witness. Now listen I'm not trying to be involved in anything. But your Uncle Ronald and I go way back. And I know that Money Cola was like your father. So, I'm just pulling your coat tail. So, you'll be hip to what's what. There's no need to holler back. Just stick mirror out and look down here so I'll know that you got this. Alright Young Blood, peace. Arnie Roll.

Oh yeah? I thought, reading the kite again. This nigga Billy Lo was really trying to get at me. But I was with all that. Fighting, knife slinging, throwing shit, whatever!

I grabbed my peeper, went to the grill, and stick it out. Being sure to look both ways first, once I saw the old head's mirror, I gave him the thumbs up and he was gone.

I sat back down. I didn't really know what to do. Was it a trick? I mean, cell one was right across from the phones. So I knew that he could've definitely been able to hear Billy Lo's conversation. But still, the old nigga could be trying to fox me. Then I realized that there was no way that he would know about Uncle Ronald. Money Cola, maybe. But not Ronald. There was no way that he could know about Ronald.

I pulled out my pen and pad and wrote Murdock and Slate to put them on point. Whatever it was going to be, it was going to be, because I wasn't ducking nothing. So this is what it had come down to in the end. Me and Billy Lo. I hope he was ready because I was. If they hit my door for court Monday, I'd be ready for war.

I covered the grill back up and dug my knife out. If it was go time, I'd wanted to make sure that my hawk was super sharp.

Chapter 27

"What's up, Ock?" Wakal rolled over and looked towards the open cell door. It had to be every bit of 5 in the morning.

"I don't know." His cell buddy tossed the covers back, sat up on the bunk, and slipped his feet into his tennis. "They just opened the door."

"Close it back then," Wakal ordered.

"Hold up." He stood up, wiping cold out of his eyes. "I'ma walk down to the desk and see what's up."

Wakal pulled the blanket back up over his head and tried to go back to sleep. He'd been dreaming about uptown. Running around with multiple wives and children. Wakal knew that a conscious man of wisdom could rise above his thinking into the thinking of God. He also understood that man could operate on the level of the beast. Because the intelligence of man was unmatched by anything in Allah's creation.

"Ayo Ock! Ock!" Wakal heard his cell buddy whisper, almost as if he didn't want to disturb him. "Wakal!"

"Yo," Wakal looked up again.

"They're saying you got court," he informed.

"Who got court?" Wakal rolled over to check the calendar he had taped on the wall next to his pillow. "I don't go back to court until September, Ock," Wakal said, scanning the calendar. "I'm looking at it right here."

"Don't kill the messenger, Ock. I'm just telling you what the lady said."

Wakal snatched the blanket back and hopped down off the top bunk. "They got a nigga getting out of bed for nothing!" Wakal fired, stumbling into the wall, still half asleep, trying to find the opening of his shower shoes in the dark.

Wakal walked down the tier to the desk to tell the tier officer that she'd made a mistake. He didn't have no court date. But, when he got to the front of the tier, he learned that he did in fact have a court date scheduled for that morning.

"Everything straight?" Wakal's cell buddy asked when he walked back into the cell.

"Nah, they really got me down for court," Wakal confessed, still kind of confused. "But, I'm telling you, Ock. I don't suppose to be going to court."

"Shiddd, they may be calling you in early to cut that deal." Wakal's cell buddy smiled. "Allah knows best."

"Insha Allah," Wakal smiled back. If he could get a sweet deal, it was on. "Let me go ahead and get myself together."

"Make sure you lock the grill on the way out," Wakal's cell buddy requested, climbing back under his covers.

"I got you," Wakal assured. The community had been on high alert ever since a few brothers got jumped with some knives on the other side of the jail up the med room by some Bloods.

After making *Fajr* (morning salat), Wakal busied himself getting ready for court. He grabbed his paperwork just in case. Then, he got dressed and quietly crept out of the cell. What he didn't know, but was about to learn, was that with the wrong intentions, a man of knowledge could become as low as the snake, leaving crooked trails of betrayal everywhere he slithered.

After the usual bullpen gossip, Wakal was strip-searched, shackled, three-pieced and walked out to the Blue Bird. Wakal always found it amazing how reckless dudes talked in the bullpen and on the Blue Bird. Especially since most of them called themselves gangsters. Wakal guessed that many of them hadn't ever heard the saying that, 'real G's moved in silience'.

"—So, like I was saying, Dummie." The kid in the seat in front of Wakal with the orange jumpsuit on continued to run his mouth and tell all his business. "You already know how I get down. I don't give a fuck. So we're up medical and I'm asking Dummie what's up. And you already know it's g-season with him all day. So we worked them niggas up in there."

The kid's last statement got a few Muslim brothers on the Blue Bird's attention. Including Wakal's.

"Oh, that's what you're going to court for today?" the kid's friend inquired. "I was wondering where the fuck everybody else was at."

"Nah." The kid laughed before looking around. "Remember that other thing Nizzy and I pulled you up about before all that other shit happen?"

"Oh, yeah?" The other kid seemed impressed. "How you pull that off?"

"Nah, yo thought he was rocking me. But I was already on point. They just never hit yo door this morning. I was going to wear his old ass out too."

"You still crazy as shit, Charm."

"You already fucking know," the kid bragged.

Charm? Wakal thought, leaning up against the window to get a good look. Oh shit! It was really Charm. Wakal instantly started looking around for a familiar face. He knew somebody had to have some kind of weapon on them.

Wakal eyed the guy sitting next to him. But, he looked so shook that Wakal knew that it was no way that he had anything on him. Wakal couldn't believe his luck. *I'ma beat the fuck out of this little nigga when we get in the strip-search room*, Wakal thought. He knew he had to make his move before they got separated into the lock-up and general population bullpens.

"When you get back, make sure you let Dummie and 'em know what's up." Charm said.

"Already." the other kid nodded.

"I don't want them niggas thinking crazy." Charm laughed. "You know, same crime, different trial. You feel me?"

"I'ma holler at Dummie as soon as I get back on the tier."

"You might not have to if I end up catching up with this old nigga in the bullpen." Charm gave the kid a gesture Wakal understood all too well.

Wakal couldn't believe that Charm didn't recognize him. Then, he thanked Allah that he didn't. Wakal just sat there and continued to listen to Charm talk shit as the Blue Bird was loaded. He was really something else. And his little ass was in everything except a hearse. He was even responsible for the shit up medical with the brothers; an incident that Wakal now knew that dudes were running around mistakingly blaming them crazy ass Bloods for.

As the Blue Bird drove towards the courthouse, Wakal got himself mentally ready. He already knew that Charm had a joint on him. So he knew that he had to strike first. The chances of Billy Lo being in the bullpen with them again was slim to none. Especially while he was in trial. He'd gotten lucky the last time and that was before he decided to try to take some snitch nigga's head off inside the courtroom.

When the Blue Bird turned into the underground courthouse parking garage, Wakal was still trying to figure out how he was going to play things. He knew he had to do something. Not only had Charm crossed him and his brothers—Black, Lil'Dray and Mumbles. But, he'd also gave Billy Lo up to the mob. On top of that, Wakal had given Billy Lo his word that if he ever got the chance to touch Charm, he would. He'd even swore by Allah.

When the bus completely entered the underground parking garage and got dark, Wakal got an idea. Moving quickly, Wakal brought his shackled legs up over Charm's head and wrapped the chain around his neck before he even knew what hit him.

Charm instantly began trying to get free. But it was no use. With his hands restrained by the three-piece and his feet shackled, he couldn't even begin to defend himself. Actually, the more Charm struggled, the tighter Wakal pulled the chain into his throat, cutting off his oxygen.

"Allahu Akbar! Allahu Akbar!" Wakal shouted, choking Charm until he was blue in the face. "Allahu Akbar!"

Once the bus finally came to a stop, Wakal was able to lift his legs back over Charm's head. Charm's body fell forward and slumped up against the window. At that point, everybody jumped up and started trying to get off the bus before the body was discovered. The first person hadn't even stepped foot off the bus before niggas started telling. In fact, it was actually why everybody had began lining up. They all wanted to be the first one to snitch. Most of them were just tired of the crudy Muslim brothers' power. Some were just looking for an early release date, and the others just wanted a way out. Before long, Wakal was located, read his Miranda rights, and taken into custody.

***

"Has the jury reached a verdict?" The Judge looked directly at the foreman after the case was read into the record.

"We have, Your Honor," the foreman replied, nervously standing up.

Billy Lo watched as the heavy-set bailiff took the folded up piece of paper from the foreman and handed it to the Judge to read. The judge unfolded the paper, read it and handed it back to the bailiff to pass back to the foreman without changing his expression in the least.

The courtroom was packed wall to wall. And Billy Lo knew that most of them were there to see him go down. Shaneeka and India were probably the only two people inside the courtroom besides Susan rooting for him.

"Mr. Foreman, would you please read your verdict into the record," the Judge instructed, and waited as Billy Lo's heart began to pound in his chest.

"As to count one, murder in the first degree, we find the defendant Anthony Izzard, not guilty."

The courtroom exploded with moans and groans when they jury dropped the 'not guilty' bomb. But Billy Lo remained calm. He knew that he wasn't out of the woods yet.

"Order in the court!" The Judge banged his gavel repeatedly. "Order in the court. I'll not tolerate interruptions in my courtroom. Is that understood?"

Billy Lo stood there like a true soldier. Ready to take his hit on the chin. No matter the verdict. Because honestly speaking, it was just another day in the game called 'Street Life'.

Once the Judge was sure that he'd gotten his point across, he signaled for the foreman to continue.

"As to count two, murder in the second degree, we find the defendant Anthony Izzard, not guilty." The foreman continued to let the air out of the courtroom. "As to count three, handgun in the commission of a crime of violence, we were unable to reach a verdict, Your Honor."

"Do you need more time?" the Judge inquired.

"No, Your Honor. We've tried. We're just deadlock," the foreman admitted. "Nobody's budging."

"Okay," the Judge finally spoke after a long pause. "Thank you for your service, ladies and gentleman. You're free to go." The Judge banged his gavel, dismissing the jury panel. "We'll reconvene in two weeks from today to see if the state wishes to proceed further with this case," the Judge continued as the jury began falling out.

So that was it. In two weeks Billy Lo would find out if the state wanted to retry the case or let him walk free.

"I'll see you before you leave." Billy Lo's lawyer Susan Kerin quickly gathered her belongings and rushed out of the courtroom behind the jury.

Billy Lo saw Detective Baker talking to Carilyn Cosby and another suit as the bailiff handcuffed him to escort him back to the lock-up bullpens. By the time Susan got down to the holding cell, Billy Lo had already heard that an inmate had been strangled to death on the prison bus. He just didn't know that it was Charm until Susan told him.

"Man, that's crazy." Billy Lo shook his head like he really didn't understand what was going on.

"What's crazy is that the suspect was down as one of your character witnesses too," Susan Kerin glared at Billy Lo intently. Almost as if she was trying to read him. "I am warning you, Anthony, if you know something about this shit, I'll see to it that you never get a good defense in this city again."

"I'm clueless on this one," Billy Lo lied. "All of us fuck with each other."

"I am serious. This is my career we're talking about," Susan argued.

"I wouldn't do that," Billy Lo said sincerely. He honestly would've never put D.W. and Charm on his witness list had he thought for a second that it would jeopardize Susan's career. He had too much respect for her. "So what's the other thing you got to tell me?"

"Oh darn," Susan cursed. "I almost forgot. I talked to the jury. Turns out you were right. The fact that men and women don't enter the through the same doors at the church most of the time really made a big difference. That and they just couldn't imagine you putting your life on the line by going after that witness for nothing when he was on the stand"

"I told you!" Billy Lo smiled at the memory of breaking his cane over the state's lying ass 'jailhouse' snitch's head. "So what now? You think the state gonna want rumble go again?"

"Carilyn's tough," Susan admitted. "But I think that I can get her to deal you out. Especially now, with all the madness surrounding your case."

"What are we talking?" Billy Lo looked at Susan and prayed that she wouldn't say nothing crazy. "Eighteen months, two years?"

"More like five years tops," Susan corrected. "Let's not forget you're a convicted felony, Anthony. But, I can have you back in front the Judge in eighteen months on a modification."

"What about the Feds? You think they're coming?"

"It's a toss up," Susan answered honestly. "They may charge you. They may not. Either way, if they do, you aren't looking at more than ten years."

"A'ight, fuck it," Billy Lo said, ready to let the chips fall where they may. "See if you can get the deal."

"I think that's the best move, Anthony," Susan declared. "That way everybody feels like they won."

"Yeah, I heard that, Miss Susan Kerin," Billy Lo grinned. "Make it happen then."

"Consider it done." Susan nodded and started for the door.

"I hate to see you leave. But I love to watch you go," Billy Lo teased, licking his lips with his eyes glued on Susan's little, tight butt. He couldn't help himself. It had been a long time. "I told you you're my favorite white girl!"

"See you in two weeks, Anthony!" Susan looked over her shoulder with a smile, shook her head and disappeared out the door.

Chapter 28

Detective Baker had sat inside the packed courtroom two weeks ago, thinking that the state's top D.A. Carilyn Cosby was about to score a victory for the department as the jury began to read the verdict in Anthony Izzard's case. But, things didn't go as planned. Once again, another criminal had tricked the jury and convinced them into believing that he was another innocent black man being tried by an unjust system. It felt like another chapter of what seemed to be a very bad book. Especially since he had promised Lashaun before she took her last breath that he'd not sleep, nor retire until every last one of the deadly 'Dummie Squad' members were brought to justice.

If that wasn't enough, Baker still couldn't figure out exactly who the other little mask-wearing shooters in Lashaun's case were. And Donald White had somehow managed to find a way to stop him from ever being able to question Calvin Johnson about it. Baker had been so angry when Detective Malone had leaned forward and mumbled something about poetic justice before patting him on the shoulder inside the courtroom when word of Johnson's death began to circulate.

Detective Baker did not want poetic justice. He wanted real justice. He wanted Jonnson, Izzard and all the rest of those little bastards to rot away in prison cells. Instead, most of them got off easy. James Tanner had succumbed to multiple gunshot wounds in route to the hospital. Frank Lance was shot down outside the Clarence M. Mitchell Jr. Courthouse, and Calvin Johnson was found unresponsive inside the underground parking garage. The only good news was that the FBI seemed to have a solid case.

"All rise!" The court clerk alerted the moment the Judge's chamber door began to open. "The Honorable Timothy Player Sr. presiding," the court clerk continued. "You may be seated. Your Honor, this is case number 198261014 on the docket. State of Maryland versus Anthony Izzard."

"Carilyn Cosby for the state," the fine District Attorney informed.

"Susan Kerin for the defense," Billy Lo's lawyer seconded.

Detective Baker shook his head. He never understood how some attorneys could call themselves United States citizens, yet represent street terrorist.

"Thank you." The Judge glanced from the defense table to the D.A. "I understand that there's a plea agreement on the table?"

"A plea agreement?" Detective Baker shot to his feet. "You're going to offer that bastard a deal?"

"You may want to have a seat before you find yourself being held in contempt, detective!" the Judge warned sternly.

"That's correct, Your Honor," Carilyn Cosby looked back at Detective Baker understandably. She knew they'd spoken about retrying Izzard on the weapon's charge and hitting him with the maximum punishment. But, things changed once she received a call from the DEA's Office. "The state is willing to offer Mr. Izzard four years for the handgun violation."

Baker saw the little smirk spread across Anthony Izzard's face and wished for a moment that he could stand him up in front of a firing squad. He had wanted Izzard to be found guilty and sentenced to death so bad. That way, he could personally observe him going gray and bald from worry as he filed appeal after appeal until all his remedies were exhausted and his number was called. Then, he could get a seat in the execution chamber and witness Izzard walk the 'Green Mile' like so many other animals before him whom had committed heinous crimes. This was, of course, after he'd eaten his last meal. If he could stomach it.

"Miss Kerin," the Judge addressed Izzard's attorney. "What is the defendant's position?"

"He's very grateful, Your Honor. But, he just wants to put this entire situation behind him—"

Detective Baker sat there and listened to the Judge, D.A. and Defense Counsel go back and forth. Then the Judge questioned Izzard to ensure that he understood what pleading guilty meant, before getting him to state on record that he was knowingly and intelligently doing so.

After it was all said and done and Billy Lo received his four-year sentence, Carilyn Cosby made her way over to Detective Baker and tried to explain why she'd made a deal with the devil.

"That's easy for you to say, detective, when all you have to do is arrest them," Carilyn Cosby argued when Detective Baker questioned her ability to do her job. "I am the one who has to convince a freaky jury of their guilt! And trust me when I tell you detective, your department hasn't made my job any easier."

"Yeah, but I have!" Baker reminded. He'd practically given her Anthony Izzard on a fucking silver platter.

"One bad apple always spoils the bunch, detective."

"So, that's it, huh?" Baker questioned. "He gets off with a measly four years that he probably won't do another year on."

"Some times we got to take what we can get," Carilyn Cosby defended. "But like I said, I spoke with a friend of mine in the D.E.A. office. And they assured me that they're looking hard at Izzard."

"Thanks for nothing, sister." Detective Baker shook Carilyn Cosby's hand and left her standing there. Because honestly, in the end it wouldn't have mattered how much time Izzard, Johnson, Lance or any of them have gotten. As far as Baker was concerned, no amount of punishment could bring back the love of his life. No victory would make him feel any better about losing Lashaun. No matter what, he would never feel that sense of joy again.

"You okay, Baker?" Detective Malone inquired the moment Baker stepped outside of the courtroom.

"I actually am," Baker removed his gun and badge, took Detective Malone's hand and placed the badge and gun in her palm. "Tell the chief I quit," he added with a sinister smile. "Because if I ever decide to pick up a gun again, it won't be for this city."

The End

Submission Guideline

Submit the first three chapters of your completed manuscript to ldpsubmissions@gmail.com, subject line: Your book's title. The manuscript must be in a .doc file and sent as an attachment. Document should be in Times New Roman, double spaced and in size 12 font. Also, provide your synopsis and full contact information. If sending multiple submissions, they must each be in a separate email.

Have a story but no way to send it electronically? You can still submit to LDP/Ca$h Presents. Send in the first three chapters, written or typed, of your completed manuscript to:

LDP: Submissions Dept
Po Box 944
Stockbridge, Ga 30281

DO NOT send original manuscript. Must be a duplicate.

Provide your synopsis and a cover letter containing your full contact information.

Thanks for considering LDP and Ca$h Presents.

Coming Soon from Lock Down Publications/Ca$h Presents

BOW DOWN TO MY GANGSTA

By **Ca$h**

TORN BETWEEN TWO

By **Coffee**

BLOOD OF A BOSS **VI**

SHADOWS OF THE GAME II

TRAP BASTARD II

By **Askari**

LOYAL TO THE GAME **IV**

By **T.J. & Jelissa**

IF LOVING YOU IS WRONG… **III**

By **Jelissa**

TRUE SAVAGE **VIII**

MIDNIGHT CARTEL IV

DOPE BOY MAGIC IV

CITY OF KINGZ III

By **Chris Green**

BLAST FOR ME **III**

A SAVAGE DOPEBOY III

CUTTHROAT MAFIA III

DUFFLE BAG CARTEL VI

HEARTLESS GOON VI

By **Ghost**

A HUSTLER'S DECEIT III

KILL ZONE **II**

BAE BELONGS TO ME III

A DOPE BOY'S QUEEN III

By **Aryanna**

COKE KINGS V

KING OF THE TRAP III

By **T.J. Edwards**

GORILLAZ IN THE BAY V

3X KRAZY III

De'Kari

THE STREETS ARE CALLING II

Duquie Wilson

KINGPIN KILLAZ IV

STREET KINGS III

PAID IN BLOOD III

CARTEL KILLAZ IV

DOPE GODS III

Hood Rich

SINS OF A HUSTLA II

ASAD

KINGZ OF THE GAME VI

Playa Ray

SLAUGHTER GANG IV

RUTHLESS HEART IV

By Willie Slaughter

FUK SHYT II

By Blakk Diamond

TRAP QUEEN

RICH $AVAGE II

By Troublesome

YAYO V

GHOST MOB II

Stilloan Robinson

CREAM III

By Yolanda Moore

SON OF A DOPE FIEND III

HEAVEN GOT A GHETTO II

By Renta

FOREVER GANGSTA II

GLOCKS ON SATIN SHEETS III

By Adrian Dulan

LOYALTY AIN'T PROMISED III

By Keith Williams

THE PRICE YOU PAY FOR LOVE III

By Destiny Skai

I'M NOTHING WITHOUT HIS LOVE II

SINS OF A THUG II

TO THE THUG I LOVED BEFORE II

By Monet Dragun

LIFE OF A SAVAGE IV

MURDA SEASON IV

GANGLAND CARTEL IV

CHI'RAQ GANGSTAS IV

KILLERS ON ELM STREET IV

JACK BOYZ N DA BRONX III

A DOPEBOY'S DREAM II

By **Romell Tukes**

QUIET MONEY IV

EXTENDED CLIP III

THUG LIFE IV

By **Trai'Quan**

THE STREETS MADE ME III

By **Larry D. Wright**

IF YOU CROSS ME ONCE II

ANGEL III

By **Anthony Fields**

FRIEND OR FOE III

By **Mimi**

SAVAGE STORMS III

By **Meesha**

BLOOD ON THE MONEY III

By J-Blunt

THE STREETS WILL NEVER CLOSE II

By K'ajji

NIGHTMARES OF A HUSTLA III

By King Dream

IN THE ARM OF HIS BOSS

By Jamila

HARD AND RUTHLESS III

MOB TOWN 251 II

By Von Diesel

LEVELS TO THIS SHYT II

By Ah'Million

MOB TIES III

By SayNoMore

THE LAST OF THE OGS III

Tranay Adams

FOR THE LOVE OF A BOSS II

By C. D. Blue

MOBBED UP II

By King Rio

Available Now

RESTRAINING ORDER **I & II**

By **CA$H & Coffee**

LOVE KNOWS NO BOUNDARIES **I II & III**

By **Coffee**

RAISED AS A GOON I, II, III & IV

BRED BY THE SLUMS I, II, III

BLAST FOR ME I & II

ROTTEN TO THE CORE I II III

A BRONX TALE I, II, III

DUFFLE BAG CARTEL I II III IV V

HEARTLESS GOON I II III IV V

A SAVAGE DOPEBOY I II

DRUG LORDS I II III

CUTTHROAT MAFIA I II

By **Ghost**

LAY IT DOWN **I & II**

LAST OF A DYING BREED I II

BLOOD STAINS OF A SHOTTA I & II III

By **Jamaica**

LOYAL TO THE GAME I II III

LIFE OF SIN I, II III

By **TJ & Jelissa**

BLOODY COMMAS I & II

SKI MASK CARTEL I II & III

KING OF NEW YORK I II,III IV V

RISE TO POWER I II III

COKE KINGS I II III IV

BORN HEARTLESS I II III IV

KING OF THE TRAP I II

By **T.J. Edwards**

IF LOVING HIM IS WRONG…I & II

LOVE ME EVEN WHEN IT HURTS I II III

By **Jelissa**

WHEN THE STREETS CLAP BACK I & II III

THE HEART OF A SAVAGE I II III

By **Jibril Williams**

A DISTINGUISHED THUG STOLE MY HEART I II & III

LOVE SHOULDN'T HURT I II III IV

RENEGADE BOYS I II III IV

PAID IN KARMA I II III

SAVAGE STORMS I II

By **Meesha**

A GANGSTER'S CODE I &, II III

A GANGSTER'S SYN I II III

THE SAVAGE LIFE I II III

CHAINED TO THE STREETS I II III

BLOOD ON THE MONEY I II

By J-Blunt

PUSH IT TO THE LIMIT

By **Bre' Hayes**

BLOOD OF A BOSS **I, II, III, IV, V**

SHADOWS OF THE GAME

TRAP BASTARD

By **Askari**

THE STREETS BLEED MURDER **I, II & III**

THE HEART OF A GANGSTA I II& III

By **Jerry Jackson**

CUM FOR ME I II III IV V VI VII
An **LDP Erotica Collaboration**
BRIDE OF A HUSTLA **I II & II**
THE FETTI GIRLS **I, II& III**
CORRUPTED BY A GANGSTA I, II III, IV
BLINDED BY HIS LOVE
THE PRICE YOU PAY FOR LOVE I II
DOPE GIRL MAGIC I II III
By **Destiny Skai**
WHEN A GOOD GIRL GOES BAD
By **Adrienne**
THE COST OF LOYALTY I II III
By Kweli
A GANGSTER'S REVENGE **I II III & IV**
THE BOSS MAN'S DAUGHTERS I II III IV V
A SAVAGE LOVE **I & II**
BAE BELONGS TO ME I II
A HUSTLER'S DECEIT I, II, III
WHAT BAD BITCHES DO I, II, III
SOUL OF A MONSTER I II III
KILL ZONE
A DOPE BOY'S QUEEN I II
By **Aryanna**
A KINGPIN'S AMBITON
A KINGPIN'S AMBITION **II**
I MURDER FOR THE DOUGH
By **Ambitious**
TRUE SAVAGE I II III IV V VI VII
DOPE BOY MAGIC I, II, III
MIDNIGHT CARTEL I II III

CITY OF KINGZ I II

By **Chris Green**

A DOPEBOY'S PRAYER

By **Eddie "Wolf" Lee**

THE KING CARTEL **I, II & III**

By **Frank Gresham**

THESE NIGGAS AIN'T LOYAL **I, II & III**

By **Nikki Tee**

GANGSTA SHYT **I II &III**

By **CATO**

THE ULTIMATE BETRAYAL

By **Phoenix**

BOSS'N UP **I , II & III**

By **Royal Nicole**

I LOVE YOU TO DEATH

By Destiny J

I RIDE FOR MY HITTA

I STILL RIDE FOR MY HITTA

By **Misty Holt**

LOVE & CHASIN' PAPER

By **Qay Crockett**

TO DIE IN VAIN

SINS OF A HUSTLA

By **ASAD**

BROOKLYN HUSTLAZ

By **Boogsy Morina**

BROOKLYN ON LOCK I & II

By **Sonovia**

GANGSTA CITY

By **Teddy Duke**

A DRUG KING AND HIS DIAMOND I & II III

A DOPEMAN'S RICHES

HER MAN, MINE'S TOO I, II

CASH MONEY HO'S

THE WIFEY I USED TO BE I II

By Nicole Goosby

TRAPHOUSE KING **I II & III**

KINGPIN KILLAZ I II III

STREET KINGS I II

PAID IN BLOOD **I II**

CARTEL KILLAZ I II III

DOPE GODS I II

By **Hood Rich**

LIPSTICK KILLAH **I, II, III**

CRIME OF PASSION I II & III

FRIEND OR FOE I II

By **Mimi**

STEADY MOBBN' **I, II, III**

THE STREETS STAINED MY SOUL I II

By **Marcellus Allen**

WHO SHOT YA **I, II, III**

SON OF A DOPE FIEND I II

HEAVEN GOT A GHETTO

Renta

GORILLAZ IN THE BAY **I II III IV**

TEARS OF A GANGSTA I II

3X KRAZY I II

DE'KARI

TRIGGADALE I II III

Elijah R. Freeman

GOD BLESS THE TRAPPERS I, II, III

THESE SCANDALOUS STREETS I, II, III

FEAR MY GANGSTA I, II, III IV, V

THESE STREETS DON'T LOVE NOBODY I, II

BURY ME A G I, II, III, IV, V

A GANGSTA'S EMPIRE I, II, III, IV

THE DOPEMAN'S BODYGAURD I II

THE REALEST KILLAZ I II III

THE LAST OF THE OGS I II

Tranay Adams

THE STREETS ARE CALLING

Duquie Wilson

MARRIED TO A BOSS... I II III

By Destiny Skai & Chris Green

KINGZ OF THE GAME I II III IV V

Playa Ray

SLAUGHTER GANG I II III

RUTHLESS HEART I II III

By Willie Slaughter

FUK SHYT

By Blakk Diamond

DON'T F#CK WITH MY HEART I II

By Linnea

ADDICTED TO THE DRAMA I II III

IN THE ARM OF HIS BOSS II

By Jamila

YAYO I II III IV

A SHOOTER'S AMBITION I II

By S. Allen

TRAP GOD I II III

RICH $AVAGE

By Troublesome

FOREVER GANGSTA

GLOCKS ON SATIN SHEETS I II

By Adrian Dulan

TOE TAGZ I II III

LEVELS TO THIS SHYT

By Ah'Million

KINGPIN DREAMS I II III

By Paper Boi Rari

CONFESSIONS OF A GANGSTA I II III

By Nicholas Lock

I'M NOTHING WITHOUT HIS LOVE

SINS OF A THUG

TO THE THUG I LOVED BEFORE

By Monet Dragun

CAUGHT UP IN THE LIFE I II III

By Robert Baptiste

NEW TO THE GAME I II III

MONEY, MURDER & MEMORIES I II III

By **Malik D. Rice**

LIFE OF A SAVAGE I II III

A GANGSTA'S QUR'AN I II III

MURDA SEASON I II III

GANGLAND CARTEL I II III

CHI'RAQ GANGSTAS I II III

KILLERS ON ELM STREET I II III

JACK BOYZ N DA BRONX I II

A DOPEBOY'S DREAM

Delmont Player

By **Romell Tukes**
LOYALTY AIN'T PROMISED I II
By Keith Williams
QUIET MONEY I II III
THUG LIFE I II III
EXTENDED CLIP I II
By **Trai'Quan**
THE STREETS MADE ME I II
By **Larry D. Wright**
THE ULTIMATE SACRIFICE I, II, III, IV, V, VI
KHADIFI
IF YOU CROSS ME ONCE
ANGEL I II
IN THE BLINK OF AN EYE
By **Anthony Fields**
THE LIFE OF A HOOD STAR
By Ca$h & Rashia Wilson
THE STREETS WILL NEVER CLOSE
By K'ajji
CREAM I II
By Yolanda Moore
NIGHTMARES OF A HUSTLA I II
By King Dream
CONCRETE KILLA I II
By Kingpen
HARD AND RUTHLESS I II
MOB TOWN 251
By Von Diesel
GHOST MOB II
Stilloan Robinson

MOB TIES I II

By SayNoMore

BODYMORE MURDERLAND I II III

By Delmont Player

FOR THE LOVE OF A BOSS

By C. D. Blue

MOBBED UP

By King Rio

BOOKS BY LDP'S CEO, CA$H

TRUST IN NO MAN

TRUST IN NO MAN 2

TRUST IN NO MAN 3

BONDED BY BLOOD

SHORTY GOT A THUG

THUGS CRY

THUGS CRY 2

THUGS CRY 3

TRUST NO BITCH

TRUST NO BITCH 2

TRUST NO BITCH 3

TIL MY CASKET DROPS

RESTRAINING ORDER

RESTRAINING ORDER 2

IN LOVE WITH A CONVICT

LIFE OF A HOOD STAR

CPSIA information can be obtained
at www.ICGtesting.com
Printed in the USA
LVHW082008121021
700249LV00014B/369